Little Wrecks

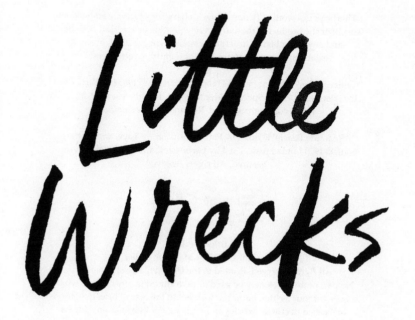

MEREDITH MILLER

HARPER
An Imprint of HarperCollinsPublishers

"Gates of Eden" Written by Bob Dylan. Copyright © 1965 by Warner Bros. Inc.; renewed 1993 by Special Rider Music. All rights reserved. International copyright secured. Reprinted by permission.

"Redondo Beach" Written by Patti Smith, Lenny Kaye, and Richard Sohl. © 1975 Linda Music. Used by permission. International copyright secured. All rights reserved.

Little Wrecks
Copyright © 2017 by Meredith Miller
All rights reserved. Printed in the United States of America.
No part of this book may be used or reproduced in any manner whatsoever without written permission except in the case of brief quotations embodied in critical articles and reviews. For information address HarperCollins Children's Books, a division of HarperCollins Publishers, 195 Broadway, New York, NY 10007.
www.epicreads.com

Library of Congress Control Number: 2016960407
ISBN 978-0-06-247425-4 (trade bdg.)

Typography by Torborg Davern
17 18 19 20 21   PC/LSCH   10 9 8 7 6 5 4 3 2 1
❖

First Edition

This book is dedicated to its readers

I too have bubbled up, floated the measureless float,

　and been wash'd on your shores;

I too am but a trail of drift and debris,

I too leave little wrecks upon you, you fish-shaped

　island.

—WALT WHITMAN

Little Wrecks

RESISTANCE

one

PEOPLE GET FROGS in their pools. The frogs think the pools are ponds, jump in, and can't get out again. Invisible chlorine seeps through their skin and kills them. On spring mornings, the more fortunate citizens of Highbone wake up to find their swimming pools full of dead or struggling frogs. They stand in their bathrobes with pool nets, fishing them out while their coffee gets cold.

Only Isabel and the frog-fishers are awake now. She walks barefoot through the empty streets around Harbor Ridge, spreading her toes and pushing off the ground with every step, trying to feel everything at once. It's early and the grass is still wet. The sun slants along the ground and the drops on the spiderwebs are glinting in the bushes. She's wearing her blue cotton skirt, the flouncy one that shows her thighs and reminds her of the sky.

Over that, she has on a secondhand Navy sweater that's almost as long as the skirt. One of the frog-fishers stands there with her pool net dripping and stares at Isabel's sweater and her bare feet. Isabel just laughs.

Doesn't the lady realize how she looks, doing ridiculous frog maintenance on her perfect life that looks exactly like the perfect life next door? Factory-made and totally meaningless, pretending to be paradise and full of road kill.

Everyone pretends the water is clear. Those pools might as well be full of girls instead of frogs. Bleeding, barefoot girls, floating facedown with the soles of their feet staring up at the sky. The collateral damage of all that pretending.

She turns her back on the frog-fishers and heads towards the heavier air down the hill. The onshore breeze is full of salt and the smell of ocean green blowing over Highbone Harbor. The pavement is gathering heat from the early sun and sending it up through the soles of Isabel's feet. She breathes. It could always be like this. If everyone would just take their shoes off and breathe in, the day could stay like this. But already the traffic is starting up. Slamming car doors echo down Main Street. She has to move out of the way so a Highbone cop can drive past her. He turns his siren on, drives through the red light at the bottom of the hill, then turns it off again.

Mariner's Maps and Books isn't open yet. Mr. Lipsky is never too worried about being on time. When he shows up, she can get the copy of *Under a Glass Bell* he ordered for her. One day, Isabel is going to live on a houseboat like Anaïs Nin. Right now, she can hear the shackles on the sails in the harbor, ringing like bells against aluminum masts. She can feel the shelves of poetry behind the window at her back, the thousands of miles there are to travel in every direction. She knows how beautiful it all is, and that's what makes her different than everyone else in Highbone. She'll never understand why people trade in their souls for pool nets and sprinkler systems.

The cop parks between Isabel and the sun, then gets out and stands looking down at her legs.

"Waiting for someone, young lady?" he says to her thighs.

"Yep." She stands up and pulls her skirt down. "Is that a problem?"

The cop jerks his head away from her sixteen-year-old legs like suddenly they offend him.

"Where are your shoes?" he says, as if her bare feet are what he was staring at.

"Don't have any. Pawned 'em for a train ticket out of this hole."

The cop just stands there for a while, looking at the harbor and doing his cop silence.

Whatever. Isabel is going to get out. They're all going to get out, her and Magdalene and Ruth. None of them are supposed to be here. They all know it, and that's why they get each other; that's why they're friends.

Isabel has a plan. As soon as she's eighteen, she'll get a job working at the Lagoon. They have bouncers, and the girls wear cutoff shorts, so it's just topless. They rake it in; that's what Vicky says. Vicky works at Dunkin' Donuts now, because they won't let her work at the Lagoon anymore. She won't say why, but she did say when she was there she brought home a hundred bucks after six hours, on a good night. A year of that kind of money and Isabel could live for ages on a houseboat.

The cop is inside the diner now, sitting at the counter drinking free coffee and eating free pie. He's so arrogant he left the car window open with a wallet sitting right on the passenger seat. Isabel looks both ways before she reaches in and grabs the wallet. She puts it under her skirt and sits back down in the doorway. Then she laughs.

After her heart stops pounding she scoots farther into the doorway, pulls the wallet out, and opens it. Inside there are two five-dollar bills and a picture of some boring kids with braces. That's it. What was she hoping for? Something to make her feel better about being leered at and then made invisible by a cop, whatever that might be. There isn't even a badge, which would have been cool.

The door of Mariner's Maps and Books opens at Isabel's back and the little bell tinkles.

"You coming in, or what?" Mr. Lipsky says.

When Mr. Lipsky turns his back to head inside, she pulls out the ten bucks and throws the cop's wallet over the curb. It falls right between the grating of a storm drain and down into the deep dark underneath Main Street.

Perfect shot.

Inside, Mr. Lipsky looks down at Isabel's sweater like it

worries him. Well, it has a couple of holes where she ripped the Navy patches off, and it is much too big. So obviously he doesn't get it. The Navy sweater is like armor, or maybe like wearing your bed all day. It makes her feel safe, anyway. Besides, Mr. Lipsky can't really look at her like that, since his khaki pants are always too big for him and his shirts hang out at the back. He dresses like he can't quite handle being a grown-up, which is nice.

"Come on in. I'll make coffee." He disappears into the back.

Isabel climbs all the way into the bay window and pushes up one sleeve so she can pet Gaius Pollio, the cat. She just robbed a cop; maybe Saturday morning isn't so bad after all. You get one life; it's full of things that taste and smell and make people feel. Your mission, obviously, is to taste and smell and feel as much of that as you can. Daydreaming should be a job. People should be paid to do it for the good of society.

It takes a lot of daydreaming to counteract Highbone, though. Stay here long enough and you're certifiable, that's for sure. Isabel's mother is living proof of that. One day, Isabel will have a mooring on a river somewhere, maybe in France, maybe in Mexico. The boat will have a musty cabin and a single bed and a typewriter. Little waves will rock her and sound will do comforting things at night, traveling over the surface of different water.

When Mr. Lipsky comes back out with two mugs in one hand and a half-pint milk carton in the other, Isabel is sitting with Gaius Pollio in her lap. He hands her the coffee and puts *Under a Glass Bell* down in the bay next to her, then pulls up the captain's chair from behind the counter for himself.

"Tell me again about the kinds of hell," Isabel says.

"Let's see . . . for the flatterers, there's this pit where they're all plunged up to their necks in excrement. What do you think?"

"For saying something nice to someone when it isn't true, you spend eternity swimming in shit? That's a little much."

"I think Dante was worried about people who fawn over politicians and corrupt people with lots of power. Why don't you let me order you a copy and you can read it yourself?"

"I like listening to you tell it. Also, the coffee is good. My dad's coffee sucks."

"Any time, kiddo. But you should read Dante before you go to college."

"I don't know about college. And anyway, I need to get through these first." She holds up her new book. "Anaïs Nin and those people weren't all caught up by money and jobs. They just lived. They paid attention to everything."

"They had trust funds."

"That's why I need to go straight to work, Mr. Lipsky. I need money."

"You need to read everything you can. Trust me. How's your mother?"

"My mother is the same. You know, fine. She just sits around all day in Castle Gloom, eating cheese and crackers and reading about some fat guy named Nero Wolf."

"Castle Gloom?" He raises his eyebrows. "Your mother is a very smart lady, Isabel. I learned more from her in high school than I learned from some of my teachers."

"My house is kind of dark and depressing. My friends named it Castle Gloom. Magda and Ruth seem to think it has fairy-tale potential. They don't have to live there, obviously. And yeah, my mom knows lots of stuff. Sometimes she tells me it, but mostly she doesn't say anything."

"All right, well. I just know it'd make her happy if you read the important stuff."

"Okay, okay, but it's not gonna be today, Mr. Lipsky. I need to meet Magda."

"Magda is Magdalene Warren, right? Your friend? My dad knew her grandparents."

"We're going up to the mall. Fucking mall named after a poet!" He doesn't even blink when she curses. That's one reason why Isabel decided to be friends with Mr. Lipsky.

"Don't worry, Isabel. There is an extra special hell for town planners who build shopping malls and name them after poets."

"I already decided. I'm voting for the one where they're buried upside down in the rock with their feet on fire."

People out on the sidewalk are looking twice at the front window of Mariner's Maps and Books, wondering why there's a teenager dressed like a homeless person sitting in it with a cat and a cup of coffee. Mr. Lipsky stares straight back through the glass and smiles.

two

COMING DOWN THE hill on Seaview Road, Ruth can
see everything stretched out below her, the water shining in
the Sound and the traffic on 25A, cutting the village off from
everywhere else. You can see the dividing lines, the different
worlds of Highbone. Ruth lives on the other side, away from the
beach and the bluffs and the old arts and crafts houses. When she
looks down on Highbone from here, everything seems clear and
inevitable. The divisions between herself and everyone else are
just part of the pattern of the world. In the fading light, it all looks
as fixed and distant as the end of time.

Sometimes lately, the veil over everything falls away and
the meaning is suddenly obvious. Ruth's stomach lurches; she
loses her breath and the world comes into a new kind of focus.
For the first time, she doesn't need anyone else to see things for

her. Turning onto Main Street, she comes up behind Isabel and Magda, heading towards Highbone Harbor in the almost dark.

"My space goes two ways together, twilight's forever," Ruth sings out behind them, and Isabel joins in without turning around. Ruth falls into her usual place, three steps behind.

They're all way too old and way too cynical for jump rope songs, but this one is special. Isabel says it's actual poetry, whatever actual means. What about the girl who first made up that rhyme though, maybe a hundred years ago? It's like she was describing them. Was her life just like theirs, if you leave out the details? Can't be denied; those words fit the situation.

The three of them pass by the weird mix of preppies and homeless people sprinkled around outside Flannagan's Bar, and walk, singing, past the floating docks by the playground. They pass all the broken men returned from Vietnam, twitching and hallucinating on the benches at the bottom of Main Street. It's four years since the war really ended, but the human wreckage is still lying around everywhere. It doesn't match with the Rhode Island types in their sailboats, moored in the harbor, the picture-postcard park and the Victorian shop fronts.

Ruth watches from behind, dragging her old lace dress on the sidewalk while Magda and Isabel move right through it all without paying attention. None of it is new. They see it most days, but to Ruth it's impossible to ignore, impossible not to feel it all the time. *Two ways together, twilight's forever.*

She waves at Lefty, on a bench reciting poetry into the air while his friend Robert looks for cigarette butts along the curb.

Lefty waves back with his one whole arm, and Ruth follows Magda and Isabel behind the bushes at the back of the park.

"This is the worst possible spot. We are so gonna get caught," Magda says. But even as she says it, she throws down her Army Navy Store backpack and sits on the grass.

"The cops are too lazy to check back here," Isabel says. "Anyway, it's time for a bonfire; we all agreed. Safety valve. Escaping steam. Not exploding, that's the plan. You know that as well as I do, so what did you bring, Magda?"

Magdalene reaches into her backpack, takes out a book, and hands it over to Isabel.

"*The New Eden: Mythopoesis and Westward Expansion*? Cool title." Isabel turns the book over. "And this book deeply offends you why? I'm not sure how I feel about book burning."

Magdalene jabs a finger at the cover. "Read it."

"John W— Oh! I kind of knew your dad wrote books, but I didn't know they were cool books. Mythopoesis, I love that word."

"Fuck you, Isabel."

"Okay, your dad's an asshole, I get it. No reason to be nasty. Remember our first bonfire?"

"Yep," Magda says. "It was at Fiddler's Cove. We made a fire at the beach, like normal people. That must have been before you turned into a crazy person and convinced us to start a fire in the park."

"That was only about two months after we met." Isabel lights a match for no reason, holding it up until it burns her fingers.

"After we met *you*, Isabel. I met Magda before I could talk."

Ruth checks behind her and then lies down, closing her eyes so all she has to deal with is the sound of them. It's enough.

"I'm just saying, we weren't even halfway through ninth grade. Ruth was still in middle school. This is bonfire number six. Six, in not even two years. I think they're getting more frequent. Does that mean things are getting worse?"

"No," Magda says. "It means we notice more, we're fighting back more. We're not as oblivious. Especially you, Isabel. If it weren't for us, you'd still be floating around two inches off the ground thinking the whole world is wonderful and all made just for you."

"And that would be a bad thing why? You're bragging because you made me mad at everything? You jaded me?"

"I'm not bragging," Magda says. "I'm just pointing out that because of us you started noticing what really goes on in this place and why we need to get the hell out."

"Ruth, where'd you get the cool dress?" Isabel tugs on the hem. She can't stand anyone not looking at her. Ruth opens one eye.

"Stole it from Attic Antiques."

"You went without me? No fair! Anyway, you guys liked me, admit it. You liked me right away."

"It's true," Magda says. "You have some excellent qualities. You just needed a push in the right direction."

"Yeah, also, I have resources."

Isabel pulls a half pint of blackberry brandy out from under her sweater and waves it at them.

"See?" Magda says. "Always prepared, that's an excellent quality. Girl Scouts've got nothing on you."

"I was thinking more cowgirl than Girl Scout. Fire, flask of moonshine. We could be cattle rustling."

"Does moonshine taste like cough syrup?" Ruth grabs the bottle, leans on her elbow, and screws off the cap.

"Cowgirls in the wilds of Highbone." Isabel draws a pretend six-shooter and aims at Ruth, straight between the eyes. "The Highbone Gang, thieves and guns for hire."

"Westerns never have chicks in them," Ruth says.

"Yeah, also"—Magda reaches for the bottle, but Isabel grabs it first—"the Indians are always white guys with terrible makeup and a three-word vocabulary."

"So, we need to make a new kind of western." Isabel blows the smoke off the tip of her invisible gun, then pours some brandy down her throat.

"Slow down there, Stagecoach Mary." Magda takes the bottle. "So the heroine of our movie will start out all demure and proper, then her parents die and she turns into a bank-robbing saloon singer."

"Dibs on the title," Ruth says. "It's gonna be *Tulip*. That'll be the main chick's name."

"That'll have to be you, Miss Blonde-with-Tits," Isabel says. "I'll be a dime novelist, touring the West to soak up the atmosphere. Then I fall in with you and get drawn into the life of sin I've always written about. What about Magda?"

"Well." Ruth squints her eyes at Magda. "I guess you grew up in a Lakota camp on the move with twelve brothers, so you never learned to be domestic in the first place."

"As long as I can shoot and cure snakebite, I'm good."

The three of them lean forward with their elbows on their knees, imagining themselves in painted deserts and badlands, sitting on bedrolls under the stars. It's like there's a fire they're all staring into together, even though they haven't actually lit one yet.

"So, Ruth," Isabel says, "what did you bring?"

Ruth reaches into her back pocket and pulls out a heavy, embossed piece of paper. It still smells like the cabinet she lifted it from, like chamomile and her mother's patchouli. Magda grabs her hand and leans over to look at it.

"You can't burn your birth certificate, Ruth! You're gonna need it when we get driver's licenses. I'm not driving all the way to California myself while you lie back in the passenger seat spacing out."

"I don't know," Isabel says. "I kind of get it. I mean, why let them make you get a piece of paper to prove you were born? We're here, aren't we? What difference do the details make? They just want to keep pieces of us in filing cabinets."

"Read it," Ruth says. "There *are* no details. In the place where there might be some useful information, it's just blank. I mean, everyone already knows who my mother is and that I'm from Long Island. Those are both kind of annoyingly inescapable facts. The rest is blank space."

"You're not the only one with a blank space where your father is supposed to be," Isabel laughs. "I live in a house with my father. Trust me, it doesn't make a difference."

"I don't want to come from anywhere," Ruth says. "I don't want to be a collection of facts. I'm burning it. Deal. Your turn, Isabel."

"I'm burning this, but I'm not opening it." Isabel holds some papers, folded and folded again, six or seven pages' worth. "You just have to trust me."

"This is exactly why people *don't* trust you," Magdalene says. "Come on, ante up, O'Sullivan."

"We're all pouring out our deepest shit here, Isabel. You're supposed to throw in with us; otherwise it isn't fair."

The imaginary fire has gone, leaving Ruth feeling naked and chilly. Alone again in a world full of people who don't see what she sees.

"I don't care if it's fair," Isabel says. "Fair is not the point. Catharsis is the point. It's like Mr. Driscoll said about *Antigone*."

"I think what Mr. Driscoll said was that *telling the story together* is what makes all the people better." Magdalene reaches for the papers and Isabel rolls away onto the ground, clutching them underneath her.

"Do you want me to stay or not?" she says. "If you want me in, I'm burning these without opening them. End of the story."

Ruth has never seen that look on Isabel's face before. She shrugs and holds out her birth certificate.

"Well, got a match, Magda?" she says.

They all laugh because that is the magic incantation. They can say it whenever they need to, in school or at the beach with a bunch of ridiculous cheerleaders, or in the street when some construction worker offers them five bucks for a blow job. *Got a match?* And the thought of everything catching and burning will take whatever it is away. Fire makes them feel clean again, takes the wrongness of everything and the blindness of everyone around them away.

The heavy paper of Ruth's birth certificate makes a green-and-yellow flame. They use that to light the unknown papers, burning Isabel's secrets in their folds. Over those, Magdalene holds open her father's book, pages down so they will catch, until the flames come up and nearly light her sleeves. The cover takes ages to burn, and they have to use more matches and some paper bags from the garbage pail behind the bandstand.

Turns out they don't get caught. Either no one sees the fire behind the bushes at the back of the park, or no one cares. When they're done, they climb the bank at the side, up through the bushes onto Baywater Avenue.

Ruth leaves Isabel and Magdalene at the top of Seaview Road by the elementary school. The wind kicks up last year's leaves along with the bottom of her lace dress and a lot of dust from around the goalposts. She turns her back to the water, and the wind blows her hair forward in front of her eyes. They all squint against the grit blowing off the football field, and Ruth shouts good-bye to the world and her friends flickering in and out of view. Magda and

Isabel disappear into the dark. As soon as she's alone it all comes back. The green-and-yellow flames of the bonfire are burning in her head, and the world drops away from under her feet. Minus the birth certificate, she feels lighter, cleaner, like someone's cut her anchor and she might just lift up and away any minute, flying out over the houses and the sea.

She turns down the hill towards the highway where Highbone divides, leaving behind the boats and the harbor and Baywater Avenue, where the man whose name is missing from her birth certificate lives. Over 25A and down into South Highbone, Ruth's house sits in a dusty yard in front of a patch of trees. On a good day, it's just her mother and herself in the little ranch house. On bad days, it could be anyone. There might be a dozen people getting stoned in the living room, excited that she's home and acting desperate to hear what she thinks about everything. For Ruth's mother and her friends, the secret to life is never thinking like an adult. They act like Ruth is some kind of guru, possessing the secret of anti-wisdom.

Or there might be a boyfriend. They usually arrive without warning, or without warning Ruth, anyway. The first one was pretty harmless. He mowed lawns and played drums and thought being with Ruth's mom was like winning the lottery. She dumped him. Then Stevie showed up. He started by slapping her mother's ass and saying, "Who's that?" in a stern voice whenever someone called on the phone. At the end, there was a lot of yelling and throwing things. For the last few weeks he was around, Ruth spent Saturday nights awake in her room, listening to things hit the walls. Then one Sunday morning, her mother was alone at the table wearing too much makeup, and Stevie was gone. He never came back and they didn't talk about it. For a few weeks her mother's friends came around a lot, checking on her. There were no boyfriends for so long after that, Ruth started to relax. They watched movies on Saturday nights, or went out to the beach together with her mother's friends. The house went back to its good smell, like dust and patchouli and whatever it is they pack the bedspreads in when they ship them from India.

When Danny Pavlich showed up, it took Ruth a few weeks to realize he was staying. Him and her mother laughed a lot in the stupid way people do right before they start sleeping together, and after a while he was there in the morning, smiling his goofy smile and offering Ruth tea in her own kitchen. But why? Her mother knows about what happened to Mrs. Warren, Magda's mom. Jesus, she knows what it's like to crouch in the corner trying to protect your face with your hands. She can pretend she doesn't, but Ruth was there. Even after all that, does she really have some kind of fairy-tale blindness that makes her think things will stay like this, that Danny will stay like this? Didn't she learn anything?

The sudden sick clarity comes back while Ruth is heading down the hill into South Highbone. Looking down at the landscape of their lives, she knows everything in one sharp second. It all fits together, her and Isabel and Magdalene, her mother and Danny and the whole shape of the land around them. Like a saint from the middle ages, she can see fire and flood and angels descending.

Worlds are grinding together tonight, ripping into each other. Separate circles, meshing and turning like gears. Maybe like a riptide. Ruth feels dizzy and clairvoyant. There is a change washing over everything, and only she can feel it. The sea wind blows something into her, a shiny new soul that was meant for her all along. She is a vengeful spirit, a protector, burning with a halo of green-and-yellow flame.

Danny's white Dodge is shining out of the dark in Ruth's front yard when she gets home. Her mother will be in her room with him, music playing, and their voices underneath it, just a constant, rhythmic murmur without meaning, all night long.

Somebody has to save her.

Ruth goes through the house and into the kitchen to find one of the steak knives her grandmother gave them for Christmas. She doesn't need to turn on any lights. Her body knows the house like it's inside her own head, like inside and outside her head are no different anymore. Sometimes in the middle of the night, she goes out to smoke in the trees behind the brake repair shop, half-asleep. In between asleep and awake, she tries to walk into the world without her own body, feeling her way in the dark, trying to stay in her dreams and move through the world at the same time. It feels like that now.

When she goes out the kitchen door into the backyard, the security lights from the brake repair shop shine through the trees, and she sidesteps them, staying in the shadow. She walks around the house to Danny Pavlich's car and sticks the knife into a front tire. It's harder than she thought it would be, but satisfying. She leans into it, and then falls suddenly forward as the air hisses out. The other three tires are easier. When she steps back, Danny's Dodge slumps down onto its rims, first on one side and then the other. Ruth crumples down on the grass next to it.

The air goes out of her, too, all at once. She settles back into her body and starts to feel a little sick. There is the earth again, solid underneath her. The sky has emptied out, leaving her sitting by herself in a world without visions or sense.

three

MAGDA LEAVES ISABEL and walks on up the hill to her house. It sits back on Sycamore Avenue behind two oak trees and a gravel driveway with a carriage house at the end of it. The porch light is broken, and the front windows all stare back at the night, reflecting nothing. In the yard, light shines onto the lawn from her father's study. Magda comes through the back door and stops to take off her shoes so she doesn't make noise on the kitchen tiles. She hangs her Swiss Army trench coat on the newel post. The coat is much bigger than Magda and has all kinds of inside pockets, in which she keeps paperback books and silver cigarette cases and bird feathers and things made of metal. She doesn't go anywhere without the coat until the full heat of summer forces her to.

Magda crosses the hall into the den, but she doesn't turn

the lamp on. She knows the order of all the books by heart, even though she can't read the titles in the streetlight coming through the window. Mostly they're New Modern Library editions that her parents collected in college, translations of French stuff and editions of James Joyce. But there are other books too, mystery novels and Tolkien, because everyone has those.

Magda smiles with satisfaction at the hole where her father's great opus used to be. She didn't tell Ruth and Isabel that she can remember him throwing that very book at her mother. He was yelling at her while Magda stood in the doorway, thinking she was old enough now, maybe she should try to get in between them. He swung his arm with the book in it and her mother's head snapped sideways. He went quiet then, and Magda's mother opened the kitchen door and puked off the back porch. By the time Magda went to bed there was a lump on her mother's forehead and the whole house had that sickening after-a-fight hush.

Three days later Magda woke up with her little brother, Henry, standing over her. He was hungry, and Magda's mother was gone.

It's been two years since Irene Warren left Magdalene alone in the house on Sycamore Avenue with her brother Henry and her father and the New Modern Library. People say she went to Mexico, but Magda never heard that from her father. He doesn't talk about it. Since running off to the border like a fugitive cowgirl is obviously the most interesting thing anyone's mother has done, it isn't easy for Magdalene to hold it against her.

She takes down a Dashiell Hammett and lifts it to her nose while she climbs the stairs, wondering if it smells like anyone or just like time and dust.

"Magdalene!"

"Hi, Dad," she says to the top of the stairs without turning around.

"Where were you? Henry had to go to bed by himself."

Well, no, he didn't, did he? But she doesn't say it out loud.

"I was at Isabel's. We have a math test on Monday."

"Next time, do it here." He slams the door to the study and her body flinches without checking with her first. What's the point of flinching? Whatever is coming comes anyway.

On her bed there is a pile of paperbacks she got at a yard sale, some Asimov classics and a manual for a two-way radio. Magdalene doesn't have a two-way radio and doesn't plan on getting one. She has a lot of manuals for machines she's never owned. There's usually one in the pockets of her coat. There is a book for everything, and Magda likes to make things with moving parts. On her desk there's something that's kind of a cross between a reel-to-reel tape deck and a set of balance scales. Her dad thinks it's art, but really she just likes little closed systems that do the same thing every time. They don't need to have a purpose to make sense.

In Henry's room, everything is almost in the right place. He tried to pick up before he went to bed. She leans over to breathe in the smell of his six-year-old hair and then bends down to turn the nightlight off.

"Magda?"

It's been over a year since Henry woke up in the night and said Mommy.

"Hey, man." Magda comes back to sit on the bed. "Having a dream?"

"No. Sorry, Magda."

"It's okay, little guy. You'll have dreams someday. I promise. It'll be good for you. Dreams clean your brain out."

Henry keeps all his little fears on the outside. Even though he's only six, and Magda and Isabel and Ruth all look out for him, he still casts his eyes sideways in both directions whenever he walks into a room. You can see how jumpy he is all the time.

The difference is at night when they're both in bed. Magda spends lots of time staring wide-eyed at the dark, but whenever she looks in on Henry he's curled up on his side with his eyes shut and his mouth open, his whole face relaxed. He never dreams. She asks him every morning while she makes his break- fast. *Nada*. He needs to dream. Buffer dumping, that's what they call it. She read about it; it's how you process and store away everything that happens all day. If anybody who's six needs that shit, it's Henry.

"Will you stay till I'm asleep, Magda? Please?"

"Lemme get my book, big guy. If you don't care about the light, I can stay and read."

By the time Magdalene settles in under the blanket with *Red Harvest*, Henry is breathing happily into his hand, lost in his com- fortable darkness, dreaming of nothing.

*   *   *

Inland, at the mall up on Herman Road, Monday afternoon is stuffy and gray. Magdalene sits back-to-back with Charlie Ferguson on the base of a light pole in the parking lot, waiting for Isabel to make her way towards them through the maze of cars. Outdoors feels so close it seems like indoors, but made of metal.

"So, where's the little brother, Warren?" Charlie says.

"Playing at his friend's house. I try not to commit felonies when he's here."

"Pretty sure shoplifting's a misdemeanor," Charlie says.

"Oh, really? That's cool. I'll bring him next time. That'll be a big hit with my dad."

"Unless it's, like, a car. Or a bunch of diamond jewelry. That's probably a felony."

"Got it, Charlie. Thanks."

Charlie is Isabel's friend; Magda has nothing to say to him. Can't he tell that, by the fact that she has her back to him? They've already been inside the mall, because it wasn't like Magda was going to sit outside and make conversation with Charlie for an hour while they waited for Isabel to show up. So now Magda has a nine-volt battery with snap-on contacts and a brand-new crescent wrench in her coat pockets.

Two people are yelling in one of the cars in the next row. Either they're fighting or something worse is going on, something Magda doesn't want to think about. So she draws into herself and imagines the whole scene from above, from the sky. Magdalene learned to do that when she was as little as Henry. Gazing down on the world is kind of her specialty.

Charlie is still talking.

"So when we break into people's cars, I think it's still a felony. Even if all we're doing is getting warm and having a smoke."

"Okay."

Magda can never tell whether Charlie is pretending. Someone is using fabric whitener on his clothes, and odds are it isn't him. On the other hand, whoever washes his clothes didn't stop him from getting those jail tattoos. They're the kind you make with a sewing needle wrapped in black thread. It takes hours to do them and it's got to hurt. Other kids have them, but not the ones who live on their side of the highway. Magdalene and Isabel's side.

And that is why Isabel is making her way towards Charlie now, like she's lost and he's magnetic north. She thinks he has a lifeline to something less boring than Castle Gloom, something dangerous from South Highbone.

The voices coming from the car in the next row keep getting louder and higher, but the words aren't clear. There is a sound of scraping metal and then a bang, as a car door opens and slams shut again. The woman's voice goes up an octave.

"What's up with those people?" It's Isabel, standing over Magda and craning her neck to see into the next row.

"Whatever, Isabel. Leave me alone. I'm thinking."

"What do you mean, whatever? Is that woman okay? Is he hurting her?"

"Probably. Why don't you go check it out, Isabel? . . . No, of course not. So stop talking about it, then."

Everything Magda says comes out sounding like that. She can hear herself, but she can't seem to stop it. She's like Patty Hearst, everyone looking at a scary picture of her toting a machine gun, and all the time she's actually wondering how the hell it got into her hands and whether someone's going to shoot her because she's holding it. Yep, Magda looks like the tough one. People don't notice the flinching.

Charlie walks up and down, looking through the windows of cars. Magda stands and turns her back to the two people in the next row, where the noises coming from the woman are no longer words. The parking lot stretches out around them, empty except for that voice. The rows of cars close in, all that metal right in the way of her perspective.

After a minute, Charlie calls them and jerks his head at a blue Chevy Nova with a mother and son getting out of it. The kid leans on the roof and talks to his mother over the car for a minute before they disappear into the mall. The bank of chrome-and-glass doors moves in and out to swallow them, slicing up the reflection of the cars and the metal sky. Charlie pulls a slim jim out of the side of his jeans and does the driver's-side door, then leans through to let Isabel in.

"No, let me use that." Isabel always whines when she's with Charlie.

"Don't be an idiot, Isabel," he says. "The door's already unlocked."

He opens the glove compartment to see what's in there, and Isabel slides in under his hands while Magda makes a flat-out dive, landing facedown on the backseat. Charlie pulls Jackson Browne's *The Pretender* out of the tape player and frisbees it onto the asphalt. It skids along under the row of cars and he puts in a copy of *Houses of the Holy* he got from between the seats, slamming the driver's-side door.

Magda lies down in the backseat, while Charlie rifles through the glove compartment and Isabel looks around the floor in front. She hands Charlie a newspaper and he spills some buds out onto it. None of them seems to have anything to say. They just let the car fill with quiet smoke while the air outside the windows gets heavier. If it were July there would be a thunderstorm coming, but the world hasn't built up enough heat and tension for that yet.

After a while, Charlie says, "I know where there's three pounds of Colombian and half a pound of Thai stick just sitting under a bed."

Isabel is reading, so it's Magdalene who has to answer.

"Uh, okay."

"I'm just saying, it seems like kind of a golden opportunity."

"Anyone with that much weed doesn't just leave it sitting under a bed, Charlie. They'll have a gun, you know that. People with lots of weed also have guns."

Hasn't he read a single book? The big guys have guns, and they shoot you for getting in the way of their cash flow. Anyone who ever read The Saint knows that. But, then, it isn't likely that Charlie's read anything since *Curious George*. Did anyone even read him that? Which brings Magdalene back to the question of the white T-shirt and the jail tattoos. Contemplating Charlie is just too much work for no reward. If she had to guess, she'd say no one ever read him bedtime stories.

"Are you listening back there, Warren?" Charlie taps her and holds out the joint. "This guy I'm talking about just got some money from somewhere. He knows some other guys from Nassau County and they hooked him up. He's a total amateur. He doesn't know what he's doing."

"Neither do you, Charlie," Magda says, still lying back and looking at the roof of the Nova, fake black leather with little holes pricked in it.

Isabel turns the page, blows smoke out of her mouth and sucks it back in through her nostrils. Nothing to add.

"Right, well," Charlie says, "Matt Kerwin and his friends always go out for beers at the same time, right before *The Twilight Zone* and *Dr. Who* come on channel 13 and . . ."

"Jesus, Charlie! Matt Kerwin? No way." Magda rolls over and raises her voice. "He may not have a gun, but he can kick your skinny ass."

Isabel looks up from her book. "He's Ruth's mother's dealer."

"Also he's twenty-two, and his friends are all landscapers and construction workers." She sits up and rests her chin on the back of the front seat. "You'd be so dead, man."

"Ruth feels sorry for Matt," Isabel says. "She thinks he's brooding and tragic. He's the kind of guy my mom calls Byronic."

"Well he's gonna need consoling after next week, so tell her to get ready."

"And you're gonna need a plain pine box. Should we order

it now? Anyway, why are you telling us this? Isn't it your big-secretmasterplan? If you go telling everybody you know, you're definitely gonna die. I mean, loose lips sink ships, sweetheart."

Charlie isn't any smarter than them, but of course he assumes he is.

"I'm telling you because you're girls," he says. "And I need to tell someone, in case something happens. If I tell any guys, they might get there before me, 'cause it *is* the perfect crime. I mean what's he gonna do, call the cops on me?"

Well, he isn't wrong about that.

Before they leave the car, Magdalene leans over into the front and pops *Houses of the Holy* out of the stereo. She pulls the shiny brown ribbon of tape from the case and ties it to the handle of the blue Nova, then carries the cassette with her. Charlie and Isabel are walking side by side a few steps in front of her. Isabel holds her new book like it doesn't matter, because it doesn't matter to Charlie.

And there, on the way out of the parking lot, is the woman from before, from the other car. She's outside now, leaning against the light pole where they started, holding an unbuttoned cotton shirt tight around her and staring at a point somewhere just above the horizon. Her makeup is weirdly perfect and her expression is as empty and as heavy as the color of the sky. She looks like there are no words inside her at all, like language has taken a vacation from her life and left her alone.

If Magdalene could just lift up from the parking lot, look at everything from the sky, she would be able to see it all as a pattern that makes sense. Now she just feels surrounded, by Charlie and Isabel and the endless parking spaces, and by the memory of that strangled, desperate voice coming from the car in the next row. That's the condition they're all in, most likely. Magda, Charlie, Isabel, and the woman from the car, feeling it from both angles. Their bodies are surrounded, but inside they're looking at it from the sky.

Isabel doesn't see the woman standing there, Isabel who was so concerned about desperate strangers an hour ago. She's completely absorbed in looking at Charlie like he's going to give her something she needs. He isn't. It's an old story, and Magdalene is bored with it. She goes back to watching the plastic cassette empty out as she walks, noticing the two tiny Phillips-head screws that hold it together and thinking what she could make with the spooling mechanism inside. The tape flutters down and sticks to the ground behind them, all the way from the car out to the traffic light on Herman Road.

"I need to meet Ruth," she says. "We're picking Henry up from his friend's house. Coming, Isabel?"

No response. No sound from the parking lot now, either.

From the sky, the three of them would look like giant snails, leaving an iridescent trail of audiotape. Once they get near the bus stop, Magda puts the empty cassette with the other things in a pocket of her coat. All of it rattles together when she walks.

four

THERE IS DANNY'S Dodge when Ruth gets home from school on Monday afternoon, sitting in the front yard with four shiny, new tires. Danny has a lot of friends with useful jobs, and his car insurance is up to date. For a pothead who can't keep his hair out of his eyes, Danny is really organized. He thinks somebody just came off the road and slashed his tires for no reason. "It happens, flowergirl," he said to her on Sunday morning. Just like that, with the same goofy smile as always. Anyway, there is his car, sitting on its nice new treads and letting Ruth know there's no point going inside.

She'd like to say it's her house and he should get out, but it isn't her house, really. Never has been. Everyone thinks it would be so great to have Ruth's mother, because her mother hangs out with longhairs and listens to cool music. Nobody ever stops to think what it would mean to try to figure out what you are when your mother is already it. Nobody ever asks how it feels when you see that kind of mother crouching in the corner trying to protect her face. Her mother and all her friends, with their wide-eyed looking at Ruth like they're *really listening* to her, don't actually leave her any room to say anything at all. Nobody ever says, do you want to live with this guy? What about this one? What about the next one?

Ruth wishes she could set Danny Pavlich's car on fire and stand in the front yard, shouting out the truth while a crowd gathered, awestruck and terrified of her. Mostly, she wishes she could be like Magda. Except if she had that kind of conviction, she wouldn't waste it.

She walks around the house and through the woods to the brake repair shop. Do not pass go. Do not collect two hundred dollars. Do not stop to be gravely listened to by stoned people who pay way too much attention to you.

Driving in a car, you'd think the brake repair shop is ten minutes from Ruth's house, but really they share the same little set of backyard trees full of old beer cans and poison ivy. The same family of raccoons steals shiny things from both yards. Mr. Macanajian owns the shop and the only other person who works there is a young guy who is maybe related to him. The young guy is the creepy one. Mr. Macanajian is skinny and talkative and his hands are always clean, which is weird for a mechanic. He has a blue union suit with a perpetual pack of Marlboros in the breast pocket, and he doesn't seem to think it's wrong for kids to smoke.

That's how Ruth got to know him, bumming cigarettes. She goes to Macanajian's brake repair shop a lot, when home gets to be too much. Break. Repair. Today, though, she is on a mission.

Ruth wants to know about the brakes on Danny's car.

Mr. Macanajian has one of those square pits someone can stand down inside of while somebody else pulls a car over it. A light on a cord hangs by a hook in the side of the pit. It would take a lot of trust to stand down in there while someone parked a car on top of you. What if they slipped? What if they pulled that light cord out of the socket? What if they were busy trying to feel up the girl who lived in the house behind the shop and they forgot about you and left you in there with two tons of Cadillac parked on top of you? That pit is like a grave that isn't quite big enough for a car to be buried in, but it's big enough for at least fifteen bodies.

Anyway, it's just Mr. Macanajian in the shop right now, no creepy, touchy-feely kid, and he isn't using the pit. He's flushing the brakes on some guy's Lincoln. Ruth asks him for a cigarette, and they stand out front because he won't smoke near the cars.

"So," she says. "What does that mean, flushing the brakes?" She maybe should have led up to it, but he doesn't seem to think it's a weird question.

"If the system gets water in it, your brakes can fail when the water burns off," Mr. Macanajian says. "Anyway, what are you learning at school, then, kid? Why don't you tell me what they teach you in history or something? You're not gonna be a mechanic when you grow up, are you?"

He means it as a joke. Ha, ha, girl mechanic. He never met Magda.

"Why not?"

"You look like the college type."

Ruth laughs out loud. "Are you serious? You can see my house from here, Mr. Macanajian. So, how does the water get in there?"

"Finish that cigarette and I'll show you." He isn't creepy, but there aren't that many men who won't show Ruth whatever she asks them to. Usually, Ruth wishes she had someone else's body, but today she'll use what she's got. Or maybe Mr. Macanajian actually just likes her as a person, who knows? Weirder things have definitely happened.

By the time they come out of the garage, Ruth is pretty sure she can find the master cylinder on Danny's car. She looks up into the bright sky, soaking in the blankness through her eyes. Mr. Macanajian says he has to go back to work, so she sits down on the side of the road in front of his shop, trying to keep her mind still by staring at the oil making rainbows in the road. Half of her is making a plan, and half of her is trying not to. She grips the cement curb with both hands, trying to breathe herself into its weight, trying to quiet down the argument that's always going on in her head lately. Is she the person who messes with someone's brakes to make them go away? Is she the person who just hides in her room while her mother gets hit in the face by some shithead? Well, yeah, she is, because she's already done that. Is there some kind of middle ground between those two things? Is she a middle-ground kind of person?

A shadow falls over Ruth, and a big, white thigh stretches out next to her.

"Hey." It's Doris, who lives with the bikers across the road.

"Hey," Ruth says. She can't think of anything else.

Doris has cutoffs on and overly blond hair, bleached and curled like a waitress in a truck stop.

"You again, eh?" she says.

"Nope, actually just one continuous me since last time I saw you."

"Very funny. Cute. What've you been up to, girlie?" She actually says that, *girlie*.

Ruth met Doris a couple weeks before. She's pretty much the most interesting thing that's happened in South Highbone in ages. Maybe ever.

Around Easter-time, Doris and her biker boyfriend and the rest of them just dropped into town from someplace else. All of the sudden they all seemed to live in the old garage across from the brake repair shop. Well, it's a garage now that they've moved into it, anyway. It looks more like an old barn, clapboards and huge yellow doors you could drive a tank through. Now it opens up every day around noon and a dozen motorcycles pour out, roaring towards the beach. Doris rides in the sidecar of her boyfriend's pink trike.

It would have been pretty hard not to notice her. Everything about Doris is big. Not fat, big. Big thighs, big eyes, big, matronly tits, and enough blond for three truck stop waitresses if it came down to it. Doris talks to Ruth like them talking is just normal.

She looks at her straight, not up or down.

"Know any place they're hiring in Highbone?" She doesn't seem to notice that Ruth is barely old enough to have working papers.

"You can pretty much always get a job at the supermarket," Ruth says. "People don't stay long."

"I'm not too good at sitting still and smiling at housewives." Doris squints her eyes with a little, sarcastic smile. "What else?"

"My mom cleans houses in the village. Sometimes I help her. Could you do that?"

"Rich people don't tend to feel comfortable giving me their keys for some reason. What else?"

Ruth just laughs. "Does your boyfriend drop you off? Maybe it's the trike."

"Then they're just stupid. That trike is the ultimate possession. No one who gets to ride around on that needs to steal anything."

"Except maybe gas."

"I like you, girlie." Doris slaps Ruth on the thigh. "You look like a forties movie star, but you're not stuck-up. How does that work?"

"Uh, I only just turned fifteen. I live in South Highbone. There's a 90 percent chance my dad is some married guy from the village, but my mom seems to be living with a clammer who's about ten years younger than her. I'm only guessing he lives with us, though, 'cause she hasn't actually told me yet. I don't really have that much to be stuck-up about."

"Your dad get visits?"

"Are you kidding? People in Highbone Village don't admit they knocked up their cleaning ladies. And if the cleaning ladies talked about it, they'd never work again. Anyway, I'm not 100 percent sure it's him. It's not like anyone ever bothered to explain it to me."

"Look, girlie, in a few years it won't matter. You're smart." Doris looks Ruth up and down like maybe smart is something that shows on you somewhere. "I can tell that already. And, shit, I wouldn't leave you alone with *my* boyfriend. Wanna see my new tattoo?"

She pulls the leg of her shorts up an extra inch to show it off. On the inside of her thigh, all the way up, it says *just a kiss away.*

Ruth takes a minute to figure out what to do with that image.

"So, where did you move here from, anyway?" she asks.

"Around," Doris says. "We stay moving."

Somewhere, there is a place where women get tattoos like that. Ruth would like to live there, whether Magda wants to or not. That makes her a little dizzy. It's the first time she can ever remember wanting to go anywhere without Magdalene.

"You wanna come in for a smoke?" Doris waves her hand at the bikers' garage.

"I have to meet my friends." Ruth gets up, hesitates, then holds a hand out for Doris to grab on to.

"You don't have to be scared of us, girlie. Don't you trust me yet?" Doris nearly pulls Ruth over when she grabs her hand and heaves herself off the curb. "We don't steal kids, I swear."

"No, really. My friends get bitchy if you stand them up. I'll come another time. Promise."

There are a lot of things circling around Ruth's head. She needs somewhere quiet to think about everything she's learned today—master cylinders and the boiling point of brake fluid and the new self that seems to be struggling to take over her body. And Doris. How does she get to have a life like that? She can roar down roads on a giant pink trike, live in barns with guys everyone's scared of, and tattoo instructions for them on the inside of her thighs.

One thing Ruth noticed right away: none of Doris's friends are girls.

Later, out on 25A, Ruth watches Isabel running towards her with Henry riding piggyback.

"Flap your wings, Henry! Flap as hard as you can!" Isabel shouts.

Magda is behind them, watching them like Isabel might drop her little brother and break him. Isabel pretends it's Henry making them go faster. Henry isn't laughing. He flies past Ruth with a look on his face like he's actually making the physical effort it would take to carry them along. Henry is so little he can believe anything, which is a kind of magic all by itself. What does it take to make that go away? Ruth wants it back, that little-kid belief.

The road out of the village has the junior high school and the public library on it. The trees that line the sidewalks thin out and then disappear at the highway. There is a gas station that sells cigarettes, a Dunkin' Donuts, and a twenty-four-hour supermarket. This is the road of real life. The village by the harbor might as well be on the back lot at Universal. They put all the ugly stuff, the gas and the junk food and the shocking pink doughnut shops, up here on 25A, out of the way of their sailboats and their nice old houses. And the people who clean their houses and mow their lawns, they stick them up here, too.

Henry laughs now, lying with Isabel on the last patch of grass before the supermarket. His tinkling voice comes back to Ruth and Magda, and Isabel shouts.

"We flew! Did you guys see that?"

Right now it's sunlight and six-year-olds laughing, but in a few hours, it will be dark and the streetlights will come on. Ruth can picture the days opening and closing on that strip, and the stream of people who move through it, always on their way to somewhere else, some pretend place like Highbone Village. She can see the nights and days flickering past like a speeded-up film, and the people moving through them. In fact, you never really get to the other place. You may be on your way somewhere, but you always circle back, for milk and cigarettes and plastic crap you don't need. Right up here is where everyone is actually going, all the time. People move through this gasoline wilderness like the coming and going of the light itself.

It has no poetry in the daytime. Just oil stains on the asphalt and women in flowered housedresses buying frozen peas. At night, the normal people are gone, safe in their houses. The fluorescents in the supermarket send their green tinge out to meet the yellow of the sodium lights along the road. Together, they make a light that's like carnivals and slot machines and strip joints. It has a kind of sick romance. Demented syphilitics from the VA hospital outside Carter's Bay are drawn to it like moths. They stash their medications and sneak out at the midnight staff change for coffee and doughnuts and cigarettes from the gas station. Sometimes, Ruth and Isabel and Magda come out through their bedroom windows in the small hours and sit at the counter in Dunkin' Donuts. They buy bottomless coffees and watch the trucks go by, listening to the adrenaline ranting of broken men in mismatched uniforms and planning their escape from Highbone.

At Ruth's house, Danny's car is still in the front yard. Inside, Danny sits on the couch eating granola and watching something black-and-white. He smiles and says hello, combing his hair out of his face with his fingers and casually sliding the ashtray under the couch with one foot.

"Smooth, Danny," Ruth says. "Where's Mom?"

"I haven't seen her; I was just going to ask you. We're supposed to go to the beach tonight for a bonfire. I was gonna help her make tabbouleh and teach her how to make *stangle*." Then he notices Henry. "Hey! How's it going, li'l man?"

Ruth stops in the kitchen doorway to breathe everything in. There are pictures of Leslie West and Janis Joplin on the refrigerator and a green enamel teakettle on the stove, and it smells like spices and old linoleum and dust. That is their smell, hers and her mother's. Couldn't they have just a few months without some sweaty pothead covering it up?

Isabel fills the kettle and lights the gas burner with a match from the box on the counter. "I like it here," she says. "Everything just fits. When I have a house, it'll be like this. No one will have to pretend to be different than they are."

"Grass. Greener," Ruth says.

"I love you, Isabel." Henry stands in the doorway next to her, looking torn between their conversation and Danny's TV movie.

"I love you too, Henry."

"I love you, Ruth, but I'm going to marry Isabel. Dad says I can't marry Magda."

"No one is going to marry anyone, Henry." Magdalene is washing out mugs at the sink. "Marriage is an outmoded patriarchal institution invented to sustain capitalism and control women. It's a sucker's game for everyone involved. Got that?"

"But I want to marry Isabel."

"You better tell him, Isabel."

"I'm not marrying anyone because . . . what Magda said. But I can love you forever, Henry. How's that?"

"Can we live in the same house?"

"Maybe. We'll see."

Henry turns to walk through to the living room, where he hauls himself up on the couch next to Danny and settles in. Isabel is rifling through an inlaid wooden box full of tea bags and herbs at the kitchen table.

"Ruth, why does your mom have wormwood in here?" Isabel waves a baggie at her.

"She tried to make absinthe. It's illegal."

"Way to go, putting a label on it," Magda says to the window over the sink.

"I like your mom for trying to make absinthe. I like Danny. He's cool."

"He's temporary, Isabel. Don't get attached," Ruth says.

"Should we take bets?" Magda puts three mugs on the table. "I'm going for six months."

"He cooks and he's already been around for six months. I'll give him eight, tops. And I should know; I live here. Anyway, if he doesn't go by then, I'll throw him out myself. I'm sick of this boyfriend shit."

Isabel throws three Sleepytime tea bags at Ruth. "Have some of this and chill out. It's kind of like Valium, but cheaper. Anyway, Henry likes Danny."

"Because he watches bad TV all day," Magda says from the floor in front of the sink. She's tightening the handle of a cupboard with a butter knife. "You'd never catch my dad watching Laurel and Hardy. Danny is Henry's idea of the perfect man. There's no pressure about the guy."

"Yeah," Ruth says, "but how useful do you think he'd be on one of those days when they've turned the electricity off and delivered an eviction notice and the school is calling to see where I've been for the past two weeks and there's nothing in the house to eat but rancid tofu and dry spaghetti? He's too young."

"Young can be good," Magda says. "He's not remotely scary."

"Yeah, well, scary kind of sneaks up on ya, in case you two

haven't noticed. You guys go in my room. I'll check my mom's room for some cigarette money."

"What about them?" Magdalene looks through to the living room, where Henry has carefully arranged himself in a slouch identical to Danny's.

"Watch me deal with Danny," Ruth says. "See how it's done. You go through first."

She stops as they pass through the living room and makes urgent, stifling gestures at Danny with her hands. "Isabel is having an . . . um . . . emergency. I'm gonna go in Mom's room and see if I can find something."

"That's cool," Danny says. "Leave the little guy with me and Stan and Ollie so he can learn to be a real man."

Magda and Isabel are already stretched out on Ruth's bed when she comes in with a handful of nickels. In her room, stolen clothes from Attic Antiques hang from hooks on the walls, and there are prints of old paintings taped up everywhere.

"See?" She shuts the door and leans against it, whispering. "Just suggest the idea of menstrual blood and you get all-areas access and free babysitting thrown in." She opens the lid on a portable record player and moves the needle straight to "Gates of Eden" while Isabel counts out the change.

"So, Ruth," Magda says, "check it out. Charlie thinks he can rob Matt Kerwin."

"I do actually like Charlie, you know," Isabel says. "Have you noticed that, Magda?"

"You don't like Charlie, Isabel, you need him. He fucks you and then doesn't call you for three months. Now he's back around, and you're acting like his lapdog again. It's boring."

"You don't sound bored, Magda. You sound pissed off. How is it any of your business who fucks me and what they do after?"

"Will you two stop it?" Ruth puts a hand up between them. "Of course it's her business, Isabel. That's who we are. We watch out for each other."

"No we don't. What about the bonfire? Isabel obviously doesn't tell us everything, Ruth."

"If you're talking about what I burned, forget it. I'm allowed to have a private life."

"Yeah, Isabel, okay. So what is this about Charlie and Matt?"

"At the mall Charlie told us he was gonna rob Matt Kerwin's house." Magda has rolled on her side to look at a print of Rembrandt's *Anatomy Lesson*. She speaks to the wall. "If he steals all the pot, Matt can't call the cops on him. How's he gonna get caught? Even for Charlie, it has a certain elegance."

"No, wait," Ruth says. "You guys don't understand about Matt. He's complicated. His life, I mean."

"Yeah, yeah. We get it, Ruth. Hey, big guy, please could you use me like a condom and toss me out of the car into a badly lit parking lot? It fulfills me."

"No, Magda. I'm not an idiot, and I'm not into Matt Kerwin. I'm saying he's actually a cool person and he's had a hard time. He's my mom's friend. I don't want Charlie to screw him over for no reason."

It isn't really any of that. It's just that the sound of Matt's name coming out of Magda's mouth makes all the things in her head start circling around again. Matt lives in South Highbone, too. Hearing Magda and Isabel open up his life and talk about it gives her a sick jolt, like a piece of her skin's been turned inside out.

"What, you think we should warn him? Why do we have to be the ones with the standards? Don't you think that's kind of a scam?"

This can't be Magdalene, because for the second time today Ruth doesn't like what she's saying, wants to argue with her. Magdalene Warren is the kind of person you follow without thinking about it. When they were little, playing at the Warrens' house while Ruth's mother cleaned, Magda was the one who could fix the broken toys and open the locked doors. She could touch the world and make it do what she wanted. When Ruth first learned about magnets, the word made sense to her right away because it sounded so much like Magda. She doesn't have any memories from before Magda was there, rattling around next to her.

Dylan says, *There are no kings inside the gates of Eden.* The room spins a little and then stands still.

"There's no 'have to,' Magda," she says. "Since when is Charlie Ferguson your moral compass? You're just not that mean. Not even close."

Ruth puts "Gates of Eden" back to the beginning and climbs under an old piece of tulle she has tacked across one corner of her room. There is a big pillow on the floor behind it, where she lies down to listen. Behind the veil she can just drift, because she believes she can. Like Henry. Isabel and Magda are still there on the other side, smoking and talking over each other, but now she doesn't have to believe they're real.

"The truth just twists. Its curfew gull it glides," Dylan says.

She wants to think about Doris, where she's from and where she'll go next. What it would take to be like her. Maybe not with a biker boyfriend, but definitely with the guts to just ride away whenever you feel like it, and tattoo what you want on your body for the world to read. Sometimes, people drop into your life and change the way you see things. It's only after it happens that you realize how ready you were.

She needs to think about Danny and brake systems, too. And what kind of person she actually is now if she isn't just someone who follows Magda around.

They're still talking on the other side of the veil. They might be talking to her, but it doesn't matter. The space inside Ruth is opening up, filling with people and things that belong to just her. It's giddy and breathless, suddenly having a purpose and a reason. When it rises up and takes over, nothing outside of her matters.

She is light and separate, in a world inside the world. Turns out it isn't that things don't make sense without Magda; it's just that Ruth speaks a whole other language.

"All and all can only fall, with a crashing but meaningless blow."

five

WHEN MAGDA GETS home on Thursday afternoon, Jeff Snyder is in her driveway with the hood up on her father's Volvo. It's Magda's job to keep Henry away while Jeff works on the car. But why would Henry stay away when the hood is up and someone is revving the engine by pulling a pin inside? He is fascinated; he's never seen the guts of a car. Kids never think about the insides of things until they see them.

Isabel and Ruth don't know Jeff, and that's pretty much what's good about him. She could mention him, but she doesn't. She saves up all the days when she comes home and Jeff is there, working for her dad. She keeps them to herself like the rest of the stuff in her pockets, because they shine and have a mechanism all their own. The rules are different. She doesn't have to be Magda. It's like having a life inside her life, one where she doesn't have to be in charge.

Jeff's hair isn't long, but it isn't short either. It falls down sideways while he leans over the carburetor. She holds Henry up to see the engine.

"It looks like one of your toys, Magda," Henry says.

"That's the fuel line," she says, "where the gas goes into the carburetor and gets mixed with air."

Jeff twists his head around and raises his eyebrows, but then he smiles at her, not Henry.

"You should have a car, Magda," Henry says.

"You're not wrong, small guy," she tells him.

"Just hang on to him so he doesn't stick his hand in here." She can't help liking him then. Someone else stopping to think about whether Henry might get hurt is such a relief it almost makes a sucker out of her.

"What are they making you read in English?" He doesn't turn around or raise his voice. Like if she hears him that's good but if not that's okay, too.

"*Sister Carrie*. It's good," she says, because she isn't going to pretend not to like English just to impress Jeff Snyder. Leave that to Isabel.

He knows all about *Sister Carrie* and about how Chicago grew at the end of the nineteenth century and how big businesses moved out there and the people flocked in, looking for work. Jeff works at Speedy Mufflers, but he's taking two history classes at Stony Brook. One on Immigration from 1880 to 1920 and one on Westward Expansion and the American Myth. The titles of college classes have actual meanings. Not like "English" or "Math." Why can't high school teachers use their imaginations like that?

"You know, those big dirty new cities were exciting because people actually believed all that American dream crap. They actually thought they could roll the dice and wind up like J. P. Morgan, right up until they wound up living in Hoovervilles with their babies dying of lung disease." He's all excited now, waving his hands around. He's on a roll.

"Cigarette?" He holds out a Player's Navy Cut and she likes him a little bit more.

She looks up at the house. "Um, can't right now."

He nods. "Let's take a little walk with the small guy."

He kind of saunters, so she and Henry can follow him around the corner. It's afternoon, but the light is still pale, and the maple leaves are that crazy new green they always are in May. She pulls one off a tree to show Henry the caterpillar rolled up inside. The new leaf is thin as a bat wing and tears easy. Around the corner in the Kennedys' side yard there's a pussy willow, and Henry wants to touch it.

Jeff looks up at the corner to make sure the Warrens' house has disappeared, then smiles with half his mouth. "Cigarette?" he says again, and she takes one.

Henry is on one of the Kennedys' swings, pumping his little legs and going nowhere.

"So, why'd they name you Magdalene?" Jeff asks.

"It's a combination of my mother and father. She's Italian and he's a snob, so they needed something Catholic, but artsy. I guess

Magdalene was it, but it's a little like a label of doom."

He laughs. He gets it. "Smart *and* funny," he says.

She pushes Henry's swing and tells him about her grandparents stomping grapes in Calabria and coming here to have a farm in mid-island and then a restaurant on 25A. She can't stop talking because she can see him looking sideways at the details of her. His eyes stop on her hair and then her hands, resting on them like a guy with plenty of money looking at a new car. She can barely hear what she's saying herself, because all she can think about is what her own body is doing. She feels dizzy and sick and she just wants to get away from those eyes.

"So, you know why people came here from Italy, don't you? It's like I was saying before—"

"I gotta go," Magda interrupts him, and Jeff looks like she slapped him. Then he looks a little insulted.

"What, I'm talking too much for you?"

"No, I just have to do stuff."

He isn't looking at her anymore. He's looking at the end of his cigarette, and Magda has a little, uncontrollable sense of loss.

"You coming back tomorrow?" she says before she can tell herself not to.

"Maybe. Depends whether I finish."

Magda feels like she stole ten thousand dollars then dropped it off a cliff, just because she didn't have the guts to spend it.

Well, that's another reason not to tell Isabel and Ruth about him. Turns out Magdalene is as desperate as anybody else for somebody to pay attention to her.

six

NONE OF IT adds up. Isabel stands with Henry at the entrance to Highbone Park and everything that's wrong is right in front of them. What does it take for people not to notice? At the other end of Main Street some kind of afternoon service bells are ringing on the Methodist church. There are two perfect rows of maple trees stretching down each side of the park, two paths of asphalt, and one bandstand making the end of the vista, perfectly placed to mirror the end of the pier out in the harbor. And it's full of bodies.

Not dead bodies, exactly. Partially present, partially mobile, and they have, in most cases, the majority of their limbs. They are all men, they are all breathing, and several of them have words pouring out of their mouths in steady, free-associative streams. They have been to Vietnam.

There are other, overlapping, sets of bodies. Like the 'Nam

vets, they're sitting in circles on the grass and draped over the bandstand steps. The difference is, none of them are over twenty years old. They haven't been anywhere at all. Most of them never will go anywhere. It's all so sick and tragic, Isabel can't understand how people pretend it isn't.

"Where's Magda, Isabel?" Henry pipes up, and she remembers it's her job to distract him while Magda and Ruth have a smoke behind the bandstand.

"She went with Ruth for a minute. Come on, guy, let's see if we can spot a water rat."

"Do they bite, Isabel?" Henry looks askance at the rocks piled at the edge of the harbor.

"Not when you're with me they don't. Look, it's Lefty!" Isabel waves.

"He doesn't have a hand, Isabel. I don't like it. Magda says one day I'll start to have dreams about stuff I don't like."

"He does have a hand. Look, the right one is still there. Come on. You won't dream about Lefty because you'll talk to him and your little brain will be satisfied. You only have nightmares about stuff you're chicken about. If you're ever worried you'll have a nightmare about something, just walk right up to it and start a conversation. 'Dark Shadow,' you say, 'what's it like being you? You should know, Dark Shadow, Isabel says you're not allowed to bother me.' Try it. It works."

Isabel holds out her iced tea for Lefty, because he likes the lemon ice cubes.

"Hey, Lefty, have you met my friend Henry?"

"Henry the Fourth," Lefty says, taking Isabel's cup with a little old-fashioned bow. "Henry the Fourth estate. Henry the Fifth column." Lefty is mostly there, and also someplace else at the same time. Nonstop poetry, but most people don't see it that way.

"Hi," Henry says.

"Hi, small person. Magdalene is your sister, your Holy Harlot Mother, mister. Isabel is nice, too. She's a good friend to have."

"I'm gonna marry her."

"You're a little short, aren't you? Short change, Mr. Strange. You can't get married yet."

"When I'm taller, I mean." Henry doesn't miss a beat. Lefty makes perfect sense to him.

He does make perfect sense, in the context. He breaks the spell of Highbone. He sees everything they see, but he's never mad. Gentleness wafts off him. Considering everything, it's weird that Lefty isn't scarier.

Ruth is calling them from the bandstand steps, pointing to the shrubs behind and waving them over. "We gotta go. Oh, Henry, we forgot to look for water rats."

"That's okay. It was nice to meet you, Lefty."

"Nice to meet *you*, Oh Henry," Lefty says. "Henry the Eighth wonder of the world."

Once they're out of earshot Isabel says, "You're a good little man, Hank, a very nice guy. Don't you forget it."

"I'm not scared of him, Isabel. I won't have a dream. Why doesn't he have a hand?"

"I told you, he does have a hand. Always be accurate, little guy. What you mean is, why doesn't he have two hands?"

"You are the smartest one, Isabel. Why doesn't he have two hands?"

"No, I am not the smartest one. Your sister is. Everyone knows that. You need to ask *her* about Lefty's hands."

Behind the bandstand, Magda is sitting in a patch of slanting sun unscrewing a cassette case with the screwdriver on her Swiss Army knife.

"What are you making, Magda?" Henry says. "Why doesn't Lefty have two hands, Magda?"

"He lost one. Don't worry, it can't happen to you. I don't know what I'm making yet. I'm still dreaming it."

"Cop," Ruth says, looking over Isabel's shoulder towards the entrance to the park.

"Where?"

Isabel turns around, and it's him, the one with the thing for teenage legs. The one who thinks Isabel is meaningless and disposable just because she isn't a cheerleader whose dad owns a bank or something.

"So," she says, "this is probably a good time to tell you guys."

Magda looks at her like she's already decided it's stupid, whatever it's going to be. The cop is making a beeline for them.

"Uh, I kind of stole something from his car the other day."

"From who?" Ruth looks around at Lefty.

"Not Lefty. The cop."

"You what?!" Well, the look on Magda's face isn't superior and dismissive anymore. Ruth just gets up and walks away towards the water. Henry follows her.

"Well, I was kind of pissed off. He was weird to me. Anyway, he's so arrogant he just leaves his wallet sitting in the car with the window open. He thinks no one can ever touch him."

"No one can, Isabel. Welcome to America. So, I just wanna check, you stole a wallet from a cop?"

"Yeah. He deserved it."

"Okay, good. I'm sure that'll really teach him a lesson about the basic humanity of people like you. Where's the wallet now?"

"I threw it away."

"Well, there's a silver lining. Here he comes; try not to do anything stupid for the next five minutes."

"I see you're wearing shoes today, Miss . . . ?"

"Ferguson. I'm Isabel Ferguson."

The cop turns around to watch Ruth skipping stones with Henry by the water. It's some cop tactic, pretending Magda and Isabel aren't there. Also, all guys look at Ruth. All the time.

"You didn't see anyone hanging around my car the other day, did you, Miss Ferguson?" Subtle. He obviously thinks he's Columbo.

"No. Why?"

But he is already walking away, without looking at them or saying good-bye.

"So which part of 'don't do anything stupid' did you not understand?" Magda spreads out a bandanna and lays the open cassette and its little screws out.

"What?"

"You told him your name was Ferguson. That seemed like a plan?"

"Yeah. I didn't want him to look me up."

"This isn't the Bronx, Isabel. It's Highbone. He doesn't have to *look you up.*"

"You know what, Magda? Never mind. I have an idea."

"Another one. Great?"

"Ruth! Come back."

Henry comes first, and Ruth walks half backwards, still staring out over the harbor.

"So," Isabel says, "this robbery plan of Charlie's. What if we do it?"

"Henry, can you go over there and throw this away?" Magdalene hands him some tissues from one of her pockets. "Just to fill you in, Ruth, Isabel thinks she's a criminal mastermind now. She stole a wallet from that cop."

"Yep, I heard the first time. What does that have to do with Matt's weed?"

"Nothing," Isabel says. "Well, I mean, no one ever thinks we matter. No one even thinks we're important enough to be in the way. Charlie thinks we can't do anything remotely useful or dangerous because we're girls. If we stole the weed and then surprised Charlie with it, he'd have to admit we're as good as him."

"Oh, I get it. Charlie's about to dump you. Again. So you think me and Ruth should go to jail so you can impress him enough to make him keep paying attention to you."

"Okay, look," Ruth says. "Matt's mother is sick. In the head, sick. She goes all catatonic. He used to have to spoon-feed her, until they took her away. He lives by himself, watching *Twilight Zone* and reading about outer space. He's a person. This idea is messed up."

"Everyone is a person, Ruth." Magda points to the edge of the park, where an English Ford swishes past the shrubbery on Baywater Avenue. Behind the wheel is Mrs. Hancock, who's married to the guy who owns the yacht club. She has orange lipstick and big round sunglasses on. If Isabel had those glasses and that car, she wouldn't waste them on Baywater Avenue.

"That," Magda says, pointing at Mrs. Hancock, "is a fucking person."

Henry runs back full tilt from the garbage pail and Magda puts out an arm to keep him from stepping on her bandanna.

"Mrs. Hancock is the person I never want to be," Ruth says. "Which, you know, is my point."

"What's so wrong with Mrs. Hancock?" Isabel cranes her neck to see over onto Baywater Avenue. "She looks kind of cool, for a suburban wife, I mean. Maybe she's just trapped."

"Ruth's mother works for her, Isabel. She's married to Harold goddamned Hancock, Mr. Big Man Yacht Club Owner. She's climbed the pathetic social ladder of Highbone and now she thinks she can spit on us from the top. She's not remotely *cool*."

"One of the first things I remember," Ruth says, "is trying to sit perfectly still in that woman's kitchen while my mother was cleaning. Mrs. Hancock always noticed me, though, no matter how still I sat. She has freaky weird eyes that kind of gather up light and use it on you like a knife."

"Her and my mom hung out," Magda says. "I wonder if she sends her letters."

"I used to sit on a chair in their kitchen and Mrs. Hancock would come in and cut right through me with those eyes. When I was little, I had dreams where she was standing in my bedroom doorway, staring at me and sucking all the air out of the room, like in the movies when there's a hole in an airplane. She's just messed up, Isabel. Trust me."

"It looks like bicycle wheels!" Henry says, reaching for the pieces of Magda's cassette.

"Don't touch, big guy. I'll let you play with it when it's all done." Magda stands up and slips the tiny screws into the watch pocket of her Levi's.

"We're not helping Charlie rob Matt, Isabel," Ruth says. "If you try, I'll tell him it's you."

When did Ruth stop being the sidekick? She stands there in the falling sun looking full of scary purpose, like she just slew a dragon or robbed a bank and got away with a million dollars and not a scratch on her. Actually, maybe two million. Ruth already looks like a million dollars anyway. All the time.

seven

RUTH WALKS INTO Old Mr. Lipsky's living room and finds him sitting on the couch under the picture of his beautiful, dead wife.

"All done, Mr. Lipsky," she says. "Everything's shipshape. Even my mom would approve."

Manny Lipsky's apartment is above his son's bookstore. You get to it up the stairs in the alley behind Main Street. She took the job off her mother because Old Mr. Lipsky is probably the coolest person in town. You can talk to him about pretty much anything. Also, he gets that most people in Highbone are boring.

"Sit down. I'll make coffee. And call me Manny or you'll get me confused with the kid."

"Nah, I definitely won't. And let me make the coffee." Ruth puts her cleaning bucket down by the door to the stairs.

While the coffee is percolating, she stands in the kitchen doorway and watches him. He looks like he forgot she's there at all. In the picture above him, his wife has that hair that people's grandmothers had when they were surprisingly beautiful in black and white. Even though she is long gone, Ruth can see that she hovers over Manny like some kind of angelic ghost. Ruth brings two coffee cups out from the little kitchen and puts coasters on the glass coffee table.

"So, what is it today, little movie star?" He always calls her that.

"I don't know, Mr. Lipsky. Everything seems like it's shifting around lately. It's like I woke up from a dream where all the crazy stuff made sense and in the awake world it doesn't. Sometimes, I'm just really mad. I mean, why do people keep going around in pointless circles? It just gets to me."

"I told you, call me Manny."

"Sorry, Manny. I think I just want to start taking charge of stuff, you know? I mean, it doesn't seem like anyone else is gonna do it right."

"You know what I think? I think you're meant for bigger, faster places. You were born sparkling. Life should be like one long roller coaster for you. If you like roller coasters, I mean. I don't think it's this place moving around; I think it's you."

"I used to think that about Magdalene's mom," Ruth says. "You knew her, didn't you? I always thought she wasn't supposed to be here. Now she isn't. I keep trying to imagine her new life."

"Irene, you mean? Irene Buonvicino she was, before she got married. Your little friend, the daughter, looks just like Irene used to look."

"Milk or black, Mr. Lipsky?"

"Milk. Stomach goes when you're old. Black coffee could kill me instead of waking me up."

"Oh, I don't think so, Mr. Lipsky. You have too much left to say. You can't die yet."

"It could happen midsentence; don't kid yourself." He chuckles and puts both hands around his coffee cup. That's what Manny Lipsky has decided to do about age and death, laugh in its face. He does it all the time.

"Little Irene was a looker," he says. "You know, all the boys wanted to take Irene Buonvicino out on Saturday night. Her parents were old-world though, and the boys had to get past her brother, little Tony, too. It was gonna take guts to marry that girl."

"You know, Mr. Lipsky." He points a finger at her. "Manny, I mean. I used to think Magda's mom was a queen or an angel. I've been going to their house since I was really little. When my mom read me stories like 'Bluebeard' or *The Lord of the Rings*, I pictured all the women to look like Mrs. Warren. I thought Professor Warren was the ogre."

"Well, yeah."

"Mrs. Warren had something shining out of her, you know what I mean? Like your wife." She points to the photograph, and Old Mr. Lipsky beams at her. "Luminous," she says.

"Yes," he says. "Luminous."

Isabel is friends with the son, the bookstore man, but the dad is the one with the soul in the Lipsky family. Why can't she see that?

Ruth shouts good-bye and closes the door at the bottom of the stairs behind Mariner's Maps and Books. It'll be dark soon, half-way Highbone all over again. She heads down to the end of the pier and sits where she can't see anything but water. No Danny, no Isabel, no Magda, no kid from Macanajian's garage. No lurching terrible visions of how the world really is. No decisions to make about whether she's brave enough to change anything at all. If you can just let go, all the thoughts get washed in sea and sky.

When the orange is gone from the clouds Ruth stands up and heads in, just in time to see Doris and her boyfriend roar up to a parking space at the end of Main Street. They're not on the trike, they're in a green Impala. Doris opens the passenger door and shouts hello. Her hair and her pink fingernails stand out on Main Street like colors from a different movie. Her boyfriend cranes his neck out the driver's window to look Ruth up and down. Doris says, does Ruth want to go to the beach, and waves at the backseat.

"This is Marvin." Doris points at her boyfriend. Marvin? Really? "Come with us down to Fiddler's Cove." It isn't an order, but it isn't a question either.

Doris throws herself over the front seat and opens the back door for Ruth, then sits back down, puts Golden Earring's "Leather" in the tape deck, and starts singing like she forgot about Ruth already. Once they're moving, Doris throws her head back on the seat and sings louder.

They park at Fiddler's Cove, and the three of them sit smok-ing and looking at the water like people do, acting like the beach is a drive-in movie. It's too loud for conversation anyway. Ruth tries to think what to do about her mother and Danny, about this new language that the world seems to be speaking to her, and about how no one else is going to understand it. Not even Magda, who has been telling her what everything means for so long, it's like she's inside Ruth's head, even when Ruth is alone. The water here is not as comforting as the harbor was, not as empty somehow.

When a voice comes from the seat next to her, Ruth actually jumps. She was spacing out and didn't hear the car door, but there he is. Doris and her boyfriend are still facing the sea and sing-ing with their eyes closed. Marvin, the boyfriend, is doing a little head-banging against the driver's seat.

"Seen you with those other kids downtown," the guy next to Ruth says. "You don't belong there."

She looks over, and the first thing she notices is his hair. It shines, like Magda's. Only this guy's hair is fine and straight, and it looks like he brushes it a hundred strokes a day. The color, though, that black with secret browns and reds in it when you look up close, that's the same as Magda's. His hair is like Magda's hair would be if it belonged to some kind of unholy angel.

"I looked at you and saw you right away," he says. "It's like you're lit with a different light." When he says that, she can see a rip in the fabric of space and time, with light shining through it.

An eerie gold light, falling only on her.

When she asks him his name he looks into her for a long minute, then tells his last name first. "Mackie."

"That's it?"

"My first name's Virgil, but that makes me sound like a cracker. My parents are from South Carolina. People just call me Mackie."

And that's how it starts. Before she knows it, she's telling him things she's never told Magda, things she's never even made into language before. Words are coming out of her so fast; she keeps on making sentences that don't really say what she wants them to.

"Sometimes I feel like there are two layers to everything, and I'm the only one who can see them both," she says. "Does that make any sense at all?"

He just nods and looks at her, while the music keeps blasting out of the front speakers. In the backseat, Ruth and Mackie are in a bubble where the noise in the car can't reach them. Mackie hears every word she says.

"I draw pictures, but sometimes it doesn't feel like I'm doing it. It feels like they force themselves out of me."

Saying that out loud makes the air around her turn suddenly cold, like there is no atmosphere, no earth under her, no right or wrong. It feels good. Stuff just keeps coming from her mouth into the waiting space Mackie seems to make. When she finally runs out of breath, he leans over and whispers to her.

"You're mad, aren't you? You're mad at all of them."

How does he know? She says she guesses she is. Maybe. Sometimes.

"That's because you're better than this," he says. "You're *supposed* to be different."

"You're kind of the second person to tell me that tonight."

"None of those other people are really paying attention, though. I can see you. Keep talking to me."

"How come I can, though? Why are you so easy to talk to?" He doesn't answer that. He doesn't seem to answer anything, but he knows everything before she says it.

"You want to stop things from just happening to you. That's not crazy. It makes sense. You should be in charge for a change. You want people to pay attention. I'll listen. I can help." He puts his finger to his lips. "Don't tell anyone else."

He gets out of the car then. When he stands up, his black coat falls down around his knees and the things in his pockets clink into place. He walks away without a word, leaving Ruth there in the backseat, feeling his absence. It's another five minutes before Doris stops singing and turns around.

"How you doing all by yourself back there, Lana Turner?" Doris says.

"Doin' good, Mae West."

Doris's sharp laugh goes out the window, filling up the salty dusk.

And Ruth won't. Tell anyone. She feels light and strange ever since the night of the bonfire. Changed. Like she's the kind of insect that goes to sleep and wakes up in a different shape, with shocking new abilities. It's as if Virgil Mackie appeared on the crest of a wave. She can feel it, sucking the air from around her as it rises, moving towards them all. It keeps rushing at her when she isn't looking. For the first time since she can remember, she just knows Magda and Isabel wouldn't understand.

eight

ONLY FOUR O'CLOCK on Saturday and Isabel has to stop when she comes through the door to let her eyes adjust to the darkness in her front hallway. A maple tree throws shade over most of the front lawn. Dark wood furniture and Chinese silk wall hangings make it even gloomier. Then there's the hideous wallpaper. Ruth says Isabel's mom is talking through the furniture, and they should all listen. She doesn't have to live here, obviously.

"Isabel, where is your mother?"

"Hello to you too, Dad."

"Hello, honey. Have you seen your mother?"

Her dad is so chipper; it really doesn't go with the house. Right now, he looks a little unhinged.

"I don't know; I'm not her keeper. Can I call Elizabeth?"

"I haven't seen her since I got up. She's usually right here all day on Saturday." Her father casts his eyes around the living room and then passes through the door to the garage. He looks lost.

"Dad!" Isabel follows him. "Can I call Elizabeth?"

"What do you want to call your sister for?" He says it with his back to her, staring at the garage door.

"Uh, to talk to her. What are you doing in here? You think you're gonna find Mom under the car or something?"

"It's expensive calling all the way upstate, Isabel. You need a good reason."

"Okay, you really want to know? I think something is wrong with Ruth and everything seems weird lately. I can't tell whether things are finally beginning to happen or we're just all falling apart and starting to go a little crazy."

"Ruth Carter?"

"Yes, Dad, Ruth Carter. One of my best friends for the past two years. Pay attention."

"Honey, Ruth Carter has had a tough upbringing. You know, you should be careful with her. Why don't you talk to your mother?"

"She's not here, remember? And even when she is, she isn't. You know that."

"Don't talk about your mother like that! Of course she's here for you. She's a good woman and she loves you. Imagine if Caroline Carter was your mother. Then you'd have something to complain about."

"There's nothing wrong with Ms. Carter. You are such a snob."

This is why Ruth is wrong about the house. It's all just sick, the sideboards, the wall hangings, the tacky wallpaper. They have it right there in the hallway just to announce their up-to-the-minute taste to anyone who looks in the front door. It's like these big black-and-white flowers say, "We're hip, we're cool, we're *so seventies*."

The thing her parents hate more than anything is reality. That's why her father looks so uncomfortable right now, because she told him how she actually feels. No one yells at you for it; they just space out and leave you hanging. You can *try* to tell them what life is actually like. Mostly they'll just look away at that wallpaper and pretend they didn't hear you. At least Magda's dad gets mad. It sucks, but it's something.

"I just thought maybe I could talk to Liz. I feel a little worried about stuff. She might listen to me."

"Are you sure you haven't seen your mother today?"

When it's time to go out to meet Magda at Dunkin' Donuts, Isabel puts on her big, old army pants and ties them with a long piece of nylon webbing her dad brought home from his job at Davis Marine. Then she puts on a pink satin bed jacket Ruth got her at Attic Antiques. Then her Navy sweater, since she never feels safe in the dark without it. She gathers the ends of the sleeves up in her clenched fists and heads down the stairs. There is no light on in the living room and the empty couch startles her. It's Saturday:

her mother should be there in the corner of the couch, reading Rex Stout with a glass of Dubonnet and exactly eight slices of orange cheddar on saltines filling a plate next to her on the side table.

Good she isn't there, though, because it means Isabel can get enough money for doughnuts and coffee out of the big brandy snifter full of change that sits on the sideboard. Her dad throws the coins from his pockets in there every night. To get to them, Isabel has to lift up a scrap of paper that says, "Stop stealing my change. Yes, this means you."

Something about the dark room makes Isabel shudder. She opens the front door in slow motion, like she's sneaking out, even though she isn't. Just before she closes it, she hears a scratching behind the couch. A mouse maybe, or branches on the window.

After Isabel's dark living room, the light in Dunkin' Donuts is like violence itself. From the night road it's a box of glass and chrome shining like a sick beacon, drawing the dispossessed in from the night. Them and the cops who feed off them. Everyone looks green and deflated in there, and later it's always hard to remember the details of what you've seen under the humming tubes of those fluorescents.

It's Vicky working the counter. Her hair is bleached like Jean Harlow, but with inch-deep roots as dark as FBI shoes. The pink uniform makes her look even paler than she is. She has two scabs on her chin, and you can see the scar on her upper arm from the time she ran away to the city and got cut up by a john in the subway. Vicky still has that deep, dead junkie look in her eyes. That's what makes every guy that sees her want to touch her, no matter how many other guys have been there before them. Something about that crazy emptiness turns guys on.

Whenever Vicky comes back to Highbone, she's sad and dry and clean. After a while, she has a relapse and leaves town, then reappears a few months later with another piece missing. The manager at Dunkin' Donuts always gives her the job back. He takes it out of her in trade. Everyone knows that, too.

Isabel likes to imagine the places Vicky has been to and the things she's seen, what it's like on the highways and in the train stations. She wonders who are the poets Vicky sits next to on all-night bus rides to Florida and Chicago. What kind of things have been written about the sad, beautiful junkie without a name?

"Hi, Vicky. You seen Magdalene?"

"No, honey." Vicky leans in close over the counter. "Just me and Officer Krupke tonight." She throws a glance towards the smoking end of the counter, where a motorcycle cop sits with his mirrored shades next to his coffee cup. Not Highbone Police— county cops hang out in here. The highway is the village border.

Isabel laughs. "Guess I'll sit down here and wait." No way she's sitting at the smoking end next to that guy. "Will you make me a soul coffee, Vicky?"

"Yes, Isabel, you weirdo."

"No one will make them for me when you're away."

Half coffee, half tea. She read somewhere that Thelonious

Monk drank it. It's good once you get used to it. Isabel looks out at the road.

"Charlie working tonight?"

"Yes," Vicky says. "And I'm pretty sure you knew that, missy. Think I've never been you?"

He'll be here at midnight for his baking shift. He'll work until four in the morning, and if they come back around two when he's done making the doughnuts, he'll fry them special shapes out of the extra dough. They'll ask for airplanes and Saturn and tulips, anything they can think of to stump him.

The cop at the other end of the counter raises one finger at Vicky. "More coffee, sweetheart."

"I know," Vicky answers, "just the *thought* of milk."

He thinks that makes him tough, like he's fucking Easy Rider or something. Like extra milk makes you a pansy. Isabel makes a wide circle around the back of his stool on her way to the bathroom, looking at him like he might get her dirty. Vicky smiles over the cop's shoulder with just her eyes.

There is a swing door into a little vestibule with three more doors, to the kitchen, the men's room and the ladies'. The air back there is saturated with powdered sugar, acid and invisible. After you hang out in the back with Charlie, all your clothes smell like that.

When Isabel comes out of the bathroom there's a vet from the hospital in the way, just standing outside the men's room. He has greasy bangs hanging down over his eyes, and the nervous energy that's trapped inside him is making one of his feet tap the floor fast as a roadside drill. She turns sideways to get around him, thinking about where Magda is and whether when she gets there, she'll help her find Charlie at the firemen's fair.

The guy is so quick he's under her Navy sweater before she even realizes he's moving. One hand grips her left arm like a claw and the other one is groping like a priest's, kind and soft and searching for her breasts. He's holding her just below the elbow and it shocks her how strong his hand is. A minute ago, he was practically invisible, now she can't even move to put any space between them. His jacket is three inches from her face. The words *PROTECTIVE AGAINST VESICANT GAS* are stamped over the breast pocket. He smells like Night Train and coffee and cigarettes and disinfectant.

Isabel goes still, gathering all her strength up to use in one sharp burst, then twists as hard as she can around to the right and into the swing door. She says, "Take your fucking hands off me, pig," but quietly, so the cop won't hear. Every girl knows the last thing you need after some creep tries to feel you up is a cop. The force of breaking free makes her stumble a little, but she tries to come through the door like normal. Luckily, the cop has his back to her.

Her soul coffee is waiting on the counter near the front door.

"Thanks, Vicky. You are, hands down, my favorite waitress."

Isabel's voice surprises her by shaking. Everything looks a little too big and too bright and she gets distracted by the traffic for a minute before she sits. Once her breathing slows down, her body starts speaking into the silence. There will be finger-shaped bruises on her arm. One side of her shivers like spiders are crawling up under her sweater, memory working its way out of her muscles. She picks up the mug, but her soul coffee sloshes out and she puts it down again. Vicky looks at her, then sideways at the door behind the cop, where the guy from the VA hospital is just coming through.

He sits down and tries to catch Isabel's eye, smiling a sly smile like they share a cool secret. Vicky sighs and puts a Bavarian cream down in front of Isabel without saying anything. Their eyes meet and they both know everything. Vicky's are blue and watery. Not dead, clean. Everything just washes out of them, nothing sticks.

"Magda's late, man. Where the hell is she?"

Magdalene is late. She shuts the kitchen door and walks around to stand for a few minutes in the dark under Henry's window. Isabel will be waiting at Dunkin' Donuts, wondering why Magda hasn't appeared exactly when she wanted her to. It won't occur to her that maybe Magda had to spend the afternoon and half the evening keeping Henry occupied in his room, counting whiskies until her father shut the door to his study and quieted down. They made a library out of Lincoln Logs and told a story about a librarian who kept a dragon and could knit rivers. That was Henry's idea, knitting water into a long river like a scarf. There is a lady who knits at Highbone Library. That must be what gave him the idea. He definitely has the equipment for dreaming.

She cocks her head, listening for her name, but Henry is

swimming in his own empty darkness. He won't surface until morning. The carriage house hulks in front of her at the end of the driveway, with her mother's stuff piled inside. For the past two years, Magda's father has thrown in whatever he's found as he's found it. He's still doing it. There's always a box at the bottom of the stairs in the front hall. He tosses in whatever he finds that annoys him and, when the box is full, carries it out and puts it here. Every box is a random collection of clothing, cookbooks, jewelry, exercise equipment, shoes, photographs, and makeup.

The carriage house is made of painted green planks, and there is a door near the roof that once went to a hayloft, but it's all one high-ceilinged room now. It's so full of boxes and trunks that her dad parks his Volvo in the gravel driveway. She can feel the dead piles of clothes and shoes and pictures, saying nothing at all in the dark.

"Fuck you," she says to them, and heads out towards 25A.

From the road, Magda can see Isabel sitting near the door of Dunkin' Donuts with her sneakers tucked around the back of the stool and her elbows in their tattered sweater sleeves resting on the counter. Magda comes into the light and through the door, setting off the electric bell in the kitchen.

"So, Isabel, about those papers you burned the other night?" She hoists herself onto a stool.

"Drop it, Magda. For real. Private. Life."

"While we're on the subject of private lives, you need to stop talking about how cool Mrs. Hancock is in front of Ruth."

"Why?"

"Because, Isabel, Mr. Hancock is probably Ruth's dad."

"Probably?"

"No one ever talks about it, but everyone kind of knows. It's weird. It's been like that ever since I can remember."

"Shit. I had no idea."

"You never do, O'Sullivan."

"Fine, I do now. What about Matt? What about my plan?"

"Oh, yeah, good idea, Isabel." Magda looks sideways at the cop at the end of the counter. "Let's talk about that *now*." She smiles at Vicky. "Hi, Vicky. When did you get back?"

"About a week ago. I was in Florida. I went with this guy who manages racehorses."

"Bitch!" Isabel says. "Was it warm?"

"Yeah, warmer than here. We were on the west coast, though, by the Gulf. It's nice there, but no tourists. Kind of boring, and the horse thing is really sad. They have these little spindly legs that won't heal if they break. It's like they're not supposed to be made the way they are but someone glued the wrong parts together. They have tragedy eyes."

"I wish I could go to all the places you go," Isabel says.

Vicky just laughs.

"Well, Isabel, sorry to disappoint you, but there's just the firemen's fair. No epic drama there. Nice you're back, Vicky. See you later."

There's a low, sickly sky over 25A, but it clears out into stars as they get closer to the water. Cars are moving past on Seaview

Road, all heading in the same direction they are.

"We should talk about the plan before we see Charlie."

"There is no plan, Isabel. Here's the weird thing: impressing Charlie is not a big priority for me and Ruth. Go figure."

"Fine, but I'm not giving up. We need to expand our repertoire. Develop our talents. I want Vicky's life," Isabel says. "Florida all winter, man."

"Vicky is a junkie prostitute, Isabel. What is she gonna do when she's thirty-five? That is, if some guy doesn't kill her first just 'cause that's how he gets his rocks off. It's not exactly a long-term, low-risk game plan."

"This is America, hon. Short-term, high-risk built this country. Guys will pay to look at you naked. How nuts is that? They're always gonna be grabbing us and shoving their hard-ons up against us. There's no stopping 'em; we might as well work somewhere with a bouncer and charge them for it."

"Yeah, that's really working for Vicky. 'Cause she isn't covered in scars or anything. Her life is not your amusing fantasy. Show some respect."

It never lets up. Even at night when Henry is asleep, there are Isabel and Ruth flinging themselves at destruction. She still has to be the one standing in the way. Magda flicks a cigarette butt under a passing car, wishing it would shoot up the tailpipe and explode, just to give them something else to think about. But Isabel won't let go.

"All I'm saying is, it seems like to me we're just as likely to get cut up here as Vicky is in the city. Highbone isn't exactly a psycho-pervert-free zone. How do we make the best of it, is all I'm asking."

"There is no best of it, Isabel. It's a big nasty machine, like a book by Dashiell Hammett. We're gonna get dirty."

"Yeah, Magda, but I'm thinking maybe we can get dirty without being the ones who get hurt."

Looking down on the firemen's fair makes Isabel dizzy. She and Magda lean out over the edge so they can be even dizzier. Like every year, the rides and the shooting booths and the towers of goldfish bowls and teddy bears are down there on the scrubland between the sea and a half-built executive development. You can still see it was an old gravel quarry. Isabel looks at the high sides of the pit, covered with shale, and at the expensive houses, with their acres of sod, spread out below them. There's a bare concrete slipway that was supposed to be the marina, but no boats.

Heading down the hill with all those people and all that neon underneath her, Isabel feels like she's walking down out of the sky, like one of those dreams where gravity doesn't apply. Someday her whole life will be made of moments that feel like this. When people ask "What do you want to do when you grow up?" how do you tell them that?

"What kind of sucker buys a house down there?"

"You know who buys houses down there, Isabel," Magda laughs, "the kind of people who would actually move to a town like this on purpose."

Kids are shuffling up and down the hill to the firemen's

fair, filing past each other with their fishnet stockings showing through the holes in their jeans, and their painted stencils of Jim Morrison glowing on the backs of their sleeveless denim jackets.

"You know what? I'm not knocking these idiots. At least when the bus can't get up that hill in the winter, they cancel school."

"Yeah," Magda says, "we have these superficial morons to thank for half our snow days. Those kids, you know their parents have money, okay, but also you know they're really not that smart either. I mean, why do all these new-money idiots let them put the firemen's fair down here next to their built-in pools and their perfectly laid sod?"

At the bottom, it's all cotton candy and lots of noise. Charlie is smoking in front of the Tilt-A-Whirl.

"You two, eh?" he says. "Where's little Carter?"

"At home," Isabel says. "Don't you have to go to work tonight?"

"Come on, stop making small talk. Let's go up the cliff. I just went to Matt Kerwin's house. Scoping it out and acting like a loyal customer."

So they climb back up to the top of the pit and into the Glinnicks' backyard. The yard stretches right to the edge of the cliff, completely covered with lilies that wave now in the same wind that carries the fairground screams and the carny music out onto the water. Lemon lilies, red lilies, tiger lilies, Stargazers. Isabel knows that her clothes will be streaked with yellow pollen when she gets back to the light. She stands at the edge now with Charlie and Magda, all three of them with their arms stretched out straight to the sides, like they're either flying or dying on the cross. Below them the colors of the fair are moving in circles and spinning shapes. She can't hear the music, though. The sounds are carried away from them, out to the black sea.

"Hey, Magda." She points at the sky over the slipway. "Which star is that?"

"It's a planet, Isabel."

When you sit down in the lilies, you can't see the road, just a sheer drop to the bottom of the pit. It's like when they climb the water tower, except if you're coming from their neighborhood you don't have to climb to get here. You just walk until the road stops and the earth drops away.

"So, this house is way older than the houses in the pit," she says. "Think about it. A hundred years ago, it would have been here all by itself. The village would have been way far away, and whoever lived in this house would have been all alone on this windy cliff."

"What are you talking about now, Isabel?" Charlie sits down at the edge of the yard and reaches for the Marlboro box in his pocket.

"Change the subject, Isabel. You'll make Charlie bored. You wouldn't want to do that."

Magda thinks she's pathetic. Maybe she is, but there's nothing she can do about it. She already tried.

"Why are you girls all obsessed with old stuff?" Charlie says. "It's over. It is boring. No one smoked pot or got laid, and those old clothes you're always stealing from Attic Antiques are not sexy."

Isabel can see Magda rolling her eyes, but Charlie doesn't notice.

"Um, yes, they did. Thomas Jefferson grew pot, Charlie, and if they didn't get laid, how did we get here?"

This is what happens when Magda and Charlie are together. Magda is sarcastic, Charlie doesn't get it, and neither one of them thinks Isabel is important enough to be a full partner in the conversation.

"Hey, Charlie." She tries to head them off. "You ever been down in Underground Highbone?"

"We tried to go in once, but it was high tide. Don't you guys go wandering in there by yourselves. You'll drown and people will cry and shit. Not me, other people."

"But it's really there, tunnels and rooms underneath town where there were speakeasies during Prohibition? I've been thinking about it. We need to check out Underground Highbone. It's crazy that we haven't gone in there yet. There's an adventure right under Main Street we haven't even bothered to have. It's definitely on the list of things we need to do before we leave town."

"Bunch of flooded basements, mainly." Charlie snorts. "Anyway, you're never leaving town. In twenty years you'll be right here, sitting under a hair dryer and complaining about your kids."

Isabel falls sideways into the lilies and looks up at Charlie's silhouette against the sky.

"It almost feels like summer," she says. "Soon we'll be out all night in tank tops."

It was summer the first time she was with Charlie. Last summer. He just showed up at the beach one night with everything she needed in his pockets.

It was July, and Isabel and Ruth had stolen some of Elizabeth's acid. They decided to go swimming naked and set some paper lanterns on fire in the sea. It was hot, but a bunch of football players had a bonfire farther down, under the woods at Fiddler's Cove. Isabel and Ruth were too focused on what they were doing to be scared of them, though. The air was so humid it lay on them like wet wool. They decided to swim out and lie on Captain's Rock like two naked sirens in the moonlight. Isabel thought she could write a poem about it, and then thought how Magda would roll her eyes. Magda always says angsty and trippy are Isabel's only two poetic modes. Just yesterday, she said the worst thing about Charlie is the way he causes Isabel to write poetry.

When Ruth came up from her first dive and the two of them stood waist-high in the Sound, the drops flew off them like pieces of glass, and the mud on the bottom was silky under their feet. Ruth looked even more celestial than usual, shining black and white in the moonlight. It was all absurdly beautiful. The rock held its granite face up to the sky and sparkled, looking like their mermaid bed. Isabel dove under and kicked.

When she stretched out her hand under the water, there was a mass of slimy tentacles instead of rock. She got tangled up in the kelpy strands and gasped while she was still under. It was like one of those black-and-white horror movies they have on Sundays. Part of her was thinking *Thing from the Deep* and laughing.

She came up spluttering and stood still, trying to breathe again, shaking and staring while her skin tightened and the salt dried on her arms. The surface of the water is such a thin line between two completely alien worlds. That thought seemed really profound at the time, what with the acid and all.

Later, Charlie came down and found them with their clothes halfway on, and Ruth disappeared somewhere. After a while, Isabel wound up with Charlie on the wooden stairway that goes up the cliff. Just like now, she could see the sky through his corkscrew curls. It was a toenail moon that night. She knew which stars were really planets without asking Magda, by the difference in their colors. Red Mars and yellow Saturn. It was so clear, she wondered why she'd never noticed before.

The weird part was, when Charlie kissed her, her first thought was about her and Ruth and Magda, about how they could do anything. They could have anything they wanted. It seemed like being there with Charlie was her idea, the thing she wanted, and it would all go the way she wanted it to.

Well, it turns out you can only take what you want sometimes. Other times, you get shoved up against bathroom walls by syphilitic 'Nam vets. Everything has its ups and downs. Isabel laughs now, reaching up to grab Magda's lit cigarette.

"What's so funny?"

"I was just thinking about us."

"Ha, ha."

"No, I mean, we're as stupid as anyone else sometimes."

"No, Isabel. Not even you're stupid. You're just not paying

attention. Rose-colored glasses and everything. Whatever you end up writing, it's not gonna be anything like *Sister Carrie*. It'll be some floaty shit for people who don't have to live in the real world."

"You girls talk too much, you know that?"

"All girls talk too much, Charlie. Occupational hazard. At least Isabel is occasionally talking about something that matters. Count your blessings."

All their words are slowing down and the wind has turned and brought the tinny music up the cliff.

That night last summer, Isabel and Charlie had kissed for long enough, and she started to feel his hands on her. The muscles in her legs and back were tightening, and she was still tripping hard. She had pictures in her head of opening flowers and waving corals and jellyfish; there was no distance between her thoughts and her body. Down the beach the football players were shouting, and she wondered where Ruth was. How long would it be before Charlie put his hand between her legs and touched her?

He was having a hard time getting through her clothes.

"You wore this on purpose, didn't you?" he said, like she was trying to be shy or chaste or something.

As soon as she laughed and said no, she could tell she'd done something wrong. He turned three degrees colder and the sky kept turning behind him. In the light of the lamps coming down from the parking lot she could see his gray shadow drawing back inside itself, even though he was still touching her.

He ignored her for a long time after that night. It took months for him to look straight at her again. She spent every day wanting him to. The whole thing turned out to be a trap. They couldn't actually have what they wanted, but they could want things in ways they hadn't even dreamed of.

Now Magda and Charlie are having some kind of philosophical debate in the dark.

"I'm just saying we don't get what we deserve any more than any other idiot." Magda is looking at the sky through her crescent wrench, using it to pinch the moon. "There is no such thing as karma."

"I will," Charlie says. "I'll get what I want. You don't have to just take everything life dishes out. You just gotta be meaner than the other guy."

"Can't believe I'm saying this, Isabel, but Charlie's not wrong."

"Charlie's not a girl," Isabel says.

"That true, Charlie?" Magda laughs.

"You got a big head, little Warren, you know that?"

"Some people are just stronger and meaner than us, Magda," Isabel says. "If they want to throw you around, they will. You know that; you just don't want to deal with it."

"People can only be meaner than you if you let 'em, Isabel. Isn't that kind of what you said on the way here?"

It's so dark now that the color is gone from the lilies in the Glinnicks' backyard. Magdalene gets up and leans into the sky, holding the branch of a tree with one hand. Isabel looks at the shadow of her hair and her toolbox coat hanging out over the edge of the pit. The moon throws a pathway of light on the water and touches the top of Magda's head.

"Well, I'm going back down," she says. "You staying here, Isabel?"

"Yeah, for a while."

Magda's retreating shadow is silver in the moonlight, parting the dark flowers. After it disappears, Charlie rolls down into the lily leaves and pulls Isabel onto him. She knows how it works now. She is supposed to resist.

He is supposed to have to force her.

nine

ONCE MAGDALENE IS back in the middle of the crowd at the bottom of the pit, the air smells more like doughnut grease than the sea. Some of the music is recorded and blaring through terrible speakers, but there are still one or two old rides that have mechanical harmoniums. She stands and watches the booth at the back of the carousel, where metal levers are ringing up and down in the sticky darkness. It's connected somehow to the plate that turns the platform with the horses, but the mechanism is hidden under the floor.

Every few minutes, someone she knows passes by and she has to wave. Then she goes back to imagining the gears under the carousel. It's self-contained; that's what's so good about a mechanism. It uses the exact same amount of energy it takes. No excess. No spillage.

She runs into Jeff Snyder at one of the booths, shooting at little pop-up Hitlers with a BB gun. He puts his hand on her when he says hello, just lays the BB gun down and puts his hand on the small of her back like it's a normal thing to do. When he touches her, the invisible membrane between her and everything else disappears, like he's taking her swimming inside herself. She can feel every cell of her skin at once, the way you do when you dive into a lake.

It's like someone walking into a room uninvited, but the room is her body. People look at Ruth the way Jeff is looking at her now, and Charlie started out by looking at Isabel like that. It's the first time anyone has given her that look, though. She's pretty sure that's because neither of the other two is there to get it first.

She didn't tell Ruth and Isabel about the conversation she had with Jeff on the corner of Sycamore Avenue, or the way he seemed like he was adding up all the details of her. When Isabel likes someone she just talks and talks and talks, even more than normal. He said this; his hair looks like that; his parents are assholes and don't understand him; the last girl he was with was too ugly or too stupid; he's reading Rilke; he listens to Captain Beefheart. On and on and on. Isabel is like Magdalene's mother; they both have total conviction that other people should be fascinated by whatever they're feeling or doing. Magda would just sound ridiculous if she talked about someone the way Isabel does, so she keeps it to herself. She pretends she learned about immigrant Irish socialists and the great migration and the killing floor from the books in her parents' library instead of from Jeff.

Here and now, Jeff has his hand on her and he's nodding towards the back of the shooting gallery truck. They sneak around into the dark between the truck and the generator. Shadows made by neon are different from other shadows—dark but they still glow. There are colors in their eyes and everything they say is punctuated by the sound coming through the back wall of the truck, little metal Hitlers clacking up and down.

He talks to her about how you can do all your complicated thinking while you work on an engine, which Magda already knows. He talks about history and how it works and why people need to think about it. He asks her all kinds of questions; she feels like she's at a college interview. And the whole time he's talking to her he stays so close she can feel the heat coming off him.

"When your grandparents came," he says, "do you know why?"

"Why does anyone come to America? Money." Right away Magda can tell she was supposed to say it differently. She is the girl; she's supposed to say it as a question. But Jeff doesn't notice anyway. He's on a roll again.

"They came because they were hungry, Magdalene, and because everyone in Southern Italy was dying of cholera. So they came for shitty jobs in New York and they packed 'em in tenement buildings like sardines. In the good ol' US of A they were still hungry and still dying of cholera and the flu. When they came through Ellis Island there was a doctor standing there to check under their eyelids for diseases. If they were okay, the doctor drew a white cross on their coats, like they were cattle. If you were a kid and you were sick they just ripped you out of your mom's arms and stuck you in quarantine for three months."

"Actually Nona and Nono had some money saved," Magda says. "Nono's dad had a shop, and they sold it after he died and came over here to buy a little farm in mid-island." But Jeff isn't listening.

"The people at Ellis Island only spoke English and they just thought anyone who didn't was retarded. And speaking of retarded, they'd stop you from coming in for that, too. If you had a retarded kid, you had to choose whether to all go home or come through and leave your kid in an institution."

"They came in a berth," she says. "It was kind of different for them. If you had some money, the officials came on the boat to check your papers, and Nono could speak a little English. When he talked about it he always acted proud that he wasn't treated like complete dirt, like he was a little bit better than the people in steerage. It was kind of a messed-up attitude, but he was a good guy really."

"I'm just saying, is it really a surprise the guys down on the Lower West Side thought they'd maybe get organized a little?" Jeff says. "Take the bull by the horns, give as good as they got?"

"What, you mean by taking protection money off people who weren't as strong as them, and kneecapping the people who wouldn't pay? Not all Italians are Mafia, you know."

He finally stops talking and looks at her for a minute. "You're smart, aren't you?" he says. "Pretty and smart."

This time, when that look goes through her she can see

everything at once. Isabel on the cliff above her with Charlie, the two of them crushing down the lily leaves in the Glinnicks' back-yard. She can see Vicky and her latest scars, and the eyeliner she draws around that empty sleepiness she always has in her eyes when she comes back to Highbone. She can see her own mother, walking away, but she has to make that picture up, because her mother left when Magda was asleep. Magda has a version of that picture for every situation. Except this one. She's so distracted trying to see the picture of her mother's retreating back that it takes a minute to pay attention when he starts to kiss her.

"So," he says, "do you like me?" And he laughs, like it's a rhetorical question.

"I don't know." Which is honest. "What is that thing you feel about people? That makes you think about them?"

"You don't think about it, Magdalene Warren. It isn't about thinking."

"When you get to move out of your house," she says, "when you get to take whatever courses you want and save up and take your car anywhere you want to go, is it better? Is it as good as you think it's gonna be?"

He kisses her again instead of answering. Then he says, "So this was all a clever ploy to get information out of me, eh? I'm the older guy, all worldly and shit?" He laughs again. A lot of things seem funny to him. "So, do you? Think about me? Is that what you're saying?"

"I asked you a question first. Why do you stay here, when you could go wherever you want?"

"No, you did not. I asked you, do you like me?"

"Okay," Magda says, "so my answer is, I don't get you. Why stay here?"

"Why not? It has beaches. It has pretty girls. There's plenty of pot and four seasons. Why go anywhere else? I went to Tortola once, to surf with some guys. It's supposed to be paradise. It kind of was. There was great pot and it was hot every day and the waves were amazing. But there were big spiders and people were way poor and the cops were psychotic, even worse than here. Say what you like about the Island, it's just easier."

He hooks his hand into her belt and kisses her again. Then he slides his hand up and moves it over her, like he wants to touch every small place on her skin. She gasps and he laughs again, but softer. When he puts his other hand down the front of her jeans, she has to lean against the back of the truck and try to stop the sounds coming out of her throat. The muffled clacking of the little Hitlers comes right through the aluminum wall and into her body. She crumples up the front of his shirt in her hands, holding on so she wouldn't slide down onto the ground.

In the end, she lets him hold her up, but they wind up on the ground eventually anyway. They sit there together, smoking with their backs against the truck. When she realizes she's leaning against him she sits up. So, it is good. Better than pretty much anything. She gets it, but that doesn't mean she wants to wind up like Isabel. Or her mother.

"I need to go back, Jeff. I left my friend Isabel at the top of the pit."

"I'll walk you," he said. "You can introduce me."

"No, it's okay."

All she can think is that things shouldn't come together, Jeff and Isabel and Charlie. As long as she doesn't actually meet Jeff, Isabel won't ask. She'll just talk on and on about Charlie and whether he means that they're together again or whether he was just a bastard. She'll be so busy with all that, it won't occur to her to ask what happened to Magda in the meantime.

"No, I'll go alone," she says, and an expression flies across Jeff's face that makes him look just like her father.

Is he mad? But the shadows move and then he's smiling down at her. It's the kind of smile that makes you feel littler than you are, like there's something crucial you don't know.

Back at the top of the pit, the Glinnicks' yard is empty anyway. Isabel is long gone. Magda stands there, alone and shaky and wet between her legs. She knows she'll be up all night, redefining hunger.

ten

IN THE STREETS behind Dunkin' Donuts, Ruth feels herself flicker in and out of the almost dark, like she's walking in a country with no one in it, a place that can only hold emptiness. She told Isabel and Magda she had to stay in, just so she could walk her own streets for an hour, gather up the night and breathe it in. It's her world back here, and she wants to fade into the in-between blue of it, just for a while.

South Highbone sidewalks are made of perfect cast-cement squares with careful edges. Sometimes the spaces in between the squares have grass and dandelions, but that only makes the checkerboard feeling of everything more depressing. There are three kinds of houses on identical square plots; that's how much choice there is. Also, people have different driveways, gravel or asphalt, or grass with two cement strips, and you can tell the Italians from everyone else by the yard Virgins and the truck-tire planters.

All of that is solid. All of that is real, but Ruth could be a ghost passing over the sidewalks. Every window is emitting blue television light, falling out onto every front lawn. She could be dreaming one of those dreams where an endless succession of doors keeps opening, one behind the other.

"I want to show you something." He speaks right into her ear, then falls in next to her, moving down the sidewalk.

"Mackie," Ruth says. "I didn't hear you."

"That's why they call them sneakers." He points down to the dirty laces on his Chuck Taylors, then holds a piece of paper in front of her. When she reaches for it, he pulls it back.

"Well, how are you?" He smiles in the twilight like the Cheshire cat. "Been thinking about me?"

"Yeah, sometimes." Ruth looks down and away. "What's on the paper?"

It is a drawing of a girl, with her back bent and her body open to the sky. There are no marks on her, but Ruth can see there's no blood inside her either. Her eyes are open, seeing nothing and everything.

"Did you draw that?" It reminds Ruth of something, but she can't think what.

"This is what you see, isn't it?" He holds the paper open to the streetlight.

"Sometimes. Sort of."

"Don't be scared of it," he says. "You're different, I told you. That's a good thing."

"Did you draw that picture, Mackie?"

"Where you going, Ruth Carter?"

"A friend's house. Sort of a friend. I told Isabel and Magda I had to stay home tonight."

"But really you just wanted to be alone." He nods. "You wanted to do something yourself."

"Matt is from South Highbone." Ruth kicks at a pebble and shakes her head. "They want to steal his weed and turn his life upside down, and, you know, he kind of belongs to me. He belongs to here. I just want to talk to him. If I said that to Magda she'd be mad at me."

"Why can't you have your own ideas?" Mackie folds up the drawing. "Doesn't that piss you off?"

"Yeah, kind of. Lately. They think all kinds of stuff about me just because, you know, what I look like and who my mom is."

"When you're mad," Mackie says, "that's when you're really you. It's like you drop right down into yourself, like you're all the way there. Ever notice that about people? When they're mad, they stop hiding."

"I don't want to hide anymore," Ruth says.

"See?" He smiles again, glowing there in the streetlight. "I'm a good influence."

Ruth stops on the sidewalk in front of Matt's house, but Mackie doesn't leave. Matt's front lawn is much neater than Ruth's, even though he's only twenty-two and lives there by himself. His friend Sal is a landscaper. Girls always go on about landscapers, because they work in the sun without shirts and turn brown and have muscles. That's just one of the things Ruth doesn't get about other people.

"You know," she says to Mackie, "why is there a Highbone and a South Highbone? Never mind, actually. I already know that. My mom got born because some manager at the aircraft factory got my grandmother pregnant and then ignored her. Why aren't they pissed off? And how come no one at school but me and Magda and Isabel wants to talk about *Sister Carrie*? Also, what the hell is so hard about quadratic equations?"

Mackie just laughs, loving every word, and she feels it again. Release. Recognition. Her anger blossoms into something like happiness, or maybe it's just relief.

"What is up with those girls who spend every minute between classes brushing the Farrah Fawcett wings back into their hair? Why do they want to look exactly like each other? Why did football players cut my friend Charlie's face with can openers just because he has jail tattoos? I don't get why if there are enough listeners out there to support the Bad Music Hour on WUSB, me and Magda and Isabel feel like the only people in the world who understand each other."

"I understand you," Mackie says. "Do they? Really?"

"Magda says it isn't that complicated. People suck, she says. They suck more the closer they live to water or high ground. Other people work for the people who suck. If they're lucky. Magda sees right through a lot of things, she really does. But you're right, Mackie. Sometimes it's like they're pretending I'm there, talking to me when they can't actually see me. They think Danny and my mom are some kind of great innovation in home life, like living at my house is perfect. My mom's all right, but I don't get why she keeps moving the next man in. I don't get what they're for. I mean . . . sorry."

Mackie laughs again. "Not a problem. I'm all ears." He makes a keep-it-coming motion with his hands.

Ruth looks down at the sidewalk, where her shadow is stretching out alone in the streetlight. She thinks about the density of bodies. About floating away.

"Look, Ruth. Your body stops the light. You're here. You're solid. You're real. Those things you see, you can tell them to me. You shouldn't be scared of them. They're what make you special."

He slips the drawing into her back pocket and pulls his watch out by its brass chain. He looks at the time and then turns to walk away.

"Why don't you ever say hello or good-bye like normal people?" Ruth shouts at his back.

She stares after him until he lifts up his hand. Without turning around he waves it. Matt looks out between the curtains in his front window, then lets them go and comes to open the front door.

"What the hell are you doing shouting in front of my house, Ruth?" Matt whispers. "Get inside, before somebody sees you."

"I came to see about something?" She looks up at him from the steps.

"Uh-uh, Ruth, no. . . . You better come in, but I'm not inviting you to sit down."

"Oh, come on, Matt. Sell me a nickel bag. My money's green."

"And your *mother* is a good customer. Shit, I say it again. You can't come here for weed. Your mother'll have a fit."

"Yeah, right. If I don't get it from you, I'll steal hers. *That* pisses her off. I only want a nickel bag. Come on, let me sit down just for a minute."

The sunflowers on Matt's curtains and the old brown carpet full of burn holes wash away her anger. She thinks of Virgil Mackie, walking away into the distance.

"It's nice in here," Ruth says. "Did you get all this stuff, or was it like this?"

"My mom did it, before she . . . left." Matt misses a beat and looks away, and Ruth uses the distraction as an opportunity to sit down. She knows what happened to Matt's mom. People in South Highbone know, and anyway he's mentioned it before. Isabel and Magda don't get the whole story. Like Mackie says, sometimes it's Ruth who really sees things.

Matt looks at her now and rolls his eyes. They're nice, but not in a sex way. He's beautiful in two dimensions, like an old black-and-white movie, or an old photograph of sadness. It never seems like you could reach into his space and touch him.

"Right, I'll roll one up and smoke it with you," he says, "but if anyone else comes, you're out the kitchen door, and no whining about it, right?"

He turns the TV down and goes into his room for his stash box. The middle of the couch sags, and there's a lot of crap on the coffee table, beer cans and ash trays, a bong and an orange juice carton. Matt's house is exactly how he wants it. It must be great to live alone.

"I don't want your mom pissed off at me," he says. "She's not just a customer. I like her. She's cool."

Great. Matt, too. She came here tonight because she didn't want to be invisible. Matt is the kind of thing she knows. He's supposed to get her.

"Yeah, well I like her more than my friends like their moms, but she can be a pain in the ass. There's a definite boyfriend/no boyfriend oscillation to her. She's different at different times."

"Ruth, can I just point out you have no concept of what the school shrink calls 'maternal instability'? They put that on a statement about me, you know. You got no idea. At. All. Everyone knows where my mom is."

"I'm not gonna pretend I get it," she says, "but nobody thinks it's funny, Matt. Anyway it's only because I live over here. My friends who live down in the village don't know."

"I'm just saying, your mom is cool. Don't knock it."

"All right, all right." Ruth waves a hand and looks up at the ceiling. "I get it. She's Saint fucking Caroline of South Highbone. She does take care of business, even though I bet a social worker would say she doesn't. Even though it's my dad who never took care of anything, they'd never say that, would they? It's all on her. But we eat, we sleep, I get pens and pencils and paper for school. Whatever."

"That's a lot, man. She's on her own."

"Not at the moment. Anyway, sometimes she talks to me

about cool stuff, but you have to catch her in the right mood. She never stays still, my mom. She takes a little too much care of business, you know? Sometimes I wish she'd slow down."

"My mom used to sit in the same chair for days. Trust me, it isn't that great. I used to take care of her. After she stopped working I got the job at the hardware store, and it was all cool, even though when I came home she'd be in the same position I left her in. I had to kind of wake her up. It took a while to get her to eat and take a shower and stuff."

Matt is quiet for a minute while he opens up some buds onto a double album cover and starts to break them up. When he speaks again, it's like he isn't talking to her at all.

"Sometimes she'd wake up at night and I'd have to get up and watch her so she didn't hurt herself or break anything. She was scared, too. When she was sitting still, there was nothing behind her eyes, but if she was moving at all she'd be scared. Then she lit the shower curtain on fire while I was at work. I got home and there were cops and everything here. Social Services said she had to go."

Matt moves a pizza box to get to the lighter and the ashtray underneath it. He's quiet for so long that Ruth gets uncomfortable and speaks.

"Maternal instability? Ha! People get paid to point out the obvious."

Matt puts the ashtray down on a copy of *Astronomy* magazine that says "The Voyager Mission" on the cover.

"That yours?" Ruth points.

"Yeah, it's interesting. Whatever."

"What happened to your dad?"

"'Nam," he says. "There was a little money for that, too."

"You're due for some good luck, Matt. You need to roll the dice again."

"That's what I'm doing, little Carter. Quit the hardware store a month ago. I'm an entrepreneur now, baby. I won't keep dealing forever either, just till I can get some serious cash built up. It'll all be cool."

"So can I have a nickel bag or what?" Ruth holds out one of the five-dollar bills she got from Old Mr. Lipsky.

"No, you can't," Matt says, "but I'm smoking you up. Take it or leave it."

Matt lights the joint with a lighter that says *Coney Island* on one side. The other side has a woman in a grass skirt on it. There's a layer of liquid over her and when you turn it upside down and back again, her bikini top comes off.

Tits, tits, tits. It's always about the tits.

After a minute or two Matt starts to look a little embarrassed about all the things he's told her. When the doorbell rings he looks out the curtains again and it's like she's seeing the same moment from another angle. He says, "It's only Charlie. He called first to ask if he could stop by before work. *Called first*, like a normal, polite person. You hang out with him, don't you? You don't have to go."

"No, I will," Ruth whispers. "Please don't tell him I was here. He's got, like, a big brother thing for me and Magdalene and Isabel. He'll kick my ass. He thinks we should let him cop for us."

"Whatever." He looks at her like she's a ridiculous child.

"*Please*, Matt." Now she even sounds like a ridiculous child.

Matt has a soul. You can see it behind those eyes, but right now he's looking straight through her just like everyone else.

"All right, all right." He motions her through into the hallway.

There's a bathroom and the basement door, and then two bedrooms and the kitchen at the back. The windows are wooden and swing open from hinges on the top, just like hers. It's the same house really, except hers is turned in another direction, with the living room between the kitchen and the bedrooms. South Highbone is like a B-movie version of Levittown, all divided up by those prefab sidewalks. Turning the houses in different directions and moving the front doors around is what gives people the illusion of being different from each other.

"Listen, Ruth." Matt pushes the garbage pail aside to open the kitchen door. "I really don't want you to come back here without your mom."

Her mouth opens but nothing comes out. She can't form words because she has no breath, like someone just hit her.

"I'm not being mean. It's just . . . I'm way older than you and your mom is my friend and what if I get busted or something and you're here when it happens? It's just not cool, okay?"

She leaves through the neighbor's yard, climbing the chain-link fence at the back so Charlie won't see her from the living room window. It matters now if Charlie sees her there, because they will be back. Who cares what Isabel does to Matt's life? He's on the other side; he's the one who just said so.

Matt's neighbors have those planters that Italian dads make out of truck tires and paint brick red. These ones are full of some elephant ear things with white stripes on the leaves and the little purple flowers. There's a yard Virgin, too. These are the kind of Italians Magda's dad is always trying to keep her away from. "Your mother wasn't like that," he says to her. "Her parents were educated." As if going to college makes you not want a yard Virgin anymore. Actually, it probably does. No yard Virgins once you join the people who really suck.

Magda and her dad always talk about Mrs. Warren in the past tense, like she's dead, but Ruth imagines her new life every day. Mrs. Warren is so beautiful, Ruth likes to think of her on dance floors under Mexican stars, singing in bars with bloodred candles and dark-eyed painters. When Ruth draws her, Mrs. Warren looks like the Virgin would if she didn't have to fold her hands all the time, if she could kick off those robes and have a drink and say exactly what she thinks. Still holy, just real, too.

For a few minutes, Ruth felt like Matt was with her in the same, separate world. But that was just another dizzy trick, another piece of unsteady ground moving under her. Like Magda says, people suck. Matt knows that already; they wouldn't be burdening him with any new information by stealing his stash. They have to do something. It seems like this is the year for making things happen. The Year of Necessary Cruelty. The thing is, Ruth can't figure out whether it's the three of them who hand out justice. Is that who they are?

What would Mackie say?

There is no answer in the sky, and the yard Virgin just stares her distant stare. Maybe that is the answer.

eleven

ISABEL STANDS BY the side of a swimming pool on Harbor Ridge, feeling the sun and breathing. She lifts her arms like wings and drops of blood scatter across the cement. She bends her knees and launches herself up and out. For maybe one whole second she is moving through the morning air.

Then the smack of water and she floats facedown, looking at the twisted sunlight on the bottom of a stranger's pool. The blood from all the cuts in her wrists and thighs swirls against the medicine-blue color of swimming-pool paint. Everything feels close and bright. There are frogs floating around her, which seems right somehow. They have black, deep eyes that promise to teach her how to live comfortably between water and earth, in between one place and another. This is the real reason there are frogs in fairy tales.

Someone is screaming. She tries to take in a breath to scream back, but her mouth fills with water. Then she feels the covers pressing down on her and knows it's her father and her alarm, both going off at the same time.

Monday morning.

"Isabel!" He sounds angry or, even weirder, scared.

"I'm up!"

"Never mind pretending, just get down here."

Isabel comes down the stairs with her shoulder sliding against the wall so it can take some of her weight. Her knees aren't all the way working yet. She has to bunch up the hem of her grandmother's yellow satin nightgown so it doesn't trip her on the stairs. Through the living room doorway she can see her dad standing there with the couch pulled out from the wall.

"What?" she says. "Do we have mice? I heard something the other night."

"Come here, Isabel."

She looks over at the wall under the window, where the couch usually is, and sees her mother crouching there. She has a look on her face like Henry would make, like she knows she's doing something naughty but she thinks it's funny. Like them standing there in their pajamas freaking out is her getting one over on them.

"Jesus! Has she been there since Saturday?"

"Don't call your brother."

"What?"

"He needs to focus on college. We'll handle this ourselves."

"Dad, I wasn't gonna call Kevin. Or Elizabeth either. You need to call the freaking hospital!"

"We can't call the hospital. If an ambulance pulls up the whole street will see it."

"Oh my God, you actually just said that."

Her mother is still sitting there, hugging her knees and looking back and forth between them like she's watching a tennis match.

"She needs water," her father says. "You can't go two days without water."

"She *has* been there since Saturday, hasn't she? This is so messed up. I'm not supposed to have to deal with this."

"This is not a question of what you have to deal with, Isabel. Go in the kitchen and get a glass of water."

By the time she gets back, he has her mother sitting up on the couch, but it isn't pushed back in. The living room looks broken. She puts the water down on the floor next to them because the coffee table is shoved to the other side of the room.

She leans in and says, "Mom, I'm going to school but I'll be back later," then gathers her nightgown and runs up the stairs.

At school, it takes Isabel a long time to figure out what to say. She finds Ruth in the hallway and stands watching her rifle through the pile of markers and pastels and colored pencils on the bottom of her locker.

"I'm thinking there's an upside to Monday morning," Ruth says.

"Huh?"

Can Ruth feel what other people feel when they look at her? Not the blonde-with-tits thing, the other thing. When she opens her mouth and that mismatched, gravelly voice comes out, when you see how she holds a pencil, you just know you'll be hearing her name someday. You'll see a documentary about her on channel 13, or read about her in the *New York Times* Arts section, and think, *I wonder if her voice still sounds like that? I wonder if she remembers me?*

"You don't have a pencil that's kind of brick red, do you?" Ruth says now.

"Brick red? What kind of a question is that? I have a blue pen and a black pen. I have first-period math."

Or maybe Ruth will wind up hiding for two days behind a couch in Highbone. That's the other possibility. Mr. Lipsky obviously used to think Isabel's mom was destined for greatness. Look how that turned out. Days like today, though, Isabel feels like Ruth is the one who will get away, like the reason for Ruth is hope. At some point, she'll get bigger and brighter than the everyday things around her and she'll have to go somewhere with more space. All three of them say they're going to leave, but if Isabel had to bet, her money would be on Ruth.

Ruth pulls her head out of her locker, looking exasperated with people who don't keep a full range of colored pencils on their person at all times. Thank God Isabel ran into her first. It's hard to be scared or hate the world with Ruth right in front of you.

"Okay, back to the point," Ruth says. "Monday morning, we're all still wasted from the weekend, right? But so are the teachers. They've been sitting around by their friends' swimming pools drinking Rob Roys all weekend. I think Monday morning is a window of opportunity. We can get anything past these people at this point."

"What do you have in mind? What's the scam?"

"I don't know, maybe world domination? Or maybe not doing the history homework? Seriously, what difference does anything in our lives make on a Monday morning?"

Outside, there are circles of kids all over the football field, smoking. Isabel looks from the grass to the sky, takes a deep breath, and wades in, with Ruth behind her. They find Magda sitting against the wall behind the storage house, hugging her knees.

"You look like a Nazi in that coat, Magda."

"I don't think the Nazis let each other go around with their shirtsleeves hanging out of their coats, Isabel," Ruth says. "Pretty sure those guys buttoned shit right up."

"Anyway, no way Nazis had Chuck Taylors." Magda leans back and lifts up both feet. "These're the all-American shoes, girls."

Charlie is there too, in the scrub at the side of the field, beating on the chain-link fence with a sledgehammer. He swings with all his force, and the hammer bounces back in a different direction every time, wrenching his arms around. She looks at his body and tries to calm herself with the memory of what it feels like, but even that's no good anymore. The thought of him touching her makes her feel dead, cut open.

"Why are you guys wearing sweaters and coats?" Ruth waves her hands at the pitiless sun. "It's spring, people. Inappropriately dressed for the weather, that's a sign of mental illness, you know. Mrs. Kemp said so in health class. That's why the 'Nam vets in the park always have two sweaters and three jackets on in August. And *why* is Charlie doing that? He looks like something out of a bad existentialist movie."

"Guess he's letting off steam. I'm just observing the behavior of Charlie Ferguson in his natural habitat." Magda cocks her head to listen to the high, shuddering twang as Charlie's hammer hits the fence. "He took it out of the back of a truck while we were walking here. And I wear this coat 'cause I can keep lots of stuff in it. It's my house I carry around with me. Think of me as a snail, babe. Snails are a theme lately."

"Jesus," Isabel says, "is the whole world like this, or do you think we're just caught in some kind of fucked-up suburban vortex?"

"Both. Those are not mutually exclusive propositions." Magda waves a finger like Mr. Kronenberg, the math teacher. "On the upside, no one can see back here from the school windows. This is our new spot."

"There is no one watching from the windows, Magda. I said to Isabel, it's Monday. We're all constitutionally incapable of giving a shit, even if we wanted to. The teachers are just pretending better than us."

"So"—Isabel falls back to lie on the grass—"my mom's doing her Problem with No Name act again."

"The vague malaise? The suburban epidemic? Did they give her Valium? Can we steal some?"

"Way better than that. My mom doesn't mess around. Betty Friedan has nothing on her, man. She was behind the couch."

"Huh?"

"Remember on Saturday my dad asked me if I knew where my mom was? She was *behind the fucking couch*. On the floor. Hiding or something, *for at least two days*."

"Right, I don't actually know what to say to that."

"See?" Isabel looks at Ruth. "Even Saint Magdalene of All Knowledge has got nothing. I guess sometimes this place is just beyond words. If we went to the next town over and told them about Highbone, do you think no one would believe us? Or do you think all the towns are like this?"

"Jesus," Ruth says.

"Yeah." Isabel closes her eyes. "I said that at the time. So, I might as well tell you it was her discharge papers."

"What?"

"At the bonfire, I burned her discharge papers. From King's Park."

"Your mom was in King's Park?" She can hear Magda slap Ruth's leg, but really it doesn't matter what anyone says at this point.

"Yep, she signed herself in. Right before I met you guys. She got them to put her in a room with a caged-in balcony to stop her from throwing herself off, in a ward with people who swung kittens around by the tail and scratched the flesh off their own arms, because she figured it was better than staying in her own house with her own family. Well, she was kind of right about that."

"What did you do?" Ruth asks. "This morning, I mean. Wasn't she hungry or thirsty or something? Can people go two days without food and water?"

"She had a bag of M&M's back there. She stashes candy all over the house, in the couch cushions, in the linen closet, everywhere. Dad said she'd be dehydrated, but maybe she came out and got water when we were sleeping. God, imagine her creeping around down there. Why does that seem spooky? It's her house."

"So, what did he do, your dad?"

"He got all focused on making her drink water. Like the whole thing was about her being dehydrated. If she just drank a glass of water, problem solved. Which one of them is crazier?"

Isabel can see Ruth searching the air for something else to say. Reaching out with her mind like there might be meaning in the ether. She wants to shout at her that it isn't there. They're never going to find it.

"There could have been a fire, and we wouldn't have known she was back there. What if there was a fire?" She stops so they won't hear the lump in her throat.

"We're not going to math," Magda says. "Ruth, you're not going to the art room either. Monday just reached a new level."

They're all still holding unlit cigarettes. Ruth taps Isabel and hands her a lighter with a hula girl on one side and *Coney Island* on the other. They're quiet for a while, just smoking.

Then Magda says, "I feel like that woman from the parking lot at the mall, like language just doesn't cover it anymore. How are we supposed to respond to this place? What are we supposed to say?"

"We can't put up with this kind of shit forever." Isabel puts her cigarette out and looks at both of them in turn. "We have to do something. You guys know we do."

"Everyone gets that, Isabel. The question is what?"

"Matt's house. Screw Charlie. We need to do it ourselves. It's wrong, but right now, I'm thinking it's necessary. Anyway, I kind of can't tell the difference between right and wrong anymore. It's a little scary, if you guys wanna know."

"Yep. I'm with Isabel." Isabel has to check to make sure it's Ruth talking.

"Really?"

"You're what?" Magda says. "I thought Matt was your personal charity case."

"Yeah, well he can call the Good Samaritans. I changed my mind."

"See?" Magda leans back onto Isabel's drawn-up knees. "Even Ruth has caved in. This place is just too fucking soulless much for us."

"Maybe 'wised up' is actually the phrase you're after?"

"What's the point of stealing Matt's stash if it makes us just as shallow as everyone else here?"

"Nah," Ruth says. "Not gonna happen. We will get out and

we will never be them. I'm getting out with my soul intact if I have to shoot my way out."

"You don't think our parents used to think that, Ruth? You don't think they sat around at soda fountains telling each other they were incorruptible?"

"It isn't about being incorruptible," Ruth says. "It's about staying alive."

That's what it is about her, Isabel thinks. It's people like Ruth who get caught up in some vision no one else can see and walk bravely into hails of bullets or freeze to death exploring the Antarctic. They never think they can die pointlessly like everyone else. Until they do.

"Well, I'm not the one who's making the plan," Magda says. "You two are some kind of knights in armor now, you figure out how to rescue yourselves."

"Already did." Isabel sits up and they all look over at Charlie and lower their voices. "Charlie thinks we can't possibly rob a house because we're girls. Magda heard him. He'll never in a million years think it's us."

Magda looks at her like she's half freaked out and half impressed, like Isabel just pulled a gun or something.

"You want to steal Matt's weed and not tell Charlie? What the hell happened to you since Saturday?"

"Um, I think we pretty much just covered that, Magda."

"We'll get caught, Isabel."

"There's a way," Ruth says. "If you two just listen to me for five seconds I'll tell you. I went to Matt's on Saturday night. That's his lighter. I took it. I can get Matt to come with me and my mom and Danny to watch this meteor shower on Friday. Mom and Danny are all worked up over it."

"You think he'll go for that? He's a dealer. Friday night is prime time for him."

"Matt thinks my mother is the best thing since sliced bread. Also, he's obsessed with planets and stuff. He'll come. Trust me."

"From where I'm standing," Isabel says, "your mom *is* the best thing since sliced bread. Anybody want a spare mother? I'm thinking I could maybe get along without mine. Shit, sorry, Magda."

"Whatever," Magda laughs. "I'm in, under one condition."

"What?"

"This is capital. We turn it into getaway money. We don't smoke it or give it away."

"Obviously," Ruth says. "This is all about focus. Life got serious lately. Don't you guys get that?"

"Also, if anyone goes to jail, it's Isabel."

"That's two conditions, Magda."

"Fine," Ruth says.

Maybe it's supposed to be a joke, maybe not. You never know with Ruth and Magda. They've had their own language since way before she showed up. Maybe the only way to find out if they'd actually save her is to get caught.

"If Matt comes with us, I'll leave you a signal." Ruth holds up the Coney Island lighter. "I'll drop this by the curb if it's all good."

The bell is ringing and the last kids are shuffling towards the school building, but Charlie is still swinging his hammer with his back to the world. Their world. The one they're about to grab ahold of. Finally the picture of Isabel's living room disappears from her mind and the sky above her opens up.

"With money we can buy a van for you guys," she says, "a houseboat for me. Whatever we want."

"And that would be the point." Magda stands up. "How are we gonna turn Matt's weed into money?"

"This is not the time for details, Magda. This is jump-now-think-later time."

"I think we should find a way to blackmail Danny into taking it off us," Ruth says.

"Danny, your mom's boyfriend?" Isabel sits up. "I like him; he's nice to Henry."

"People thought the last one was nice, remember? We're not doing that again, not on my watch. The guy is in the middle of *my* life. He deserves what he gets. Opportunity knocks, women."

"Move over, Saint Magdalene the Decision Maker. Ruth is the new mastermind."

"I thought it was you, Jump-Now-Think-Later O'Sullivan."

twelve

MAGDA STANDS IN Matt's side yard, holding his Coney Island lighter and actually appreciating the beauty of the plan. For the beginning of a career in housebreaking, this is an excellent choice. It's county on this side of 25A. Not Highbone cops, real cops, but like Charlie said, Matt can't call them. The moon isn't up yet, which is why it's a good night to see a meteor shower. Magda can just make out the truck-tire planters and the yard Virgin on the lawn next door. Matt's bathroom window is open, but it's also eight feet off the ground, with a little basement window below it.

"Only one of us can go in," she says. "I'll lift you up."

"No fucking way, Magda." Isabel backs away from her. "I'm not going in there by myself."

"Really, Bonnie Parker? Now you're chickenshit? Fine," Isabel says. "I'll go. Kneel down and let me get on your shoulders. I'll let you in the back door."

She lays her coat on the grass and kneels down so Isabel can get on her shoulders. Isabel weighs more than Henry, but less than the world.

It turns out none of the robbery is hard at all. The bathroom window is over the toilet, so she can climb down onto it, and the kitchen door comes right open. The weed is under the bed, but it's obvious there is nowhere near three pounds. Charlie was right; Matt's an amateur. They've brought one of those little army day packs and Ruth made them swear they'd only take what they could fit in there. When the army backpack is full, there's still a saltines tin full of Thai stick left for Matt.

"We are the world's dumbest thieves," Isabel says.

"No, we're sensible and humane, woman. Don't you forget it. Anyway, this is our insurance. He'll be less pissed off, more confused, and less likely to believe it isn't one of his friends."

"This is kind of meaner than I thought, though, Magda. You know, pitting friends against each other."

"So, in the middle of *me* executing *your* plan, *you* get a conscience." That's Isabel all over.

They're in the living room looking for more stuff when the doorbell rings. Isabel jumps and crouches down on the floor.

"It completely fine," Magda says into her ear. "They can't come in."

"Um . . . if it's Charlie, he's just checking. He'll be inside in a minute."

Magda waves an arm towards the kitchen hallway and starts crawling. Hopefully Isabel will have the sense to follow her. Once she's out of sight of the front windows, she stands up and Isabel runs into her. They flatten their backs against the wall and Isabel breathes big shallow breaths like she just came up from underwater.

"It was always gonna happen," Magda whispers. "You're the one who said it. He's a dealer and it's nine thirty on Friday night. Relax."

A car drives away and Isabel's breathing slows down, but they still wait fifteen minutes before they shut the bathroom window and pull the kitchen door to behind them. The best place for the stash is Magda's house; they all agreed on that. Isabel's mom might go anywhere in Castle Gloom, stashing candy and hiding behind furniture, that's for sure. And Ruth's house is smaller and already full of pot. Somehow that makes it seem like someone at Ruth's would find this, too.

They stand for a minute in Magda's driveway, looking at the carriage house. The hayloft door, high in the wall, gapes at them. When Magda's mother was still here, she encouraged the barn swallows by leaving that door open. It still lets the swallows in and out and they still nest up there. If her father ever bothers to notice, he'll probably shut it, just out of spite.

The first time Magda was left in charge of Henry, while her mother took an afternoon bath, they spent the time lying on their backs in the driveway, watching the orange bellies of the birds flying in and out. She was worried about taking care of him at first. She knew right then she could never be like her mother, all womanly and beautiful and reading poetry and giving out hugs that smelled like lilies. She wasn't made like that. Henry might get broken if she was left in charge of him. But he didn't, and she remembers the miracle of that, her and Henry both safe on the ground, with the swallows flashing over them.

It's pitch dark in the carriage house now, and they can't risk turning on the light. Magda covers the window with a blanket and turns on a big flashlight. The battery is weak, and there is only just enough light to see by.

"My dad will never look in these boxes, on principle. They are the pile of his denial. If you asked him he'd tell you he doesn't care about any of it and one day he'll just throw a match in here. It sure seems to piss him off, for something he doesn't think about."

"If I ever get as uptight as our parents," Isabel says, "just shoot me, okay? I mean, someone breaks your heart, why not just cry about it and be depressed for a while? That's normal, isn't it?"

"It wasn't his idea," Magda says. "That's what pisses him off. He didn't think of it; he wasn't in charge. She slipped out from under him and took off."

"Well, it's like you said the other day. You can't call her a bad role model, can you?"

"Nope. Hey, look, it's my granddad when he was a teenager." Magda lifts a picture off the top of one of the boxes. There are a bunch of young people barefoot in a big round wooden tub, covered in dappled shade.

"What are they doing?" Isabel grabs the picture and tilts it at the light.

"Stomping grapes, man. It was this annual festival or something. Every year everyone in the town takes their shoes off and climbs in the giant barrel and stomps on the first grapes. For luck, like. Nono said it turns your feet purple for days. My dad hates all that stuff. His friends would probably call these people dagos. He won't admit it, but he's embarrassed that we're related to them."

"I say again, why so uptight?" Isabel says. "Your granddad looks cool."

"Yeah, they had heart, those two, but my dad's never gonna get that. It's all about keeping a face on for him. Mr. Intellectual with the cable-knit sweaters from Scotland, pretending he's all about the deeper meaning."

"Okay," Isabel says, "this is what I don't get, though. Wasn't that exactly what made him fall in love with your mom? I mean, people are different from each other. They get fascinated; they have this awe and respect for each other. Then what happens?"

"Fear and need, man. That's what takes over. My dad is, like, the biggest coward on the planet."

Isabel whistles. "Wow, he does a really good job hiding it."

"Wait, let me show you this." Magda moves some boxes. "It's at the bottom 'cause it's one of the first things he threw out."

Her mother's wedding dress. She holds it up over her trench coat.

"Check out the Dior silhouette, man. It only came down to her ankles and she had these way cool shoes with beads on them. There's about forty layers of tulle under here. Some nuns in Calabria made the lace. They do this amazing thing with threads tied to all their fingers. When you go there, the old ladies are all sitting on their porches doing it."

"Stomping grapes and making lace," Isabel says. "I like these people. Maybe we should go there."

"Apparently, my parents had this big thing 'cause my mom was supposed to wear a satin bag for all of her relatives to stuff money into at the reception. That's how they do in Calabria. My dad wouldn't let her 'cause he thought it was tacky. So instead, at the reception they all just stuffed hundred-dollar bills in my dad's pockets and he stood there looking really uptight and not knowing what to do. My mom used to laugh so hard when she told that story."

Other boxes have running shoes in them that Mrs. Warren has obviously never worn, and cookbooks that tell you how to make food from India and Greece. There is a brand-new sewing machine and a brand-new exercise bicycle. And there are more family photographs of the Buonvicinos.

"Why doesn't your uncle Tony take this stuff?" Isabel waves a handful of old black-and-white pictures.

"Uncle Tony doesn't come here anymore. He can't handle any

of it, couldn't handle it when Mom was here and can't handle the fact that she left. I haven't seen him in two years."

"I only met him once," Isabel says, "but I liked him. He was fun. And he seemed like he was obsessed with you and Henry. It's weird he doesn't visit you."

"I think there's some man thing between him and my dad, you know, because of what my dad's like to my mom and me. So, you know, he won't do anything about it and he'd rather just pretend it isn't happening at all. I don't know. When Nona died Tony expected my mom to step in and start delivering casseroles every Sunday, so he could pretend he didn't want them and call her overbearing. Instead she went to Mexico to have a good time. I bet he just can't figure out why she would do that."

"Right," Isabel says. "Let's put it in the dress."

"What? Oh, yeah!"

There *is* a reason why Magda is friends with Isabel. For doling out poetic justice, you need a poet. So she wraps Matt Kerwin's pound of Colombian buds up in her mother's wedding dress and puts it back underneath the cookbooks, piling a few boxes of shoes and exercise clothes on top.

They stand side by side for a long minute, looking at the mounds of things hulking in the dark and feeling satisfied. Finally, the purpose of all this stuff has been revealed.

"Check it out." Magda stands aside and sweeps an open palm like the lovely assistant on *Let's Make a Deal*. "The wreckage of a woman's life."

"Yeah," Isabel says, "or it's just the cocoon she shed before she transformed herself and flew away."

"Call me sentimental, but I like to think she didn't have a choice about dumping me."

"No, I don't mean that, Magda. I mean, you know, from before you get your period even, guys are just sticking their hands in your clothes and pushing you up against walls. When are you supposed to have time to catch your breath and make an actual decision? By the time you can, you got at least two babies."

"You think it was like that for them, too? Weren't our mothers and their friends more protected and shit? Their parents kept them inside."

Isabel laughs. "Yeah, they kept 'em inside with their uncles and the local priest for a nice visit every so often."

"Right, but I mean, my mother didn't seem broken. She seemed stuck, but not broken." This is the thing Magda can't figure out. It's her weak spot. If either of them is ever going to be like Magda's mother, it's Isabel, not her.

"They got out of their parents' houses and married husbands who wanted them to pretend not to want to fuck," Isabel says. "Wife or whore, and all that crap."

"Are we still talking about my mother?"

"Probably." Isabel turns and looks a faraway look out the carriage house door. "Who knows? You know what? I gotta go. There's something I have to do."

"At one in the morning?"

"Yep," Isabel says. "It only just came to me. This is the perfect time."

Magda stands amid the boxes, watching Isabel's retreating shadow. Sometimes, it seems like her life is full of other people's discarded things. Discarded antique clothes, discarded house, discarded dad, discarded brother. Would it really be so much like death, living in a prefab little box house that no one else has ever lived in before? Maybe it would just feel clean.

thirteen

WHEN ISABEL GETS to the Dunkin' Donuts parking lot there are enough shadows. Only two cars and a motorcycle, but there are places to hide, places where you can't be seen from the wall of plate glass that faces the road. It's been dark for hours and there are hours of darkness left.

It will be a long wait. Isabel spends the time focusing, sharpening herself down to a fine point. It's good to be full of potential, of something real about to happen at last.

Someone has been leaking oil. The parking space where she crouches behind an old Chevy II smells strong. In the daytime it might make her feel sick, but tonight she sucks it right in. This is the kind of air she will breathe now, dirty and strong and explosive, like it's the fuel for dragon's breath. The Chevy throws a boxy shadow big enough for Isabel to crouch in and still see the end of the counter inside. There are two strangers and three vets from the hospital. Vicky moves in and out of sight behind the counter, emptying ashtrays and fending them all off with a vacant smile. When Isabel's legs start to fall asleep, she sits on the curb close to the front wheel and stretches her feet out in front of her. The piece of copper pipe she's been holding makes an echoing clang when she drops it on the ground under her legs. No one is there to hear it; the world behind the glass is a dumb show.

He is there, the one with the spider fingers and the napalm jacket. If she waits, he will leave alone through the parking lot. Everything will happen the way she saw it, flashing suddenly into her head while she stood there in Magda's carriage house. She leans her head against an aluminum fencepost, tilting it up towards the stars. They can't be seen now, anyway, through the dull orange glare bouncing off the sky. She has to take it on faith that they're up there at all.

The other two vets leave first. She shuffles closer to the side of the Chevy and breathes as they go past, soaking in the slow smell of oil until their voices fade.

"I gave it away," one of them says. "It wasn't just me. John the Jock brought back a finger. Ask him."

Then silence. The cars have dwindled down to one every ten minutes by the time he comes out. And yes, he walks right past her, heading for the tear in the chain-link fence. Heading for the woods and the streets behind Ruth's house, but he doesn't get there.

She doesn't have to think. She just lets her body do what she has already seen it doing, swings the pipe first at the back of his knees. He goes down so easily it startles her, drops to his knees and twists his body around to see what hit him. When he sees that it's her, his look of fear turns into disdain.

"What are you doing, you crazy little bitch?"

Even someone so broken he can't tell which part of his life is real knows how to say that. He doesn't even have to try not to be scared of her. It passes across his face as fast as instinct, as soon as he sees that she's a girl.

She hits him again, on the side of his head this time. There is a soft kind of thwack. His body twists around and he falls onto his ass, but he has grabbed the pipe. She can feel the physical strength of him on the other end of it, so much greater than hers. Anger now, but still no fear, still not the look she wants to see in his eyes. Then the eyes go cloudy and his grip loosens, just for a second.

She twists the pipe out of his hand and hits him again, aiming for the same place. For a weird moment she imagines him like a bruised apple, rotten surfaces and parts of him gone soft. No good for eating. He holds his head in one hand, his elbow in the oil slick on the asphalt, still looking up at her. Afraid at last.

"Crazy little bitch," he says again. But it doesn't sound the same.

Now there is fear coming off him in waves; adrenaline mixes with the petroleum air. Isabel takes a long breath, soaking it in. He gasps quietly now, his body moving rhythmically inside his jacket. Everything else freezes. The road behind them is silent.

The people left at the counter inside mime their actions behind glass under the invisible stars. The world has telescoped down into this one shadow. Inside it are the two of them, breathing.

Once Isabel feels full up with fear and power, she takes a long, last breath and time starts up again. One more swing and his head drops.

Turning her back, she steps through the hole in the fence and heads into the woods. The copper pipe falls from her hand into the scrub and she keeps walking, into the scratchy darkness between the trees. Behind her there are two dark stains on the asphalt, blood seeping into oil in the shadows.

fourteen

RUTH'S MOM SAYS Matt should take the flag home. Danny keeps lifting it out of the eighteenth hole and putting it back in. He is doing an imitation of Neil Armstrong, walking like he's wearing enormous boots and there's hardly any gravity and saying some patriotic shit in a scratchy radio voice. It isn't that funny, but Matt and her mom are laughing their asses off.

They have blankets, but Ruth has wrapped herself up in a wool Salvation Army cape, blue on the outside with red lining. Her mom has limits on how much pot and booze she can have, but there's no limit on the weird hippie food. She has hummus and tabbouleh for days. Lots of food and a little raspberry cordial have made Ruth feel dreamy and happy, even with Danny here. He'll be gone soon, one way or another.

The grass on the green is like a cop's haircut, every blade

measured to exactly the same length. While Danny steps over her, doing his Neil Armstrong, Ruth is working her way through one of her earliest memories. It's been bothering her all night. There was a day when she played outside with Magda while her mom cleaned for Mrs. Warren. They were really little, way before Henry was born. They were in the carriage house, where it was always dark and dusty. The air was gritty and comforting, and Ruth loved the loft door. There was no hayloft anymore, just that door. It had long iron hinges and swung open a square of light, up high in the front wall. Doors were for stepping through. When she was really little she imagined there must have once been people who could step through that door without falling and just float away, walking through the air. Later, she figured it out about gravity and the hayloft. Fall from grace.

They used to lie on their backs in there, watching the birds fly in and out, chattering. The straw of the birds' nests stuck out on either side of the rafters. Magda said birds could spit glue, that's how they made the nests stay up there. That might have been later, when she said that. On this day, one of them stumbled in the brightness coming out of the carriage house door, and fell into the gravel on the driveway.

This is the thing, she can't remember whether it was her or Magdalene. She can picture the knee and the red spot with the stone in the middle. It wasn't stuck on; it was flush with the surface of the skin. That made her feel sick. Skin wasn't supposed to do that with things. There was a kind of inside/outside thing about it that made her want to throw up. They didn't want to cry or tell anyone because they weren't allowed in the carriage house by themselves. In their little kid heads they thought they'd have to explain how it happened and get in trouble. Ruth can remember Magda's bathtub with the blood and the water and the piece of gravel circling down the drain. There was Mrs. Warren, beautiful with her hair coming undone, making everything safe again. She'd taken the pebble out with the sharp part of a toenail file and put Mercurochrome on the cut. But Ruth just honestly doesn't know whether the stone was in her knee or Magda's. She'll ask, and Magda will roll her eyes and tell her the answer. Magda acts like everything is as obvious as the color of the sky. Even when she doesn't know the answer, she rolls her eyes like you're stupid for not knowing she wouldn't know.

Mackie says Ruth needs to be the person she is, not the person Magda makes her. He says she's more than all the people around her put together, that she's here for a special, separate reason. It's up to her to put everything in the right place. Danny and what to do about him are up to her. If she is going to make him go away, she'll have to do it without Magda.

Her mother tugs on the corner of her cape, and she realizes she hasn't been paying attention. "Look that way," Matt is saying, pointing out over the Sound, away from the haze of light over Highbone and into the clear sky.

"You watching, Ruth?" Her mother laughs and tugs again. "Where have you been, girlie?"

"Magda's house. When we were little. I was remembering something."

"They'll come up from the northeast," Matt says, "like they're spraying up from the horizon. They call them the Lyrids because it looks like they come from a constellation named Lyra, but they don't. I guess back in the day, the old guys thought they did, before they had good telescopes and stuff. They're actually between us and Lyra. People thought they were falling stars that came from those constellations, so they named them after the constellation it looked like they were coming from. They were Italians, you know, lots of the great astronomers, like Galileo."

"I always liked the sound of falling stars," Ruth sighs. It's like the hayloft door, another thing that turns out not to really be. "So if they're not stars, what are they?"

"They come from comets. Comets sort of like carry loads of stuff along with them because of gravity."

"So, how do you know all this, Matt?" Her mom sounds all interested and motherly.

"Oh, I saw a thing on PBS."

"No, he didn't," Ruth says. "He reads about it. Don't pretend you don't, Matt. Mom thinks people who read are cool."

Matt looks embarrassed now, and Ruth realizes he doesn't really know them that well. He's awed by them because they hang out at the beach making fires and smoke pot with the kid. Her. She is an accessory to his worship of her mother's coolness.

"They're made of ice," Matt says. "In the ice there's dust and little pieces of space crap. So, uh, when the comets buzz past, some of the ice melts, and the little pieces of rock get caught in earth's gravity and burn up in the atmosphere. Mostly they burn up before they come anywhere near the ground, but sometimes they're really ginormous, and they land and make craters and stuff."

"But why are they going up?" Ruth knows her mother isn't that dumb. She's just saying it because Matt sounds nervous and she's trying to give him a reason to feel smart.

"It just looks like that because of the way we're rotating," Matt says. "In space, there is no up. The earth is round, with space in every direction. Up is only a concept if you're standing on something really, really big."

If you could speed up time, just lying still and looking at the sky would make you dizzy. Sometimes you can see that, if you lie down on your back on the football field when clouds are going by. They're all on a ride together, like at the firemen's fair. It's just that the ride is too big for them to be able to tell, most of the time.

"Anyway," Matt says, "in space terms, meteors are not coming from far away at all. They're really way closer than anything else in the sky."

Just passing sparks trapped by the atmosphere. Just prisoners of gravity disguised as gifts from the stars.

REALITY

one

THE MOON IS up, and you can't see the falling stars from here. Ruth has been drawing, and her bed is full of paper and pencils. Every time she turns over, her pictures crunch like autumn leaves, but she doesn't want to put them away. She won't sleep tonight anyway. There is a clue here; the world is trying to tell her something. The only way to get it out of her head is to draw it. Once, when they were reading Edgar Allan Poe in English, Mr. Driscoll said a clue means a ball of yarn. It's the thing you use, like Ariadne, to make sure you don't get lost in the labyrinth. Hold on and follow it; you can't let go.

Whatever it is she can feel moving towards them all lately, it becomes almost clear for a minute when she tries to put it on paper. It's like ever since she burned her birth certificate, things have started to show themselves. The pictures are whispering the truth into the dark. She can hear them.

No, it's someone outside the window, calling up at her from the yard at two thirty in the morning. When she puts her head out the window there is Isabel, standing in two kinds of shadow. Half of her face is mottled with green darkness and the other half is invisible. Is she shaking, or is it just the way the shadows are moving over her?

"Ruth, I need you," she says. "Come outside."

"Now? I was sleeping."

"No, you weren't. I heard you talking to yourself. I just need some company." Isabel is standing very straight, holding herself with every muscle. She's poised like a tightrope walker, like if she lets go of any part of herself or breathes too fast, she'll fall off of the world.

"Jesus, Isabel. What happened? Did Matt catch you guys?"

"What?" She looks confused, like she robbed someone's house and then forgot about it. "Oh. No, it's all good. The weed's in Magda's carriage house. We can figure out what to do with it later. Come outside, please."

"All right, be quiet. You're gonna wake someone up."

Ruth throws down blankets and candles, cigarettes and a sleeping bag from her bedroom, and whispers for Isabel to wait in the back by the woods.

"Bring your mom's mescal."

She puts her drawings away in the box under the bed, and then takes her mom's tequila from the dark, spicy living room. Under the trees Isabel has already spread the blankets. From the kitchen door, Ruth can see the burning ember of her cigarette and the blue-white shadow of the blanket. She can smell Isabel's smoke and the earth under the trees.

"Who do you love the most?" Ruth holds up the half-full bottle of mescal and swirls the worm around the bottom. "Me, right? I'm the one. My mom will notice, and she will be very, very scary. She's had this for, like, ten years. Her friend Susan brought it back from the Yucatan."

"Its time has come, Ruth. Trust me. And yeah, you're the one. I actually think you are."

"You gonna tell me what's the matter?"

"Can we just stay here and not talk about me?" Isabel says. "What kind of weird shit are you thinking tonight? Tell me about it."

"I was drawing. Well, I was in the dark, but before that I was drawing. Don't you think things are getting kind of weird lately, Isabel?"

"I guess." It's like someone invisible is shouting in Isabel's other ear the whole time, and she's trying to pretend they're not there.

"I want to change that flower I drew on the wall in your room," Ruth says. "I have an idea."

"No way. We're not going to my house, maybe ever again." Isabel is still shaking, but she doesn't look scared exactly. She looks full of some kind of energy, like sparks would fly off if you brushed up against her.

"Okay, I'm just saying. I was thinking about tulips, and Mrs.

Warren and your mom, and just housewives in general. I want that flower to be a tulip. Tulips are a little like housewives. When they first pop up they look all domestic and Dutch and remind you of windmills and shit, but when you bring them in the house they change. In the house, they get kind of tropical. They look like sex and danger. Tulips make me think of a dumpy housewife in her terry cloth bathrobe, stripping off and turning into some kind of Mrs. Robinson."

"Are you suggesting my mom has some secret Mrs. Robinson element to her? 'Cause that's nuts. And also, ewww."

"I just want to change that flower on your wall into a tulip," Ruth says. "But not a picture-book tulip, an open one."

By the time the false dawn comes, their cigarettes are making trails as they move to and from their mouths, and the stars won't stay still in the sky. The mescal is gone and they've split the worm. They're lying in a weird mix of streetlight and starlight, all patterned by shadows from the woods behind Ruth's house.

Then she notices Isabel's eyes, staring out of that light.

"What? Why are you staring at me?"

"You're always surprising me lately. The stuff that comes out of your brain amazes me. Seriously, I don't mean that in a sarcastic way."

"I'm surprising myself, too. It's kind of more scary than amazing, trust me."

"Ha. Ruth Carter, you have no idea how much a person can surprise themselves. Trust *me*." Isabel has another cigarette in her mouth, but she forgets to light it.

"Hang on, hang on." Ruth cups a match, and then they both have to laugh at the trails the flame makes. "Jesus, we're wasted."

"Anyway, I was just feeling a little bit of awe." Isabel pauses for a long drag, then cocks her head. "Is that an oxymoron, a little bit of awe?"

"We'll let it go."

"You know, Ruth, we could . . . I mean, no one's here. Don't you think I should just kiss you? Should I?"

"Christ, Isabel! You like guys, everyone knows that."

"I like you, too, Ruth. Don't be so suburban."

"You're addicted to male attention, Bel. That's why you're never going to live by yourself on a houseboat. There's always gonna be some skinny, brooding artist leaving his dirty socks around. Guys are your fucking vocation."

"Bel? I'm Bel all of a sudden?"

"I'm kind of drunk and tripping. Three syllables is a lot. Anyway, you're talking crap."

"Shut up," Isabel says. "I need you right now. Anyway, I want to." And she does, and all the rest of it is Isabel's idea too.

Ruth can feel the nervous energy in Isabel's body. She always imagined it would feel still and weightless, holding someone like Isabel. Like dreaming. This is like speeding down a highway while you're trying to put your hand out and touch the car next to you.

After a while she has to bite Isabel's shoulder so she won't shout and wake up the neighbors. For a second, she imagines a circle of angry middle-aged suburbanites in their bathrobes holding pitchforks, staring down at them with hellfire in their eyes.

But then Isabel whispers in her ear.

"Come on," she says. "You have to save me now."

There is a shadow over Ruth, and where the shadow isn't, she can feel the daylight on her skin. When she opens her eyes, it will be morning and there will be a third person there, so she keeps them closed as long as she can. She can hear Isabel next to her, breathing quick, oblivious breaths. At some point, Isabel was crying in her sleep, but that stopped hours ago.

It turns out to be Mackie, standing there in front of the light, just the black outline of his coat against the sun. She can't see his eyes, but she realizes he must be able to see all the parts of them that aren't covered.

"Didn't I tell you you'd be new?" he says.

"This is what you meant?" Ruth puts a hand up to shade her eyes and Mackie's face resolves out of the shadow.

"Maybe. Come and have a smoke; she looks like she's down for the count."

Ruth wraps an open sleeping bag around herself and makes her way over to sit with Mackie on the kitchen steps. The cold cement feels good scratching the backs of her calves. Mackie smells like a bar and also like the ocean.

"So, how you feeling?" He cranes his neck to look around and into Ruth's eyes.

"About what?"

"Everything, little Carter. Everything."

"This doesn't mean they're suddenly going to get me," Ruth sighs. "You can touch people without touching them, you know?"

"Why do you keep giving yourself to people, Ruth?"

"Uh, duh. Because I want them to give themselves back. Doesn't everybody?"

"You think she wants that?" He tosses his head towards Isabel.

"No, I don't. How come you know everything about everyone? You never even met Isabel."

"Seen 'em all before. There's another way to do things, you know. You could just take what you want and let everybody else look to themselves. That's what they're all doing."

"Lately I think I might do something drastic. Something I can't take back. I want to set things straight around here, but do I actually want to hurt people? I mean I would, totally, to protect my mom, but is that actually what I'm doing?"

"So," he says, "what is it you want?"

"I kind of want to know about my dad. I mean, you know, on one level I don't give a shit. But why does my mom have to lie to me about it? Everyone knows who he is, but no one will ever say it. There's a picture of me and my parents in the encyclopedia under 'Elephant in the Living Room.'"

"People are never gonna be honest, Ruth. You have to learn to see through them."

"There isn't any room for me to talk about stuff like that around those two." She looks up at Isabel. "What's the point? But, you know, people are messed up and wrong. I don't see why we have to just leave it like that."

"Well?" Mackie stretches his legs out on the steps and looks sideways at her.

"I want to make people admit what they've done. How come somebody gets to slam my mom up against the wall and then just walk away? I don't want people to get away with just screwing people over, especially not us."

"What if you're the one who's right?" he says. "Remember that time in karate when the sensei yelled at you because you turned a different way from everyone else? He wanted you to defend yourself because you were the only one who got it right. You're not crazy. You just trust other people too much. Whatever you think you might do, maybe it's the right thing."

"Even if it hurts?"

"Everything hurts."

"She won't care, Mackie." Ruth points at the blankets and the empty bottle and Isabel in the middle of the mess with her arms tossed out to the side. "It won't mean anything."

"Not to her, maybe. People don't have a right to just use you, Ruth. Maybe you're the first woman in your family who's gonna do something about it."

"I can't sleep these days, Mackie. If she didn't come, I would have been up all night anyway, just dreaming with my eyes open. I'm so tired."

"Fix things. Then you can rest." He stands up and puts his hands in the pockets of his coat, turning away from her to face the woods.

"Where were you anyway, Mackie? Have you been up all night? You just going home?"

He doesn't turn around, just raises his hand and walks into the trees towards the brake repair shop.

two

RUTH CAN FEEL the heat from under the hood of Danny's car when she climbs up to sit on it. Danny is in the deli, getting them take-out Saturday breakfast. He came into the backyard this morning and said if they wanted they could go out on the boat with him. He said the sun would burn the haze off the water and it would be warm enough to swim. Creepy the way he keeps trying to suck up to her.

"It's Saturday and I'm up at seven o'clock." Isabel slumps down onto the stoop of Mariner's Maps and Books. "This is just twisted."

"You're the one that wanted to come, Isabel. I didn't want to play the happy-families game."

She can tell Isabel isn't even thinking about what happened in the night. She won't remember it next week, probably. Matt, then Isabel, and now Danny. And still Isabel. Isn't there someone you can apply to for a break when too many things happen at once? She remembers Mackie, fading into the trees.

A little gust of summer blows up Main Street. Ruth stretches her arms out to welcome it, trying to feel that August heat that will come up off the street just to wrap around them and hold them. Spring is so merciless, the light without the heat, and the way it fools you and then throws cold breezes, so you never know what to wear or when you can relax. In the summer, days will be slower, even though they have the same number of hours. One night they'll realize they're out in the dark with short sleeves, wrapped in just the warm air.

Today, there is that mist that comes off the water when two seasons collide. Danny could feel it all the way from South Highbone, the way fishermen do. He said it meant the air would be warm over the water.

"You know there are tunnels under here, and whole rooms and stuff," Isabel says with her eyes closed, head against Mr. Lipsky's glass door.

"What?"

"Underground Highbone," she says. "It's left over from Prohibition, secret speakeasies with bars and pianos."

"That's a myth," Ruth says. "Everyone knows someone who's been down there, but have you ever actually met someone who's seen it?"

"It's not. People have been down there. We could probably get into every building on Main Street from the tunnels under there. We can move the weed down there. It could be our secret headquarters."

Why won't she stop talking? All this stuff about tunnels under their feet is wrecking Ruth's thoughts about warmth and light. Isabel showed up last night and just bulldozed her way right into Ruth's body. Now she won't shut up.

Ruth looks down to the bottom of Main Street, where Lefty is standing by the floating dock with his friend Robert. They've got their heads bent down, scanning the sidewalk for abandoned treasure. You can tell they haven't been to sleep. They've been standing for hours at the edge of the park, smoking the rescued ends of cigarettes and waiting for the air to turn from blue to yellow. Maybe Lefty is about to open up his mouth and let out the poetry that's been building up all night. It will sound slow and soft in the warm air.

"Come on." She pokes Isabel with her foot. "Let's say hi to Lefty and his friend. We can get a poem for breakfast."

"I was talking, you know, Ruth."

"Yeah, but Lefty's talk is better."

She's trying to distract herself from wanting to shake Isabel off and lean into her at the same time.

"Wanna hear a poem?" Lefty pronounces it *po-em*.

"Yeah Lefty, thanks," Ruth says. "Poem for me and Isabel, please. I'll pay you two Larks, how's that?"

He takes in a big breath and then lets go. "I cut off my hand . . ."

"Not that one, Lefty. It's a little early."

"Oh." Lefty looks confused. He's not big on choosing his words before they come out. Even though somewhere in the back of his mind there, his brain is putting them into meter and rhyme and long complicated stories, as far as he's concerned, reciting his poems is like sneezing. Unless you try really hard to stifle them, they just come out.

"Give us the one about the trip to Montauk," Isabel says. "We love that one."

Lefty brightens right up. He straightens himself a little and tucks in his chin like he's thinking, then he lets go again.

Just when he gets to, "If it was long, it was bright, and that was the morning / the road was long, black nothing with a yellow scar," Danny comes out of the deli and waves.

"Rain check, Lefty?" Ruth says. "We will definitely want the rest later. Take the cigarettes on spec."

When they walk out onto the dock, Isabel points at the drainpipe in the wall behind them. "Look at that," she says. "That's one of the ways you get in."

"Get in where?"

"To Underground Highbone, Ruth. Pay attention. You wait for low tide and walk up there."

The bottom half of the drainpipe is underwater. All of it is full of blackness, like an open mouth, shouting under the edge of Main Street.

"My sister went under there," Isabel says. "I was telling Charlie and Magda. For real, she went down with her friends and brought back this old, thick coffee mug from behind a bar. It's in our kitchen cabinet. Underground Highbone really is there."

"Okay, so?"

Ruth can feel the damp darkness under the road, the seaweed hanging from the walls and the rotting wood, waiting for half a century without light. Somewhere, stray notes from old music are hidden in corners and cracks down there. It's the kind of thing she'd like to draw, but you can't draw what happens in the dark.

"I'm just saying"—Isabel points at the drainpipe—"if one of us ever needs a place to hide out."

"Hide out? No thanks, Isabel. Actually working really hard not to be invisible over here."

Danny is talking to some guys outside the deli. Men who work on Saturday mornings are coming through the door with breakfasts wrapped up in foil, landscapers and fishermen and road workers. When Ruth looks over at Danny, he smiles and puts a thumb up at her, like they're hokey best friends. Why can't everyone just go away? Somewhere to hide? No. What she needs is the power to make everyone else disappear.

Lefty's friend Robert has found a dead pigeon in the gutter with the cigarette butts. He throws it up and catches it, over and over again, staring at it with some kind of bored wonder. All the weekend yachters sit on their decks, drinking their coffee, not noticing. From where they're standing, Robert and Lefty don't exist.

"Let's go, sunshines. Time's a wastin'," Danny says, handing her a box full of coffees and egg sandwiches in bags.

"Sunshines?"

Danny has a parking permit, and a license for one of the only sandy clam beds on the North Shore. He got those things when his father was through with them. It doesn't even bother him, doing exactly what his father did. He likes it. He's proud to be one of the only clam rakers on the North Shore. Down on Great South Bay, clammers are a dime a dozen, he says.

Doesn't he feel suffocated? Pointless?

Lefty and Robert are looking down into the water, where the pigeon is now floating next to a Styrofoam cup. Danny gets protective and steps in front of Ruth and Isabel. Just to rile him up, Ruth ducks her head around his shoulder, waves, and shouts good-bye.

Danny says, "It's no joke, flowergirl. Those are broken people." Then he jumps onto the dock.

"Yep. Broken right open," Isabel says. "It's not completely a bad thing, Danny. Turns out when you break some people open, amazing poetry comes out."

"Why didn't *you* go to Vietnam?"

For a second Danny looks like Ruth slapped him, then he mellows out again. The guy is impossible to break through. He's like liquid.

"I can't really talk about it, Ruth. It wasn't strictly legal."

It's warm on the boat and Isabel takes off her Navy sweater. Underneath, she's wearing Ruth's bikini and her jeans.

While Danny checks over the boat, Lefty's one-armed shadow falls over them. He's lured by the idea of more cigarettes, whole and entire and out of a pack. Ruth lies down and closes her eyes while Isabel hands him three Larks and half her egg sandwich, telling him to have a beautiful summer day. Just sunshine and feet two inches off the ground, Isabel O'Sullivan. What happened to the shaking and the pleading? Isabel of last night and Isabel of this morning don't add up. It's spooky.

"Not until June twenty-first. Summer's not till the twenty-first, Isabel." Lefty's proud of himself for pegging that one down. It's weird how someone can be that smart and still get worked up over what day it is. What's the difference between a schizophrenic and a mad professor?

Danny coils up his mooring rope and starts the engine. Ruth keeps her eyes closed until she feels the air around them open all the way up. The space next to her is full of Isabel. The heat of her makes Ruth feel hollow and a little sick. When she opens her eyes and sits up, they're swinging around the head of the harbor. Lefty and the drainpipe have shrunk into the distance. The sun has burned through and scattered itself in little gold pieces across the surface of the Sound.

Once they're in the cove Isabel asks if she can go in the water, and Danny nods, putting his rake together. Isabel puts out her cigarette in the can that's nailed to the engine house and says, "Watch!" Then she lays her body on the side of the boat opposite Danny. The boat pitches when she rolls off into the water.

Ruth huffs. "You do realize any other guy would curse at her, don't you? She nearly knocked you over. Only a man who refuses to throw his cigarette butts in the ocean would be that calm. It's not right."

"What's to get worked up about?" Danny shrugs. "You're only kids. And why would I throw my garbage on top of the clams?"

"Where do you think it goes when you throw it away, man? Some guys in Queens put it on a barge and dump it in here anyway."

He just leans on a section of rake handle and smiles, like he's about to tell her that everything is fine.

"Don't look at me like that. I'm serious. Now watch me. I'm far more considerate." Ruth slips over the side, feet first.

There is that wall of shock you slam into every year, the first time you dive in the water. It feels like her heart will stop, and for a few seconds her lungs are frozen. The water is cold and green. She rolls over and waits for it to go calm. Once her heart slows down and the sea is still again, she can lie there without trying. The heavy water, full of salt, holds her up. If she doesn't move at all, there will be nothing in her field of vision but sky. Blue above and the dark deep underneath her.

"Shit, it's so cold I think I'm gonna freeze up and sink." Isabel, stirring up the darkness again. She shouts over at Danny, "Didn't there used to be oyster beds around here?"

"Still are. Why do you think they call that Oyster Bay over there?"

Isabel swims closer to listen, and Ruth tries to go back to the deep and the sky. But it's no good.

"All right, smartass," Isabel says. "I mean did they used to dig oysters in Highbone?"

"Not in Highbone, but they used to land them here to get

cleaned and packed in the oyster houses. Put 'em on the train to the city every morning. My granddad was an oysterman. The oyster houses were where the yacht club is, I think."

"What happened to them?" Isabel treads water by the side of the boat.

"What happened to everything, flowergirl?" Danny lets the rake down the other side. "Shit changed. Beds got cleaned out and they closed 'em down. About as much chance of getting one of those permits now as winning the lottery."

He goes back to being quiet then, dragging his rake and pulling it up, section by section. Ruth swims around the stern to watch him. What does her mother need him for? Sex? Can't she get that in some way that's less intrusive? Some way that doesn't involve having a teenaged thirty-year-old taking up their couch, smoking joints and watching Laurel and Hardy all day?

Isabel appears from under the boat, three feet below the surface and painted in pebbly shadows. She breaks the surface next to Ruth and pushes her hair back.

"So, what would it take to satisfy you, exactly?" she says.

"I guess you're talking about Danny. Since you obviously can read my mind 'cause you channel the evil dead or something."

"Well, hmmm. You went all quiet for ages and started sending nasty glares in the direction of the boat. It doesn't take a genius. My talents are wasted, figuring you out. Look, woman, my mother stashes big bags of M&M's in the linen closet and hides for entire weekends behind the living room couch. My father pretends this is because she hasn't drunk enough water.

Are you under the impression your family is worse than anyone else's? You do realize that half the time Magdalene is afraid to go home, and she spends the other half taking care of someone else's baby?"

"I've known her longer than you have, Isabel. I get it. Anyway, you love Henry as much as we do."

"Yes, because even though he's a pain in the ass and he's taken up most of what was supposed to be my best friend's childhood, he's a sweet little guy. He sits on the steps with me and pretends we're pigeons and he tells Lefty he likes his poems, because even though he's only six he's smart enough to tell that's what Lefty wants to hear. Lotsa people suck, I grant you, but not everyone. Not Henry, and we're his good angels. We're gonna help him grow up to not suck. This is my point, woman. Danny is fucking your mom. Your mom wants to fuck Danny. But—and here's the rub, girlie—he also wants to hang out with you guys. He wants to take us out on the boat and do some kind of pretend family thing with you and your friends. It's lame, but what's the big deal? There are worse things."

"Look, whatever. Let's not play my-mom-is-worse-than-your-mom games. We all have stuff to deal with, all right?"

"And I'm supposed to be the one who's self-absorbed? Can we make a deal?" Isabel reaches under the water and grabs the string at the back of Ruth's neck. "You be nice to Danny for two hours and I won't show everyone on the water your tits."

Ruth rolls over and slaps hard, but misses. "You won't show everyone on the water my tits because you're a village pussy and

I'm from South Highbone. I'd kick your ass and you know it, Miss Head-in-the-Clouds-Everybody-Is-Wonderful-Really. Have you thought about how we're gonna sell Matt's weed?"

"What? No. I kind of got distracted."

"Distracted? Who's self-absorbed now? You ruined some guy's life, Isabel. I think it should at least pay."

"Are my lips blue? I'm freezing. It isn't remotely summer yet, is it?"

Ruth turns away and swims towards the boat. No point trying to get Isabel O'Sullivan into a conversation about consequences.

They throw themselves down on the boards at the front of Danny's boat, with their heads at the bow and their feet over either side. Ruth's arms are full of goose bumps and the salt is drying into crusty shapes on her skin. Maybe she could sleep here.

"*I* ruined some guy's life?" Isabel says. "I think you mean *we*."

"So you were listening to me."

"You're the one who did the big turnaround, Ruth. You were the one with the big 'take no prisoners' speech."

Ruth looks over at Danny in the stern. He's sorting through a rake full of creatures from the seabed, tossing crabs back and passing his clams through a ring. He isn't listening.

"Admit it," Isabel says. "You got pissed off at Matt for some reason and suddenly thought it was a good idea."

"Yeah, but it was *your* idea, Isabel. Everything that hurts is your idea."

three

MAGDA WALKS TOWARDS the water with everything at her back. Her father, her brother, the carriage house full of Matt Kerwin's weed, the inescapable riptide in her body that seems to be caused by Jeff Snyder. She turned her back on all of it this morning, got out of bed and walked away, but that doesn't seem to help these days. She can still feel it all pressing on her, pushing her on towards the harbor.

"Magdalene!" Mrs. Hancock is waving at her from the door of Mariner's Maps and Books.

No. Just no.

"Magdalene Warren! Come and say hello to me, young lady."

Jesus, it's Saturday morning. It's not even nine o'clock; nothing's open. Why does she have to deal with this? It's too late to turn around, and there's no side alley to duck into. You can't turn your back on everything when you're completely surrounded.

"Hi, Mrs. Hancock. Hi, Mr. Lipsky."

"Hi, Magdalene," Mr. Lipsky says. "Come on in."

"Get the girl a coffee to warm her up, Sam."

"It's seventy degrees, Mrs. Hancock. I'm good, really."

Old Mr. Lipsky, the dad, is leaning in the doorway at the back of the shop. He stands kind of crooked, like one leg is shorter than the other.

"Put the coffeepot on, Sam," he says. "I'll get cups."

"No, really, Mr. Lipsky. It's . . ." But he's already shuffling back up the stairs.

"I haven't seen you in ages," Mrs. Hancock says. "You're getting taller, Magda."

"Yeah, that happens."

Mrs. Hancock is impervious to sarcasm. That goes with being married to the guy who owns the yacht club. Believing you're the biggest thing in a pathetic little town like Highbone requires a certain suspension of disbelief. Young Mr. Lipsky puts an espresso pot on the hot plate in the back and they all get uncomfortably quiet until Old Mr. Lipsky comes back with three cups. There is already one for Young Mr. Lipsky on the counter by the cash register.

"Now, wait just a minute. I want to get this straight." Old Mr Lipsky points at Magda. "Your mother was little Irene Buonvicino?"

"Leave it, Pop," Mr. Lipsky says. "The kid doesn't want your reminiscences." He moves a bunch of shipping receipts and a couple of paperbacks to make room on the counter to pour coffee.

"It's okay, Mr. Lipsky. I don't mind. Yeah, my mom's name was Irene Buonvicino before she got married. She left town, though."

"You'll have to call us by our first names, Magdalene," Young Mr. Lipsky says, pouring out coffee. "We're both Mr. Lipsky. I'm Sam, this is Emmanuel."

"Like Emmanuel the savior?"

"Just Manny is fine." He leans towards Magda, taking her in. "I knew your mother when she was a little girl, playing in the back of Villa Buonvicino. Her mother and father were customers of mine. And friends. Good people."

Magda looks away at the shelves, then down at her Chuck Taylors. Manny has one of those nice, shaky old voices. He knew her mother when she was a baby. He was young then, maybe with a snuffbox and an argyle vest. Dapper, Magda thinks. Bet he was dapper.

"Where have you been hiding, anyway, Magdalene?" Mrs. Hancock has a voice like breaking glass. "I've been worried about you."

"Uh, I'm not the one hiding, Mrs. Hancock. Not the one who disappeared."

"Oh, Magdalene. I just want you to know you can talk to me. I've been around. I can listen, maybe even give you advice."

It's really hard not to laugh at that. Yeah, Mrs. Hancock was her mother's friend, but Magda can't think of anyone possessed of a smaller store of wisdom. Near as she can figure out, Allison Hancock's entire goal in life was to claw her way to the top of Highbone's little tiny snob heap. More like a social step stool than a social ladder. Magda's mom said Mrs. Hancock grew up in South Highbone. Marrying Harold Hancock is her big accomplishment, then she has to bump into his love child all over town. Now that is depressing.

The coffee is boiling hot but Magda drinks it as fast as she can. It's like a hostage situation in here. A gang of grown-ups has abducted her and won't let her go.

"I know your friend Ruth," Manny says. "Looks like a movie star, but smart, too."

"Yep, that's Ruth."

"She told me she's going to be an artist, but she said she was keeping it secret." Ruth picked the wrong confidant, obviously. "What are you going to be, little Buonvicino?"

"It's Warren, actually. My last name's Warren. But you can call me Buonvicino. It's kind of nice."

Maybe she could change her name officially. That would be cool. Her dad would flip out.

Finally, Magda makes it to the front door of Mariner's Maps and Books and opens it. They're all still talking at her, but she just keeps her eyes down and waves. The bell jangles, and the sun is so bright it makes her stumble down the step. She leans against the wall of the deli to let her eyes adjust. At the bottom of Main Street, Jeff Snyder comes into focus, standing with a bunch of guys around a Mustang.

It's like someone ripped the blanket off the top of the world today. She's naked, with nowhere to hide.

Jeff isn't looking her way, so she crosses the street and ducks down the path into the park. Lefty is lying on the bench by the bandstand, but he isn't sleeping. He's staring up at the leaves on the trees and mumbling to himself.

"Magdalene," he says. "It means harlot, you know."

"Thanks, Lefty."

"Holy harlot, though," Lefty says.

"Redeemed, my mom said. Mrs. Farrow at school said it's priestess, really."

"Wholly redeemed." Lefty makes prayer hands on his chest, pretending to be the tomb of a saint.

"You seen Ruth or Isabel, Lefty?"

"They're afloat. Left. With eggs. On a boat."

"They what? We don't know anyone with a boat, Lefty. Are you sure?"

"Magdalene Warren." Jeff comes up behind her and leans both elbows on her shoulders like she's his personal piece of furniture. "Come on," he says. "Sorry, Lefty, me and Magdalene gotta go." Jeff walks away without looking back.

And she follows him. Her stomach feels like someone dropped a rock in it.

"Didn't you see me when you came in the park?" He sounds a little pissed off.

"Yeah, you were talking. I didn't want to bother you."

"You're not gonna bother me, Warren. We like each other, don't we?" Charm now, but he put it on so fast it doesn't convince her. Or maybe it does.

"Someone was saying a dealer up in South Highbone got robbed. We were just talking about it. Anyway, it doesn't matter."

He grabs Magda by the arms and kisses her. As soon as he lets go she sits down on the grass and looks at his knees. She has to work hard to stay in her own body and keep breathing. If she stood up right now, she'd fall over.

"I like you, Magdalene Warren. You with me?"

She reaches in her pockets for cigarettes and all she comes up with is a multi-tool and an empty cassette case.

"You don't listen so good," Jeff says. "I asked you a question. You with me?"

"I . . . um . . . I don't know." The cigarettes are in her inside pocket, but if she takes one out of the pack, she might shake when she tries to light it.

"Let's go somewhere else," he says. "Come on." He isn't going to wait for an answer.

"I have to go back home, for Henry." It's kind of true.

Jeff sits down and puts his legs over hers. He kisses her again, and reaches inside her coat to put his hand under her shirt. Then he stands up and says, "I give you my number, you gonna call me?"

"I'll try." She doesn't have enough breath left to make more words than that.

"Huh?"

"I said I'll try."

Now he looks mad, for sure. He writes his number on a 7-Eleven matchbook, throws it down into her lap, and walks away.

Lefty is chanting now, on the bench by the bandstand, sounding like a medieval monk. There are sailboats passing each other at the mouth of the harbor, and someone is playing "Stairway to Heaven" on an acoustic guitar at the end of the pier. Two guys are sitting on the rocks at the edge of the water with a bottle of Night Train and a chess set. If they let Carson McCullers make tourist postcards, they'd look like Highbone Park on a Saturday morning.

four

IT'S MONDAY AGAIN, but Ruth doesn't feel like she could get away with anything. Ever since the robbery, it's like an ax is hanging over her, ready to fall. She keeps waiting for people to jump up and say they know everything, about Matt's weed and Danny's tires and her and Isabel and Mackie and the things she still wants to do.

What would Magda say? Well, she won't say anything because Ruth didn't tell her where she's going. She's been hiding in the girls' room, waiting for Magda and Isabel to leave school. When she comes out the swinging door, the marble floors are empty and shining, and her shadow stretches unbroken from the girls' room to the door of Administration.

The guidance counselor's office has spider plants in macramé plant hangers and a sign that says, *Someday schools will get all the money they need and the army will have to hold bake sales to buy bombs.* Ms. Jimenez, her guidance counselor, looks exactly like the kind of person who would have those plant hangers and that sign. As soon as Ruth sees her, she worries that her mom might know the lady. She looks like the kind of woman Caroline Carter would hang out with. She has two long braids and an Indian shirt.

"Hi, Ruth. It's good to see you," Ms. Jimenez says. "Sit down and relax."

"How can it be good to see me? You don't even know me."

Ruth stands in the doorway, wanting to leave and wanting to stay and wishing she could ask Virgil Mackie what to do. Whatever he would say, it wouldn't be, "Calm down." It wouldn't be, "Smile, everything's fine."

Why is she turning herself over to people who want to smooth out her jagged edges and slow down her breathing? She doesn't want to calm down. The situation doesn't call for calm.

Ms. Jimenez is chuckling. "Okay, but it isn't every day a student comes to see me by themselves, without somebody making them. Have a seat. Is there something special you wanted to talk about?"

Why else would she be here?

"You're not allowed to tell anyone what I say, right?"

"Well," Ms. Jimenez says, "not unless I think you or someone else is in serious danger. That's the rule." She smiles.

Why the fuck is she smiling about serious danger?

"I'm a little worried about stuff, but I don't want to be shrunk.

I'm fine; I don't want somebody to turn me into some kind of Stepford wife. I just can't always talk to my friends or my mom."

"Do I look like I'm into the Stepford wife thing?" Ms. Jimenez laughs again.

She's a little overly jolly for somebody who deals with the soul-death fallout of suburban families all day.

"There are some questions I have to ask you," Ms. Jimenez says. "They might seem strange, but it's a requirement, so let's just do them quick, and then we can talk, okay? Do you ever think about hurting yourself or anyone else?"

"Just the president." Ruth laughs now, but it doesn't sound the same as Ms. Jimenez's laugh at all.

"Seriously, though. Can you answer truthfully? Do you ever have thoughts about hurting yourself or anyone else?"

"Of course I do! Have you been outside this office lately? Do you have any idea how messed up the world is? You can't fix it with Buddhist chanting and macramé workshops, you know. It's a little beyond that." Ruth is shouting. She goes quiet and looks away out the window. "But, you know," she says, "it's only just thoughts. They're free, right?"

"I can see you're angry, Ruth. I just want to be clear. It's okay, we all have bad days and we all feel mad sometimes. So, sometimes you feel so mad you wish you could hurt yourself? Or hurt someone else?"

"Show me a woman who doesn't fantasize about hurting herself," Ruth says, "and I'll show you a liar. The whole world is designed to make us feel helpless. We can't even trust each other.

What are we supposed to do with all that? And then people like you want to make us calm down. We should be shouting and burning things down."

Outside the window, the lacrosse team is warming up, with their girlfriends standing on the sidelines in little bunches. It looks like rain, and the seagulls are circling over the football field, screaming. The sound they're making is exactly the sound she wants to make, but the world won't let her.

These days, she can't even predict her own actions. It's like she's in a big surf and trying to ride it, all the time. They say drowning is like falling asleep, once you stop struggling, once you calm down. But Ruth just keeps gasping for air, wanting to grab on to something. Here she is now, grabbing on.

"Ms. Jimenez? I read somewhere that if people are gonna go crazy, you know, schizophrenic, it happens when they're teenagers. Is that true?"

She smiles. That is her actual reaction.

"Okay, I'm asking you if I'm losing my grip on reality. I want to know whether I'm going to spend the rest of my life surrounded by dirty linoleum, playing checkers on Thorazine. Do you have maybe another facial expression for that?"

"I'm sorry, Ruth. I'm trying to let you know that you're safe here."

"Not really working. Sorry."

"The number of teenagers who worry that they have a serious mental illness is a lot bigger than the number who actually do. How's that for an answer?"

"Pretty vague. How many of those perfectly sane hypochondriacs go weeks on end without sleeping and are too afraid to tell anyone what they're thinking because most of it is completely nuts?"

"Are you having trouble sleeping, Ruth?"

"That's what I said."

"Have you asked your mother to take you to the doctor about it?"

"Seriously, Ms. Jimenez? I'm here because I don't want to talk to anybody about what's happening to me. I mean, I do, but I can't. I'm not going to the doctor with my mom. He's known me since I was born."

"Okay, listen, lack of sleep can have all kinds of effects on you."

"Can it make you see things? Imagine things happening?"

"Yes. And I think you should see the doctor about it." Mrs. Jimenez tries to look stern. It doesn't really work with the braids.

"Maybe this wasn't such a good idea," Ruth says.

She really wants to talk about her mom and Danny, about how to get rid of him and make her life go back to normal. There's a door open in her head and she doesn't know whether to go through. The way she felt at the edge of Ms. Jimenez's office is the way she feels all the time now. Wanting to go through, but also wanting to stay on this side.

"How can it be a bad idea just to talk to someone?" Ms. Jimenez thrusts her head forward and puts on a "caring and concerned" face.

"I don't want to live in Highbone, Ms. Jimenez. Not even for another year. I feel dizzy all the time, like there's no gravity here."

"Well, you'll probably have to be here a while longer, Ruth. So, what can you do to make the time go by?"

"Well, drugs and sex seem to be the preferred options. I've been, you know, exploring my dark side, which is distracting. Sometimes things are just a little much. I live with my mom, you know? She won't talk about my dad, so I kind of had to guess."

"You've never known him?"

"I sort of know who he is, but I can't talk about it to anyone. He's married to someone else and he's kind of a bigwig. I mean for Highbone. For some reason, it's started to bother me lately. It never did before. Then she has a new boyfriend and he practically lives with us now, but no one's asked me. My friends are changing and being weird. I don't get all this crap about men. Boys. Whatever. Just kind of, why would you do that, you know? Be powerless on purpose?"

"Maybe some guys are okay?" Ms. Jimenez sounds like she's trying to convince herself, not Ruth.

"I haven't seen one I'd want to touch me, that's for sure. But my friend Isabel, she's ready to give up her whole personality just so somebody will make her feel pretty for five minutes before they stop talking to her and she feels like she's gonna die. I don't get what that's about. It kind of freaks me out. I wouldn't really hurt myself, though, Ms. Jimenez. It's just sometimes I think if more girls showed people how things are, people might notice, you know?"

"I think I do, Ruth," Ms. Jimenez says.

It's nice not to have to pull punches; she can curse and talk about sex and doing acid and Ms. Jimenez will just have to sit there using the caring-and-concerned face until she gets permanent wrinkles between her eyebrows. She can't tell anyone because of the counselor thing. Still, it turns out there's a lot Ruth can't seem to say, in here or anywhere. Except to Mackie.

"My friends used to be the only thing that mattered to me. They're just not the same anymore. I feel cut off, like I'm underwater all the time. I'm talking to them, but just bubbles are coming out. I don't trust them anymore. I'm the only one left with any kind of soul."

She can feel her words ringing in the air of Ms. Jimenez's little hippie office. *Dark side. Soul.*

Soul is the part without weight. Some god puts it in the scales and it's supposed to be lighter than a feather. Bodies are heavy, subject to gravity and people's assumptions. Lately, Ruth feels like she's trying to get away from her body all the time. Following Magda, listening to the sound of her pockets or watching her build things out of spare parts, always used to make Ruth feel solid again, real. It doesn't seem to anymore.

"So, those things are making you mad? Making you think sometimes you want to hurt yourself? That's understandable, but does that reaction make sense when you think about it, Ruth?"

Maybe she should backtrack a little, before she winds up upstate in some special school or something.

"Look, Ms. Jimenez, most of what happens to girls is invisible. It's just sometimes I think, if we did the bleeding on the outside, if we showed it, things might have to change. I know that's stupid, though. I do. Thinking about it just makes me feel better sometimes."

Ms. Jimenez looks at her like she is expecting more. It's freaky the way shrinks do that, controlling people with their silences. Do they really wonder why no one likes them?

"You should go into the art room," Ruth says. "You wouldn't believe how much of the stuff kids make is about blood. Drawings, paintings, sculptures, veins, cuts, floods of blood everywhere. Mrs. Farrow says she's going to let us have a show about blood in the gallery. She says it's always like that, every year with every group of kids our age. Blood. Blood. Blood. That's kind of what I'm talking about. We all think about hurting ourselves. Mrs. Farrow thinks it's interesting. She's cool."

Out the window, the lacrosse girlfriends on the field are holding each other's legs while they do handstands. They pretend it's embarrassing when their tops fall down and their bras pop out.

"Look at that." Ruth points. "That is what girls do. How am I supposed to deal with having an actual brain in a world like this? It just gets to be a bit much sometimes."

"Would you like to come back, Ruth?" Ms. Jimenez says.

"That's your response?" Ruth would feel bad for being so rude, but Ms. Jimenez doesn't change the totally bland expression on her face no matter what Ruth says. It kind of makes you want to try and shock her. Maybe that's a shrink trick, too.

"It's important that whoever you're with you feel safe and happy, Ruth."

"Yes, Ms. Jimenez, I get that. I'm telling you I don't. Not anymore. I feel scared, all the time. Unless I'm pissed off. Really, really pissed off."

This isn't where help is going to come from. How could she have thought it was, even for a minute? This might be the actual definition of desperate, believing that the school would hire someone who could help you with real life.

"Well, I've really enjoyed meeting you and hearing what you think, and I think we could talk more," Ms. Jimenez says. "I'd like to. Would you?"

Lacrosse practice is over by the time Ruth leaves the school. Out on the empty field the world seems farther away than it was the last time she saw it. All the time now, she's looking at it through the wrong end of a telescope. People like those lacrosse girlfriends acting out things she doesn't want to understand.

Ruth didn't tell Ms. Jimenez about Danny's car, which was the reason she went to see her in the first place. Or about Virgil Mackie. No one knows about Mackie.

All the things she did say, though, have come out of her like weights. She's lighter now, cleaner. It isn't Ms. Jimenez who did that, though, it's him. The past few days, it's like Virgil Mackie took the lid off her, letting out the scalding steam.

Ms. Jimenez got distracted by all that talk about blood and suicide, and forgot all about the second question. She forgot to ask Ruth if she felt like hurting other people.

"My space goes two ways together, twilight's forever." She sings it again on the way home. This time of year, with school almost

over, night starts to tiptoe up, sparkling, instead of falling on you out of nowhere the way it does in November. And then there's everything that's happening inside her, the stuff nobody can see. She stops to lean against the empty brake repair shop and gather up enough strength to go through the trees home. Inside her head, it's all going two ways together.

"I'd offer you a joint, but I don't think you need one, little Carter."

"Jesus, Charlie. You scared the crap out of me."

"What you doing back here?" he says.

"I came back here to get away from people." Ruth shifts sideways and puts her back to the wall.

"This is South Highbone. No getting away from people here. Heard about Matt?"

"Uh, no. What?"

"The guys from Nassau County who front him stuff are pissed off. Really pissed off. Apparently he owes them a load of money he can't pay 'cause someone robbed his weed."

". . ."

"Got nothing to say, Ruthie? Isn't he your neighbor?"

"Kind of. So, um, you robbed him, huh?"

"No. Here's a funny thing. You three been smoking up all week, but none of you have bought anything off me in ages. Weird, right?"

"I stole some from my mom." That lie isn't too hard. It's pretty much the truth.

"You know where your mom keeps her stash, huh?" He looks

over at the back of her house.

"Charlie, don't rob us. It won't go well for you."

"Yeah, me and you get each other, though, don't we? I mean, we're both from up here. Sit down. Have a cigarette." He shakes a soft pack of Camel nonfilters at her until one comes halfway out.

"I don't know if we 'get each other,' Charlie." She reaches to take the cigarette and leans back against the wall of Mr. Macana-jian's garage. "I kind of doubt it. I don't really know you, but I'm guessing we don't have lots to talk about."

"No, I don't know you either, but we could fix that."

Guys really say stuff like that. No, even weirder, it usually works for them.

"Isabel's the one you should be talking to, Charlie."

"Maybe later. I'm talkin' to you right now."

And then Charlie's body is covering her, leaning into her. His tongue is in her mouth and all the shadows around them have shattered like black glass. There is a glare inside her head like someone switched on an interrogation lamp in a room full of sharp light and cigarettes. She pushes and twists out, scraping herself away against the wall.

"Okay, Charlie. See? We don't 'get each other.' Obviously. Fuck off."

"All right! Why are you being such a bitch? Calm down."

"I'm calm, Charlie. I'm so calm right now, you have no idea. Seriously, though, if you think you're gonna turn around now and start sleeping with me instead of Isabel, you're way stupider than I thought, even."

"What the hell is your problem, Carter? You walk around looking like that, guys are gonna pay attention. No need to get worked up about it."

Ruth sits on her back steps to catch her breath and make sure Charlie has really gone. She's waiting for the twilight to finish romancing everything, waiting for the good honest dark. She has a mug of tea in her hands and a cloud of cinnamon steam drifts up into her face. Next to her is a soda bottle full of water and a crescent wrench. She can't tell Magda what she's doing, but she does it like Magda would, with Magda-style precision. How did her life suddenly get so practical and mechanical? So physical? Magda doesn't have to get her past every locked door and every creepy guy anymore. Ruth is doing fine all by herself.

"Cripple Creek Ferry" is playing on the living room stereo and the sound of it comes out the screen door like a jaunty invasion in completely the wrong key. How can someone play that song on a night like this? It's so obviously time for Billie Holiday, or a Dylan piano blues. Everything about Danny Pavlich happens at the wrong time in the wrong tone. He sticks out of their lives like an extra, unnecessary limb.

Her front yard is pretending to be a lawn, but badly. Mostly it's dry yellow dust with a few tufts of switchgrass. You have to drain the master cylinder from underneath, so she grabs Danny's front bumper and slides under the car. The cloud of dry dirt that comes up makes her choke. Danny and her mother are right there on the living room couch by the window, listening to the wrong music and talking about transcendental meditation, or making their own yogurt, or whatever it is this week. If they look out the window, they'll see her. She uses her teacup to catch the fluid she drains out. Probably a bad idea, but whatever. She'll wash it.

The release for the hood is inside by the driver's seat. She checked that already. She leaves the car door open so they won't hear it slamming shut. Then she lifts up the hood, unscrews the cap, and adds the water.

If she cut the brake line or something, Danny would notice before he even got started, before he got up any speed. But also, if it happens too slow, he'll stop and get it checked. That is why the water is such a cool plan. Mr. Macanajian said it doesn't fuck your brakes until the water gets hot and boils off. Well, he didn't say fuck. And he had no idea why she was interested.

Someone drives by while she is standing with the hood propped up, using the bottom of her thermal army shirt to unscrew the cap on the reservoir. If it had been someone who knew them, they would have stopped, and she'd be busted. Once the road is empty again she feels like throwing up.

In the end, she's glad that everything she does is covered up by the sound of "Southern Man" blasting out the front window. Another annoying thing about Danny Pavlich: he always leaves the turntable on repeat, but tonight it's lucky.

Back in the kitchen, she makes more tea, then takes it out onto the steps and sits watching the dead street on the other side of the woods. Brake fluid stinks. Her shirt is covered in it, and her jeans are ruined. How the hell does Mr. Macanajian keep his hands so clean? If Danny or her mother came in the kitchen they might poke their heads out to say something caring that would show how much they noticed her and considered her a real person, just as good as a grown-up. It wouldn't really be about her, though; it would be about how cool they are. If they did that, they might notice that she is covered in grease and dirt and ask her why. It's possible, but it isn't likely. If they did ask her she'd say, someone has to be the grown-up around here. Someone has to think about the consequences.

Sitting on her poured-concrete kitchen porch, factory-made precisely like all the porches on her street, with her mother's hippie tea and her shirt covered with brake fluid and grease, she is all the way alive. The real, solid darkness has fallen now, and it makes breathing easier. This is her element. She doesn't need Magda, or even Virgil Mackie, to tell her she's right. For tonight at least, she knows what needs to be done, for herself and her mother. She's doing it, even if she can't tell anyone. She's one of those heroes that melt in and out of shadows, saving lives in secret.

five

"YOU GUYS SHOULD see yourselves," Isabel says.

Ruth and Magda are across from her at the front booth in the Harpoon Diner, facing the sun, and their two different pairs of eyes throw the light back blue and brown. It's one of those moments when you just know the reason for everything. Whatever she did on Friday, whatever those two ever know about it, this kind of beauty is the reason. How can you not know it, especially with Ruth Carter sitting right across from you? Isn't this worth killing for?

"You look like terrifying angels with the sun behind you. You're like Joan of Arc sitting next to Saint Barbara or something. Seriously, Holy of Holies. You two inspire my awe."

"Don't listen," Ruth says. "It's a setup."

"Whatever." Isabel looks over at the bookstore. "Mr. Lipsky'll close up soon; we can go over there and get him to give us a coffee before he walks his dad."

"Oh nice, Isabel." Ruth is drawing now and doesn't look up.

"I like the dad, actually. He has that old, tough way of talking, like in a gangster movie. He's cool. Anyway, Mr. Lipsky does walk him, every night before it gets dark. They have a routine. Ruth, do me a quadratic equation, please?"

"See? Told you she wanted something. Ask Magda."

"I'm not teaching her," Magda says. "Ask Charlie. He can do math. He just pretends he can't 'cause he thinks it means he's a rebel if he's taking algebra for the third time."

"Come on, Ruth, just let me look at your notebook." Isabel makes a grab for it, and Ruth slaps her hand away. "Wow, did you do that in art today?"

"They're tulips."

"Magda, you should have heard her ranting about tulips the other night. It was pure genius."

"No it wasn't," Ruth says. "It just seemed like it at the time. Anyway, it doesn't matter. I was just thinking about a new drawing. School is boring."

"For you," Magda says. "Some of us pay attention."

"Not me," Isabel says. "I'm training to be a professional daydreamer. It's a public-service vocation."

"Yeah, okay, Isabel." Ruth laughs that sarcastic laugh she seems to have picked up somewhere recently. "You keep on dreaming. Me and Magda'll just deal with all your consequences. If there's jail, we'll do it while you hang out with your typewriter being surrealist on your houseboat. Not a problem. Honest."

"Magda, do you get what's going on with her? She keeps saying there's nothing wrong."

Isabel told Ruth she was beautiful and they messed around. She needed her. Aren't your friends supposed to be there when you need them?

"Because there isn't anything wrong, Isabel." Ruth bends over her notebook and speaks through her hanging-down hair. "I don't care what you do."

"So." Magda looks down at the two crumpled-up dollar bills and the pile of change on the table. "This is what we got. This and some stolen weed you guys can't figure out what to do with and more brains than any other three people who might be sitting at a table together in Highbone. How do we translate that into an escape plan?"

Isabel scans the menu while Magda puts pennies into piles of ten and Ruth goes to work on the silver.

"Apple pie à la mode," Isabel says, "or a sundae?"

"This is the situation, on every level." Magda piles the pennies on Ruth's notebook and Ruth knocks them off. "A menu full of choices, too many women to feed, and a pile of crumpled bills way too small. It's like one of those word problems where we're on a boat, castaway with one oar and not enough food."

"Yeah," Ruth says, "now we get to decide who to throw over and who to save."

"For real"—Isabel puts the menu down—"I am dying for an egg cream. It's some kind of period thing. I just want a fizzy, chocolaty, milky thing. Please?"

"Seriously?" Ruth leans over the table and lowers her voice. "Are you paying attention at all, Isabel? What's your big plan? Magda has a bunch of Matt Kerwin's weed stashed at her house. It was your idea. So are you gonna do something with it before one of us gets arrested and has to do your time?"

"What? Calm down, Ruth. It's not gonna disappear, and no one will find it. We have time; we'll think of something."

"By which I guess you mean, *Magda* will think of something?" Magda says.

"Well, you are traditionally the mastermind."

"Four dollars and eighty-seven cents." Ruth has piled it all on the table next to the tulips in her notebook.

"So, Magda, what's your plan about the weed?"

"Shhh! First of all I just want to remind you, this was your half-cocked piece of genius. First you robbed a cop, and now Matt. As usual, somebody else is gonna get kicked by one of your knee-jerk reactions."

"Uh, you went with me, Magda. You climbed through the freaking window, remember?" But really, what Isabel sees right then is the napalm jacket guy's eyes unfocusing in the acid shadows of the Dunkin' Donuts parking lot. Right there in the air between them she can hear the crack of metal on his bone. She waves a hand to push the vision away and knocks a menu off the table.

"Well, it isn't like I expected follow-through from you," Magda says. "I thought of something."

Ruth turns her head and speaks to the window and the street outside. "Why don't you just let her get her own self out of the shit for once?"

"That isn't how we do, Ruth." Magda picks the menu up off the floor and slaps a hand down on it. "Right, bottomless coffee we can all share when he's not looking. Then we can get pie and an egg cream and fries. If he's nice to us, we can leave him the rest."

"Saint Magdalene the Bountiful." Isabel puts her hands over the money. "So, what's your plan?"

"Never you mind. I'll only try it if you don't ask me about it anymore."

"Fine," Isabel says. "No coffee. I told you, we can get it from Mr. Lipsky later. We can get two orders of fries, an egg cream, and a lemon Coke."

"*Now* you're in charge?"

"I did the math. Proud of me?"

six

AT RUTH'S HOUSE the front yard is empty. She'd worried all the way from the diner that the house would be full of people and consequences. Now she is so relieved by the lack of cars that she feels like they've been lifted away by angels. In her mind's eye, it's a junkyard assumption. The resurrection of Danny's Dodge Dart and her mom's Pinto, and the random pickup trucks of their friends. She can see the junkyard angels, covered in white feathers and engine grease, hovering with light streaming from their hands.

Danny is out driving somewhere, boiling the water in his brake line into steam. The house is theirs for now.

Ruth opens the door and takes a deep breath, soaking in the emptiness. It isn't a bad place. It just weighs her down sometimes. Too many old thoughts kicking around in here. Too many pictures she can't get away from.

"Great, no one's home and I have some macaroni and cheese stashed in my room," she says. "See what's on TV."

"What is it, contraband?" Isabel throws herself onto the couch.

"Mom would have a fit. Or probably just throw it out when I wasn't home. She thinks anything with sauce in a packet gives you cancer. It probably does. I'm up for some carcinogens. What about you guys?"

"Yes, ma'am." Isabel leafs through the *TV Guide*. "*His Girl Friday*, *Brady Bunch* reruns, or some Western?" she shouts.

"Westerns have no girls," Magda says. "We've already established this. *The Brady Bunch* has a laugh track."

"*His Girl Friday* it is, then. It's already half an hour in."

There is a minute while Ruth is making boxed macaroni and cheese when life seems perfect. She can hear the television and Magda's running commentary on sexism in the studio era, but none of it is clear. The sounds are half-defined and comforting, just like the smells of home. Someone is growing mint and basil in the kitchen window. How long has it been there?

"Ruth, you're ignoring me." Magda leans in the kitchen doorway, looking both ways so they'll both listen.

"Sorry. What?"

"My plan. We might be able to make a deal tonight. I need to get that shit out of my dad's house before I get killed."

"Make a deal with who?"

"She won't tell me," Isabel shouts from the couch. "It's some kind of secret connection. Do you have any orange juice?"

"Orange juice with mac and cheese?"

"What? It's a color theme."

"Okay, Isabel. Magda, are you gonna get us in trouble?"

"You're seriously asking me that now, Ruth? We robbed a dealer. We stashed a pound of weed in my dad's house. *My* dad. I'm trying to get us *out* of trouble."

"Do you think this is going to come back on us, Magda? I mean what are we supposed to think of ourselves now that we did all this? What's the payback gonna be?"

"Let me ask you something, Ruth. Ever wonder why it's me you're asking this stuff? How am I supposed to know about the laws of the fucking universe? I'm not the one who doles out karma." Magda rolls her eyes at the ceiling and goes back to Rosalind Russell.

While Ruth drains the pasta she looks out the back window and there he is, striding through the yard with his back to her. Mackie. She taps on the window and he turns to face her, standing at the edge of the woods. She can see the chain from his watch and something like a feather tied into his hair. He will know what to do about Matt and the weed and karma, and which part of fate is her job and which belongs to the universe. He raises two fingers to his forehead and salutes her with a smile, then turns away again. That's what she'll do, ask Virgil Mackie.

She makes three trips to the living room with bowls and glasses, then Magda says, "Eat up, women. We're going to the beach to set up a drug deal."

When *His Girl Friday* ends, it's the evening news. A nun in

Queens is claiming to have stigmata. She's there with a priest, like he's a kind of spokesman. Her handler. What if it were true, if people just opened up and bled? Not because they were hurt, because they were marked by God. It would be like your heart coming out of you, pumping your soul out into the light.

The nun's habit is just like the ones teachers have at St. Ignatius, made of polyester, blue with a white edge around her face. The priest has the whole slacks-and-cardigan thing going on. They're being filmed in an institutional hallway somewhere, and the nun is showing off her wrists with raw, bloody patches on them. Father Cardigan stays between her and the camera, talking fast without stopping. They look more like carnival hucksters than angels. Across the bottom of the TV screen is a strip of words saying *Nun Claims Stigmata* in the kind of typeface that leans drunkenly to the left and is supposed to show movement.

"This," Magda says, "is exactly the kind of craziness that is the whole reason for television."

"Yeah." Isabel sits up and puts her bowl on the floor. "Everyone else thinks the news is information."

"Why are they doing it, do you think? What's the scam?"

"Dunno"—Isabel points her fork at the TV—"but those two are so fucking each other."

Magda stands up. "Yeah, but with lots of guilt. So that's okay."

The parking lot at Fiddler's Cove is half-full. It's warm, and everyone is smiling, laughing, moving more than they do in the winter. There are buds on the salt roses and the air smells like smoke.

They're all inside a rosebud, a robin's egg. Soon the world will crack open and inside it will be July.

Magda makes Ruth sit with Isabel at the picnic tables while she goes to talk to some guy in a green Mustang. Ruth watches Magda lean into the driver's-side window, so she doesn't have to look at Isabel. That's why she sees him grab a handful of Magda's hair and kiss her. Isabel is oblivious.

"Ruth," she says, "do they have rivers in Mexico? I was thinking I could put my boat on a river in Mexico."

"They have bugs in Mexico, Isabel. Huge fucking bugs. They live in the jails where they put you when you try to buy weed. Or steal it. Be here now, woman. Just for a change. Who the hell is that?"

"What?"

"That person who seems to be entitled to your friend Magdalene Warren's body." Ruth points to the Mustang. "Obviously there's something you two aren't telling me."

"I have no idea what you're talking about." Isabel tilts her head up to look at Ruth, and the salt wind blows her hair into her eyes. She squints over at Magda, then says, "Oh, crap. Who is that?"

"Welcome to the conversation. That's what I'm asking you."

Magda turns around, leans on the door of the car, and waves for them to come over. They have to weave in between a load of football players standing around a pickup and two couples in cars trying to pretend Fiddler's Cove is romantic. By the time they get to Magda, all Ruth can feel is eyes, all over her. Someone is standing in the shadows behind the bathrooms. He's just an out-line in a long coat, but she can tell it's Virgil Mackie by the way he raises one hand, slow and somehow sarcastic. She glances to the side, but Isabel hasn't seen him. She's distracted by whatever is going on with Magda.

"Go around and get in front, Magdalene Warren," the guy says. He runs his eyes up and down Ruth, then sideways at Isabel. "Why don't you two pile in back? Magdalene says you want my advice and kindly assistance."

The air in the back of the Mustang is full of adrenaline. There's something gigantic going on and neither Ruth nor Isabel has any idea what it is. It has nothing to do with Matt Kerwin's weed. Ruth wants to say something, but what would it be?

"Hi," she says, in case Magda wants her to be nice.

"I love your car!" Isabel's ready to lie down and take it, what-ever it is.

"So, what can I do you pretty ladies for?" He looks in the rearview at Ruth and smiles.

"I think it's the other way around." Magda rolls down her window and lights a cigarette. "Like I said, we can maybe get a bunch of weed. We need somebody to pass it on to."

"Got it all figured out, eh, Magdalene Warren? Did you two know this girl can take apart a carburetor?" He's smiling but he looks annoyed.

"Hi, I'm Isabel." Isabel leans up and reaches a hand over the seat.

"Jeff," he says, and shakes. "And you?"

"Ruth. Hi." She turns her head around to try to see if Mackie is still behind the bathrooms. The sun is sharp and all the shadows have gotten deeper. She can't be sure.

"So, do you think you might be able to sell it?" Magda says.

"All business, eh?" He puts a hand behind Magda's neck and pulls her closer to him. For a minute all the sound goes out of the world and Ruth feels sick.

"We think we know where there's a lot hidden," Isabel says. "About a pound, maybe. Some people dumped it, and, um, we saw them. We could get it for you, if you think you can do something with it." She sounds hysterical.

"Dumped it, huh? Any idea who did that? How did you three find out?"

"We just did." Magda twists out from under Jeff's arm and shifts over towards the door. "Do you want it?"

"Tell you what, little Warren. Why don't we drop these two wherever they want to go and then me and you can talk about it?"

"It's kind of urgent," Isabel tries again. "Someone else might find it."

"Well, you know," Jeff says, "your friend Magdalene can take care of business. She keeps telling me that. Why don't you let us work it out? Where you two going tonight?"

"I can get out here." Ruth opens the door and almost falls after it.

Isabel will stay in that car as long as they'll let her. Watching some guy take over Magda's body won't even bother her. Ruth makes for the shadow behind the bathrooms like someone trapped underwater who forgot which way is up. The world is lurching sideways, trying to throw her off.

"Little Carter," Mackie says, and she falls against the shower tiles and slides down onto the drain.

"What are you doing back here, Mackie? I mean, I'm really glad to see you. Something crazy is happening."

"Ain't love crazy, eh?" He laughs like a crow.

"Are you serious? Is that love?"

"That's what they call it."

Ruth has two Larks crumpled in her shirt pocket. Her hand trembles when she lights one. She lifts the other hand and shakes out the match, making it burn green for a second against the purple sky.

"What about my mother? You think she calls it love? Pretty sure my father just called it a little fun. Or maybe relief, even. Isn't that what businessmen pay thirty bucks for at the Island Court Motor Inn up on Herman Road? Relief?"

"You could ask her."

"My mother? No, Mackie. I can't. That's the whole thing. The silence around that woman is like cement. Once it sets in, you can't move or breathe. You just sink to the bottom. Now Magda's doing it, just dumping us in the middle of her weird man shit so we can't say anything. We can't even ask her what the hell she did when we weren't looking, because whoever she did it with is sitting right there."

"Let's talk about you, then. What difference does Magdalene Warren make to you, anyway?"

"All the difference, Mackie. I learned to talk from her. She is the thing that's been in front of me my whole life. She's the place I'm always trying to get to."

"Maybe not anymore. Maybe you're going somewhere else now."

"If it turns out I hurt Danny, I don't even know whether I'll feel bad or not. Is that where I'm going?"

This time, when the world pitches out from under her, she leans into Virgil Mackie. The cement under her legs has held on to the warmth of the sun, but the shower tiles are cold all down her back.

"Tell me about tulips," Virgil Mackie says.

seven

ISABEL'S ROOM HAS a pitched ceiling and a window that looks out over the wooded backyard of the rented house on the corner. Outside that window is a Thursday-evening sky with the branches going dark against it. She lies on her mattress under the eaves, reading René Char's "The Library is on Fire," torn out of a book and taped over her bed. Magda yelled at her for ripping a page out of a library book. Like anyone else in Highbone besides Isabel can appreciate René Char. After a while the grays of words and paper blend too close together to distinguish. The only color left in the room is the red flower Ruth has been drawing on the wall in the corner.

She is imagining her houseboat when the doorbell rings. If it's Ruth or Magda they'll come straight up the stairs, and if it's anyone else she won't have to move anyway. There isn't anyone else she wants to see.

"Isabel?" First it's her mother at the bottom of the stairs, speaking barely loud enough for Isabel to hear. After a minute her father shouts, but it sounds high-pitched and panicky. He couldn't be scary if he tried.

The cops in the living room don't have uniforms, and they're not from Highbone, either. They're county. Her mother is curled up by the lamp with her legs underneath her, and her father sits at the opposite end of the couch with a dishtowel over his shoulder. He's been making dinner. Isabel sinks into the dip in the middle, short and sandwiched in between them. The cops are pretending to talk to her mom and dad, but the questions are for her. They're trying to trap her while they pretend to be protecting her. Cops always lie, even about the little stuff.

"We were telling your parents there's been a serious assault, Miss O'Sullivan. People have told us you might have been there."

"I don't really understand," her mother says.

The cop who's talking looks like a schoolteacher. He isn't *Dragnet* sharp or NYPD sloppy with coffee down his shirt. Just a little cheap and disheveled. The other one sits perfectly straight and doesn't say anything. He doesn't look that much older than Isabel. Outside the window behind him, the setting sun has turned half the trunk of the maple tree gold. Isabel looks at it and listens to the blood rushing through her veins. She can feel the pressure in every artery, every valve.

"Mr. Hazlett is from Social Services," the cop says, waving a hand at the guy with the peach fuzz and the perfect posture.

Isabel's father nods and coughs and then seems to decide he doesn't have anything useful to add. He looks at the carpet, and that's when Isabel notices he doesn't have shoes on. He's talking to the cops in his socks.

"Were you at the Dunkin' Donuts on 25A last Friday night, Miss O'Sullivan?" Now he sounds like a cop on TV.

"No." It comes out sarcastic and she looks him straight in the eye. *I wasn't there*, she thinks. *I know what he's talking about, but I don't know why I know because I wasn't there.*

"She's my daughter," Isabel's mother says in her high, flat voice. As if that's relevant. As if they don't already know that. She pulls her feet in and makes herself smaller, like she's just seen a mouse run under the couch. Or maybe she is the mouse, trembling in the corner and willing herself to be invisible. Great. Way useful quality in a mom.

Mr. Lipsky is always saying Isabel's mom is smart, that she taught him things and was a good friend. Isabel tries to picture her standing up straight, shouting, being excited, going anywhere at all. She tries to see her on a train to the city or on the Greenpoint Ferry. In a college class, admitting that she understands what people are saying. It's impossible. Her mother is permanently folded inward. She never breathes deep enough to say anything out loud.

The cop is standing now, handing his card to her father.

"If your daughter remembers anything, call us." His whole vocabulary is clichés.

Isabel doesn't realize they're leaving until the door shuts

behind them. She can't see them making their way down the driveway, but she sees their long shadows rolling down the lawn to the road.

The cop starts up his silver blue Ford and the roar of his engine brings back the orange sky over the Dunkin' Donuts parking lot, the sound of cracking skull, the scratching of the branches in the woods behind the fence. As soon as they're gone, it all spills over and the pictures come out into her head. She was there, of course. She pushes up one sleeve to see the whitening scratches on her arm. She plays the scene back to herself and the pressure in her veins lets up. The engine fades down the road while the blood rushing in Isabel's ears falls back like an ebbing wave.

eight

SOME DAYS, MAGDALENE can see the morning shining through the back of her eyelids, but when she opens them it turns out she was dreaming and the room is still dark. Today she has her eyes wide open, grabbing at the light like a drowning person, but it isn't helping. She almost wishes she had to go to school, but it's Saturday. She tries to fill her mind up with the empty, meaningless details around her in the room, instead of with what happened.

She should go quietly to the bathroom now, before her dad and Henry wake up. If she bumps into them, she won't be able to say anything normal.

In her memory, she can still see that afternoon in her drive-way and the night at the firemen's fair, shining like scenes from some other girl's life. There is something there she still wants. She knows she'd fall for it again, if it was dressed up right. She could choke herself for that, but there's no getting away from it.

Wednesday night, after they left Ruth at the beach and dropped Isabel off, Jeff drove up to Jenny's Head and parked. He put his hands inside her clothes while he whispered questions about the weed. She kept answering, just so he wouldn't stop touching her. When the whole car seemed full of her exhaled breath, she reached behind her and opened the door. She needed to get back inside her body so she could think of what to say. He wasn't gonna help them sell the weed, that was obvious. Looking back, Jeff has probably suspected all week what was up. That it was them who robbed Matt.

When you stand on the cliff at Jenny's Head the sand and the water are so far below, it's like looking at a map. She could just make out the twisted curves of the beach in the dark. A breeze puffed up, and she put out her arms, wishing she could fall forward and lie down on the air. Just sleep on top of all that space. Then the breeze dropped, her stomach fell away, and she stepped back.

When Jeff came up behind her and put his hand in her hair, she said, "We were wrong. Never mind. Sorry."

"What, you were seeing things? You just made it up?" He lifted up her shirt and put his hands on her skin.

It's hard now, to remember how it felt at the time. When she tries to think back past yesterday, her stomach heaves.

"You don't know Isabel." Magda gasped while she said it. "She lives in dreamland. She probably heard something and then decided she was gonna turn it into some cowgirl adventure."

"Okay, little Warren. For now." He was distracted, but not convinced.

When he parked on the corner of her street he left the engine running and pulled her over onto him. Once she felt like she would never be able to stand up again, he whispered in her ear.

"If you're lying to me I'll know, Magdalene Warren." Then he reached over her and opened the passenger door.

Now she looks down at the crotch of her underwear in the bathroom light and there's another dark, wet spot. Men just seem to keep on leaking out of you for days. She goes to the kitchen to get a pan and put some water in it, puts the pan by her bed, then locks the bedroom door.

She goes back to bed and the day just keeps moving forward. When the sun drops over the other side of the house, she realizes hours have passed and it's afternoon. Will it feel different once it's dark again?

She is alone in the house when the doorbell rings. Because the ringing goes on and on and then is replaced by loud knocking, she knows it is Isabel, and probably Ruth, too. Her body goes rigid, like holding on tight enough will keep them from sneaking into the house to check for her. She can't talk to them, not now. After a while, someone throws pebbles at the window. Magda holds her breath until it stops.

After Wednesday Jeff didn't call for two days, and she didn't use the number he gave her either. Then yesterday morning he came to get her. When he knocked on the door she thought he must be mad about the weed, that he'd figured it out and was going to tell Matt. She had already got that he was the wrong person to have asked for help. But he didn't even mention it.

He just said, "Don't go to school today. Drop Henry off and come out with me instead."

And Magda did exactly what stupid girls do, looking away past his shoulder because she couldn't stand to look in his eyes. She was flattered and scared. Not scared of what was actually about to happen. She never imagined that. She was scared that he would stop paying attention to her.

Her bedroom is full of shadows now. It's seven fifteen. The mechanism she's building is on her desk. Its moving parts are still, shining in places, catching the light from the clock. All of the objects in the room have lost their meaning. Her life has telescoped into one scene that won't let the present come through. She just goes over and over it while her body stays frozen.

She probably turned red, standing there at the door trying to catch her breath. Yep, she did everything stupid girls do, including dropping Henry off and going with Jeff. They cut through the football field behind the elementary school and Jeff said, "Let's go through the woods so no one sees you."

Under the trees it still smelled like rotting leaves, but there was new green everywhere. They even saw some Indian pipes under a pine and Jeff stopped to tell her that meant something had died there. She didn't even say that she already knew that.

"Sorry about the weed," she said. "We were wrong. It wasn't there."

"Yeah, but it was good anyway, wasn't it? Up at Jenny's Head?"

He went quiet, just waiting for that to sink into her softness.

There were blue jays screeching in the tops of the trees. They made her think about when she was little, days when it would cloud over like that. The air would get soft and the birds would start screeching. Her mother would say, "Listen, Magdalene! The birds are screaming for rain." Then she thought about how Jeff wanted to listen to her. Maybe she shouldn't be so scared of how it felt when he touched her. Why was she so scared of losing control all the time? He wasn't like Charlie, anyway. He came back.

When he grabbed her arm so hard like that, she thought it was an accident.

"Ouch! That hurts." She turned around to him, laughing, when she said it. The look in his eyes was laughing too, but it was brittle. Something shattered when she saw it. She still has the bruise smeared across her skin from where she twisted away and he wouldn't let go.

At first, that just confused her. It took her half a minute to catch up with what was happening. Her brain couldn't adjust to the way reality changed, so fast like that. Finally, she sort of woke up and felt panic shoot into her blood. Too late.

"Fuck off!" She shouted it at him, and he hit her so hard she spun halfway around. Her arm flung out behind her with the force, so it was the side of her that hit the birch tree behind.

She reaches under her T-shirt now and presses on the bruises. To make sure they're there, to make it hurt so she can put it all back together from the map of her body. Her body is the representation of an event now. It isn't somewhere she lives anymore. It isn't the house of her.

It's not exactly true that time slowed down, like everyone says. Everything got really sharp and clear, though. Thinking about it now, she can see every leaf on the ground. She can see the blue jay that squawked while it flew over her head, the daddy longlegs crawling over a rock. She must have landed on that rock at some point. The side of her leg was bleeding when she got home.

At the time she was thinking, *Don't look scared. It'll be worse if you look scared.* Where did that idea come from? She still doesn't know. He didn't seem that strong to look at, but no matter what she tried she couldn't get her arms out of his grip. Every way she twisted he was already there. All the details of Jeff Snyder were sinking into her senses. He used to have an earring. She could see the healing-over hole. Like a close-up at the movies, he took up all of her vision with sick, specific detail. The tips of his fingers were yellow from cigarettes, and there was engine grease under his nails.

Before the other night at the beach, she didn't want to tell Ruth and Isabel about Jeff, because the things her body was doing confused her. And because of the way she knew he'd look at Ruth. And he did, of course, the minute he saw her. She didn't want to tell them because he made her feel separate and definite, in the middle of her own life without them. Now it's a different kind of secret. She'll never be able to say his name to them again.

All day, everything plays on a loop in her head, trying to add up to a reason for what happened. Trying to put herself back into that special definition, to make herself matter like she did in the Kennedys' side yard. Now, though, that's just a memory of someone else's life. She gives up on trying to get back to it and throws up into the pan of water next to the bed.

She will have to call Ruth and Isabel at some point. They're looking for her, and if she doesn't, they'll know something's wrong. If she waits until tomorrow, so much silence and memory will pile up she won't be able to talk through it. Everything needs to be normal by tomorrow.

Mrs. O'Sullivan answers at Castle Gloom and when Magda hears her own voice it sounds like it does every day. Mrs. O'Sullivan practically doesn't exist. It's not like talking to anyone at all.

"Hello, Magdalene. She isn't home yet. She's with Ruth. I don't know where they went."

"Oh, when she gets home, could you tell her I called?"

"Okay, sweetie . . . Magdalene?"

"Yeah, Mrs. O'Sullivan?"

"Are you all right? Is everyone all right? I can never tell, Magdalene."

"We're all fine, Mrs. O. It's really nice that you asked." Even then, Magda doesn't choke up.

"Well," Mrs. O'Sullivan says, "having daughters is a kind of blindness. You can feel them, but you can't see anything."

For that kind of insight, she committed herself to an institution? It sounds truer than most things to Magda.

nine

THE WARRENS' HOUSE looks to Isabel like a hotel for ghosts. It has history, poetry. You can imagine the people who used to live here. You could write stories about them. The porch is half-shaded by the trees at the edge of the road. There's a collapsing cardboard box full of docksiders and cable-knit sweaters under the porch swing, and some dead brown leaves trailing from the hanging basket. It's the abandoned wreck of something Isabel would give anything to have, a house people actually feel and think in.

"No, seriously, there's something spooky," she says. "I can feel it."

"All right, Isabel," Ruth says to her, "just because you read my mind the other day doesn't mean you're some kind of gypsy-witchclairvoyant. Magda could have gone somewhere."

Isabel sits down on the front step.

"It's Saturday at two thirty. She didn't answer this morning and she's not answering now. If she isn't with us, where would she be?"

"Check me if I'm wrong, Isabel, but I think that's an insulting question. We do all have lives when you're not there."

"I'm just saying, our lives have a pattern. She wasn't in school yesterday, and she hasn't called you, right? That's weird. There's no Henry, no big bad Professor, nobody. It's spooky. People do tend to take off and disappear from this house."

"Magda wouldn't leave town without telling me," Ruth says. "You, maybe, but not me."

"Seriously, Ruth. Get off my back, will you?"

Isabel doesn't want to leave the Warrens' house. She wants to go inside while no one's home and sneak into Professor Warren's study. She could just pretend to be him, sit at his typewriter and put on one of his sweaters, breathe in the dust from his books. The cops would never find her here.

"I'll look in the back," Ruth says. "Stay here. If something happened and her dad kicked off, she might be hiding. She might come out if it's just me."

After a while Isabel gets tired of waiting and goes around to the back herself. Ruth isn't there. She tries to hit Magda's window with some little pebbles but her aim is bad. Twice she hits the bathroom window instead. There is no sign of anyone, but it doesn't feel empty. It just feels wrong.

She finds Ruth in the carriage house, lying on top of Mrs.

Warren's things with her eyes half closed. She shines out of the shadows, floating in the dust she's kicked up. Isabel would like to dress her in something long and beaded from the Attic and sit her on a couch at a party full of poets. She could be the center of something like that, the muse. It's that way she has of being half in the room, and half somewhere else all the time. Even when you take all her clothes off and touch her, you can tell there is something you're not getting at.

"One day I'm going to be able to tell people I slept with you and they'll be impressed."

Ruth doesn't answer. She's acting hurt and bitchy, but it doesn't matter. Years from now she'll understand that Isabel risked everything for them. She hit back. She lets out a heavy breath and slides her back down the wall next to the door. It's hard waiting for those two to catch up sometimes.

Now Ruth's voice comes rasping out of the shadow. "Where's the stash? We might as well grab a couple of buds and take them to my house."

They walk down the hill and stand waiting to cross 25A. The shadows of moving cars wash over them like waves and Isabel feels that same tugging vertigo you feel in the ocean. The highway sounds like surf, too. At Ruth's house, Ms. Carter is making baba ghanoush in the kitchen.

"Let's go in my room," Ruth says. "It takes ages for her to screw up the baba ghanoush. She has to concentrate."

There doesn't seem to be a lot to say. They just lie flat on their backs on either side of Ruth's veil, looking at the ceiling and filling the room with smoke. After a while, Ruth rolls over and pokes the top of her body out from under the veil, reaching for her pastels. "Put some music on." She pulls a piece of paper out from under her dresser. Isabel looks at the record player for a minute, moves the needle back to the beginning of *Horses*, and lies down on the floor while Patti Smith growls about Jesus.

"See," she says. "There are places in the world where we can say whatever we want and people will pay us for it."

"Shhhhh. I need to get this down before the picture goes out of my head. It's important."

Isabel cranes her neck over to try to see Ruth's paper, and the phone rings in the distant kitchen. A minute later, Ms. Carter knocks and opens the door without waiting for an answer. Her eyes are big and she hasn't wiped the eggplant off her hands.

"Something happened," she says, in one of those totally flat, emotionless voices adults use when someone dies or breaks a limb or leaves them for someone else.

Isabel turns the record player down. Ruth just stares at the eggplant smears on the doorjamb.

"Danny's at the hospital. I have to go. Isabel, come with me and I can drop you across 25A. Ruth? I'll be back later, okay?"

"What happened?" Ruth is using the voice, too.

"He was driving and something went wrong with his brakes. They called his parents, but his friend Sal called me."

When Isabel looks over from tying her sneakers, Ruth is drawing on the palm of her left hand with the blue pastel in her right. She says good-bye without looking up.

Outside, Isabel walks around to the passenger side of Ms. Carter's Pinto. She's never been in it without Ruth before.

"Is Danny gonna be okay, Ms. Carter?"

"I don't know, Isabel. I don't even know what I'm going to do when I get there." She says it like she forgot she's talking to a kid, like Isabel might have some advice or something comforting to say. She still hasn't washed the eggplant off her hands.

Shit. What if he's dead? Is that what just happened?

The record is playing on in Ruth's room. "Redondo Beach" now. Patti's voice comes from the open window. *Down by the ocean, it was so dismal. Women all standing with shock on their faces.*

ten

ON MONDAY MORNING, Magdalene is alone in the science hallway when someone grabs her from behind. She elbows him as hard as she can in the stomach. Her body just does it without involving her brain. By the time she turns around, Charlie is doubled over, going, "What the hell!" in a voice that would be shouting if he had any air to shout with.

"Jesus, Magdalene, I was only playin'."

"Not funny, Charlie. What do you want?"

"Do I have to want something? Let's go smoke one and sign in after homeroom." They are in the crowd outside the girls' bathroom. Classes haven't started yet.

"No thanks. Next question?"

"Okay, actually, I'm not playing." And he pushes her into the corner by the bathroom door. There is so much noise and confusion in the hallway that people don't have to notice. Magda looks past his shoulder and takes a breath.

"What do you want, then?" Her eyes fix on the banks of light above him.

"Right, Magda, I'm saying this to you 'cause you're the least girly girl out of the three of you."

"Oh, excellent, Charlie. That's great. Nice to see you, too."

"What is wrong with you today?" He growls out the words so no one else can hear them. "If you wanna know, you're actually sexy. I've discussed it with a committee of guys. You know, as part of a list. Tough sexy, that's what we said."

"Charlie, I don't care what you jerk off to, I really don't. Spare me. None of us are as clueless as Isabel. That's why she's the one fucking you."

"Right. *We* are about to start over." He brings his face closer to hers. "Someone ripped off Matt Kerwin's stash. Weird, don'tcha think?"

"Charlie, you already told us about this. How stoned were you? Congratulations, good job. I'm not helping you move the weed if that's what you're after."

She isn't even shaking. Stuff like this doesn't even make the scale of scary anymore.

"It wasn't me, Magda. I think you know that."

"You know what, Charlie? I don't need your ideas. I have my own. Anyway, you should be happy, 'cause whoever ripped off Matt Kerwin is so dead."

"Yeah, you have ideas. I know you're the one in charge. It was your idea, wasn't it?"

"Think about it, Charlie. What would I do with Matt's weed? Where would I sell it without anyone noticing?" This is so true it almost makes Magda laugh to say it.

"Tell your little friends, Warren. If it turns out to be you guys, you are worse than dead."

Then she is leaning in the corner of the bathroom alone, and she can't remember walking away from Charlie or coming through the door. Everything washes out of her, and she feels hollow and shaky. Seems like this is the thing that's going to make her cry, which is totally ridiculous, considering. She almost laughs again.

While she hides in a stall, the bathroom fills up with cigarette smoke then empties out again for homeroom. It isn't Charlie, or the weed, or Charlie's threats. It's the thing that happened in her body when he grabbed her, the way it just took over and reacted. If they were alone it wouldn't have mattered. She wouldn't have been strong enough or fast enough. There is a picture made of bruises on her body, rising up from her blank skin hours, even days, later. Ten times a day her insides just drop away and leave her like a tunnel with the wind blowing through it.

She cries and pulls her own hair and hits the back of her head against the wall behind the toilet. She is so angry it chokes her, and she sobs and coughs until she spits up everything in her lungs and wipes her mouth with her sleeve.

Then she has to sign in late after all.

In the parking lot after school, Magda and Isabel stand for a few minutes without saying anything.

"Where's Ruth?" Magda finally says.

"She left at lunchtime. Danny got in some kind of accident on Saturday. Didn't she call you?"

"I haven't really been getting the phone. Is Danny okay?"

"Well, he's home from the hospital. Ruth was really freaked, though. Why aren't you the one who knows all this?"

"I was . . . I can't always be the one holding you guys up, Isabel. Ruth needs to grow up."

"She seemed to be taking it really badly, considering how much she hates Danny."

"Look, Isabel, Charlie kind of knows."

"Kind of knows what?"

"He's pissed off. He knows someone took Matt's weed and he's pretty sure it was us. He got a little intense with me this morning."

"And you forgot to tell me, Magdalene?" Isabel shouts. "Charlie wants to kill us and you didn't think you needed to mention it?"

"I've been a little taken up with trying to clean up your mess. Sorry."

"Well, he won't really do anything. Not to my friends."

"Are you serious?" Magda kicks at a Coke can ring, then picks it up and puts it in her pocket. "He can do whatever he wants. He can jump one of us from behind a bush and cut us up. He can strangle us and dump us in a marsh in Queens. Who's gonna say anything?"

They both shuffle their feet and cast their eyes around, stuck in the parking lot with groups of kids walking away from them in all directions. Magda can feel the air stretching thin between them. The two of them are held together by some kind of centrifugal force but they each want to fly off.

"Anyway, I thought you were over him. I thought stealing Matt's weed was your big 'Screw you, Charlie.'"

Isabel doesn't answer. She is waiting. She wants Magda to tell her what to do next. Does she even realize that's what she's doing?

"I need a walk," Magda says. "You go ahead."

"Where you going, Saint Magdalene the Mysterious?"

"I don't know, Isabel. Heaven? Hell? California? I'll see you tomorrow."

There are no lights in the front windows of the Hancocks' house, but Magda knows the way around back from when she used to come with her mother. Mrs. Hancock will be in the den, the one with the harbor view.

There. Right there on the back step, her mother stood once, trying not to cry and asking if she could come in for a rum and Coke. Mrs. Hancock laughed and held the door open, and Magda's mother told her to play outside. Now it's Magda knocking, looking less perfect but still trying not to cry. Her mother could give a situation like that some kind of tragic beauty. Magda's desperation is just scruffy.

There's some fumbling before the door opens, and then Mrs. Hancock gasps and puts a hand to her chest.

"Oh my God, you look like her. You scared the crap out of me, Magdalene."

She's drunk.

"I'm sorry, Mrs. Hancock. I just . . ."

"Well, get in here. Have you heard from your mother?"

"No. I just . . ."

"I'm pouring you a whiskey. Don't argue."

They're in the den now, and Mrs. Hancock waves at the couch that faces the bay window.

"Um . . . I don't think you're supposed to, Mrs. Hancock."

"Nonsense. You look terrible, and it's my job to feed drinks to Warren women when they need them. Anyway, I can't drink alone. Women who drink whiskey by themselves are outside the pale; surely you've learned that by now."

Looks like she drinks alone plenty. Magda takes the glass, though. It's real scotch, with an unpronounceable name on the bottle.

"Women who drink alone end up in asylums," Mrs. Hancock says. "You've stepped right into the middle of a Tennessee Williams play, sweetie. Grab a chair and have a drink while you wait for act two."

Jesus, this was a bad idea. She waves at the couch again and Magda sits down. All of a sudden Mrs. Hancock looks surprised, staring at her like she just appeared out of thin air.

"What are you doing here?" she says.

"I'm sorry, Mrs. Hancock. I just . . . um . . . I didn't know who to talk to."

"Ssshhh! Listen," she says. "Hear that?"

All Magda can hear is the boats in the harbor, riggings tinkling against aluminum masts in the breeze. Then there's a creak, maybe the house settling. It's old, older than Magda's house, even.

"I wanted it, Magdalene. I wanted it so badly, the view out this window and the sounds from the harbor and the creaky old house full of the history of people who have owned this two-bit town for generations. I grew up in South Highbone, did you know that? It was different then, but still, no harbor view."

"It kind of presses on you, though. Doesn't it?" Magda takes a sip of the whiskey and tries not to cough. "The history, I mean."

"When you knocked I was thinking about *The Great Gatsby*." She points across the water. "Look over there at Carter's Bay. It's like West Egg and East Egg, right? Except there's no one over there on the lawn, longing to reach across to me, that's for sure. Not like I want that. I was just thinking about all the reasons I wouldn't make a good Daisy."

Magda has no idea what's she's talking about. She tried to read *The Great Gatsby* once, but it was written like a grocery list.

"Your mother," Mrs. Hancock says, "you know, she might have made a good Daisy. Women in novels like that are never too solid. They just hover, looking ethereal with all their thoughts halfway out of sight. They're always revealing that there's something they haven't revealed. They have to fade away when you reach out for them. It's required."

"Well, yeah," Magda says. "My mom is good at that last part."

"When people reach out for me, I'm right there. Men don't find that attractive." She looks at Magda and gets the surprised face again. "Why are you here, Magdalene? Is there something you wanted to tell me?"

"I wanted to ask you . . . I mean, I thought maybe I could talk to you. I don't know, Mrs. Hancock. It's just my dad and Henry at home, you know?"

"Let's see," she says. "Someone hurt you. A man. Boy, whichever. Physically, or just break your heart?"

"How did you know?"

"Not rocket science, sweetie. You might get to walk around dressed like a boy till ten o'clock on school nights, smoking cigarettes with holes in your jeans, but I guess the other things pretty much stay the same."

"Physically," Magda says. Really it's both but she doesn't say that.

"Well, chances are it'll happen again. I know I'm supposed to say something comforting, but what would be the point of that? The important thing, sweetie, is not to let the frayed edges show. Tuck things in when they start coming undone." She reaches for the whiskey bottle.

"I'm trying that, Mrs. Hancock, but I'm so mad. I just want to hurt someone."

"Drink up. Wearing it on the outside where people can see it just makes you look like a victim. Do that and they just keep coming at you. Trust me."

Mrs. Hancock leans over and pours more whiskey into Magda's glass. Is she gonna remember this in the morning? She's wasted.

"Yeah but, why should I have to tuck it all in?" Magda says. "I didn't do anything; why do I have to hide it?"

"It's the deal we make, Magda. Hide it or starve or wind up like one of those junkie girls who dance in the Lagoon. Those are your choices. It's a no-brainer, honey. Come here."

She pulls Magda out of the doorway and into the dining room across the hall. The curtains are open and the room is dark. Across Baywater Avenue is a row of porch lights, shining on freshly painted arts-and-crafts doors.

"What if every woman on this street got mad at the same time? What if they let it out instead of all sitting in their separate living rooms drowning it in vodka and prescriptions?" She's kind of shouting now. "We'd burn this place down, Magdalene. There'd be nothing left."

They look at each other for a minute. Mrs. Hancock's blue eyes are shining behind a layer of water, and the thin Irish skin has gone pink over her cheeks. She waves at the dining room door and waits for Magda to head back into the den. What did she come here for? Mrs. Hancock is obviously in way worse shape than she is.

"I miss your mother," she says from the doorway.

"I don't."

"Yes, you do. Don't be ridiculous."

"Could you be friends with Mrs. O'Sullivan?"

"Jeannie O'Sullivan? You're friends with her daughter, aren't you? She as pretentious as Jeannie?"

"Um . . ."

"She hangs around in Mariner's bookstore, I know that. Her mother was friends with Sam Lipsky in high school. You're not good enough for those two unless you made it all the way through *Ulysses*."

"Well, you know what my dad's like."

"Yes, Magda. I know; he's a snob too. A mean one. Your mother did the right thing. It's tough on you, but one day you'll see. It was that or burn the place down, like I said."

"I get that, Mrs. Hancock. I already get that. I should go."

Magda stands up, but Mrs. Hancock just keeps talking.

"He could use taking down a peg."

"My dad? Yeah, I know. Trust me."

"Him too, but I meant Sam Lipsky. Like he's allowed to just crush you, like everyone is a whole person but you. If I could live by myself in a stupid bookstore, I would."

What the hell is she talking about?

"I should go." Magda shrugs at her and puts the rocks glass down on the coffee table. "School night."

"As soon as you get a chance, get out of here." Mrs. Hancock comes over and grabs Magda's shoulders. Her breath stinks. Give her a match, she could breathe fire. "Take a leaf out of your mother's book."

"I intend to."

"You know, you're just as beautiful as her."

"No, Mrs. Hancock. I'm really not."

"You just carry it different, that's all." While they're walking to the door, she says, "The other one is Ruth Carter. You sure you should be hanging around with her? She's nearly as old as her mother was when she had her."

"Which I think makes your husband the bastard, not Ruth." It just comes out before Magda can stop it. Mrs. Hancock's mouth drops open, but then she closes it and smiles.

"Yes. That's what I've been telling you, isn't it? See what I mean? We can either keep quiet, or start making Molotov cocktails. There's no middle ground."

Well, it's definitely true, then. He's Ruth's father. Mrs. Hancock didn't even pretend he wasn't. Wow. She opens the back door, and a chilly smell of lilacs drifts right through Magda's body, like she's stepping through a ghost. They both shiver.

"Remember," Mrs. Hancock says. "Keep it all tucked in. Don't let them see it touch you."

Another gust of wind shakes the riggings on the boats in the harbor. The sound is like someone breaking glass in the distance.

That same wind is tossing around dust and leaves and used-up paper bags in the empty park, scooping everything up and then dropping it again. The only people around are Lefty and Robert, which is what Magda was hoping. She should have taken Mrs. Hancock's whiskey. She never would have noticed, she was so drunk, and whiskey that good would have made Robert's whole year. If her and Ruth and Isabel were going to start thieving, they should have picked on people like the Hancocks.

Lefty and Robert are using the bandstand for a theater, doing a dialogue. "I *refuse* to be seen in this light," Robert says in a thin little southern voice. Spooky.

She climbs the steps and stands looking down at him. He's being faint with an arm resting on his forehead. Lefty is trying to look disturbed over by the steps.

"Hey, cigarette anyone?"

"Magdalene, Magdalene!" Lefty says, like she's part of the act, come to save him.

She hands out cigarettes and a Zippo. She's widened the nozzle so the flame is eight inches high, but now it uses up a shitload of lighter fluid. Fun, though. Robert screeches and rolls away when the flame shoots up over his face. Maybe that was mean, actually.

"Wanted to ask you two something."

"Ask on, Mary Magdalene. You can wash my feet if you want to," Lefty says.

"That wasn't Mary Magdalene; it was one of those other Marys. You having a bad day, Lefty? You never get stuff like that wrong."

"Martha Mary. There's three Marys, you know. But only one Magdalene."

"Two, actually. Me and the one who got it on with God. So, listen, if you had a large quantity of marijuana, like enough to sell and make some money, where would you guys go with it?"

"Irkutsk," Lefty says without hesitation.

"Guam," Robert says at the same time. "You can hide it in an air force plane. Sell it there. It's cheaper there."

"I think you got that kind of backwards, Robert. The principles of capitalism have passed you by, which is cool, but anyway I was thinking of somewhere kind of closer to home."

"I got it." Robert wags his index finger like he's about to deliver the crucial point. "We could give it to cops. You know, so they could have a smoke and contemplate stuff? Get mellow. Yep. We could change the world if we gave the cops a couple pounds of weed."

"Yeah, that's a great plan, Robert. Glad I talked to you guys. Cleared stuff right up."

A Highbone police car crawls by, above them on Baywater Avenue. Mrs. Hancock will still be up there, watching out the window and dreaming of fire. Lefty and Robert will do Tennessee Williams on the bandstand until either a cop or the morning comes to chase them away. Magda will go home to play with gears and live through the darkness until it all starts over again. When the sun finally rises, everything will still be there, and it will all still be her problem.

eleven

MAGDA HUGS HER knees and watches the sun fall behind the smokestacks. It's Thursday evening, and most of the people are gone from the beach at Fiddler's Cove. Someone, Ruth or Isabel, asked a question at least a whole minute ago, but Magda hasn't answered. The threads of silence between them are so thick and tangled now, it's hard to find her way through them. Any minute, all the words the three of them are trying so hard not to say are going to just pour down from the sky and soak them.

"Hello, Magda? The machine you're making? What's it for?"

"It's not a machine; it's a mechanism."

"Oh, *sor-ry*," Isabel says. "*Mechanism*. And the difference would be?"

"A mechanism is a system of interrelated parts that has, like, a holistic function. I'm not sure I mean holistic. Unified? A unified function."

Why is she trying to explain it to them? Does it matter?

"Which is not a machine, 'cause . . . ?"

"A machine applies power," Magda says. "Like a car. Know what car is in Italian? *Macchina*. Machine. Now there's a useful thing my mom taught me before she fucked off."

More talking, but Magda hasn't said anything that matters in days. She's keeping it all tucked in, like Mrs. Hancock said. She definitely hasn't said anything about visiting Mrs. Hancock. Ruth would freak. She hasn't said how different her skin feels, either. Her body is screaming all the time, but it isn't using words. She hasn't said that there are still bruises left, or that there ever were any bruises.

"Your mom used to make you say stuff in Italian, Magda. I remember that."

"Yep. *La macchina*. Cars are girls if you're Italian."

"So," Isabel says, "you're building this *mechanism*, for why?"

"I like it. I told Ms. Farrow at school it was art. I kind of believed it. Really it's just satisfying to put parts together and make them work. It makes sense, like. It takes up your brain, all your thoughts kind of go away when you're paying attention to what goes where and how it works. In a mechanism nothing is extra; nothing gets in the way."

"Your dad doesn't care that you're building a big, greasy, pointless motor in your room?"

"It is not a fucking motor! It's a mechanism."

Someone has a burger and fries in the parking lot. Gulls are circling and screaming behind them. Any minute their screams will turn into words. *Look at her. She's the weak one.* It will echo down out of the sky and all the strangers in the parking lot will turn on her. Ruth points up at the birds.

"What do you think we look like from up there?"

"We look like crap that washed up on the beach," Isabel says. "The tide line is behind us, look. From far away we're just flotsam. Jetsam? Whichever."

"You can't see us from close up either," Ruth says. "You can't see the stuff that matters, even when you're right next to somebody."

"See what I mean, Magda? That is the kind of shit Ruth says lately."

Magda hears but she can't answer. Memory has ambushed her again, slamming down a wall between her and the present moment. Sometimes it comes in order, like a story, sometimes in flashes, like a series of snapshots. Sometimes it comes in a split second, cutting through the middle of another thought. It grabs her and won't let her pay attention to what is being said around her. Other times it just settles softly down on her like a pillow, cutting off the air.

Isabel jumps up. "Come wading, you guys."

"Wait," Magda says. "There's something I need to tell you."

"Okay, tell us in the water," and Isabel runs away into the sliding foam.

When Ruth stands up, sand and shells fall from her jeans.

Magda realizes she's staring at her. They lock eyes for a second, and all the questions are there. It's Ruth, though, so she doesn't have to answer out loud.

In the water they turn towards the red-and-white-striped smokestacks of the LILCO plant, their colors saturating in the slipping sunlight. Everything blue is fading from the world. Looking down into the shallows, the pulling waves make Magda feel like she's sliding along, even though they're all standing still with their feet sinking into the sand.

"Jeff," Magda says, and then stops.

"Yeah, when are you gonna tell us about Jeff?" Isabel splashes water in Magda's direction. "You're always sticking your nose in *my* sex life."

"Never," Magda says. "Forget it."

"So you're just saying his name?"

"No. He figured out where the weed came from. And"— Magda looks at Ruth—"Charlie thinks we did it, too."

"Let's remember not to apply for jobs at the CIA. Seems like we're not way stealthy." Isabel brings up cupped hands full of foamy water and splashes it over her face. "Also, the mass-murder part is kind of not my thing."

"Can you be serious for two seconds, Isabel? You're not going to be alive to murder even *one* person. People are gonna murder us."

"Listen," Ruth says. "I have an idea."

"Again?"

"Well, Magda, you seem kind of busy spacing out in the

middle of conversations and shouting insults at us for no reason. I just thought I'd step in."

"Fine. So?"

"So . . . what about Underground Highbone?"

"What about it?" Isabel says. "You didn't want to hear about it the other day."

"Yeah, but I asked Old Mr. Lipsky. He got me thinking. We should check it out. We could stash Matt's weed down there and wait for things to blow over."

"Oh yeah, how long do you think that'll take?"

"Uh, Ruth?" Isabel splashes her. "The harbor has tides that go up under Main Street. I don't think anybody's gonna buy the shit after it's soaked in sewage water."

"We don't know what's under there," Ruth says, "and obviously some of it must stay dry if it's still there."

"What Isabel means is Underground Highbone doesn't exist." This is why Magda always does the thinking. Those two can't be trusted to stick to reality.

"Old Mr. Lipsky said it did, Magda. He should know. He was there at the time."

"He was a kid, Ruth."

"No, it really does," Isabel says. "My sister went under there with Sal Lipardi and a bunch of other people the night they graduated. I told Ruth. She brought back this big, thick coffee cup. That's what they used to drink gin out of during Prohibition, apparently. She said there's a bowling alley under there and—"

"All right," Ruth interrupts, "but Old Mr. Lipsky said the

stairs were behind the deli. That door in the alley is all chained up. We'd need bolt cutters or something."

"You guys, listen." Isabel pulls Ruth's arm. "My sister Elizabeth and them went in through the drainpipe in the harbor. The one I showed you, Ruth, remember? You just have to time it with the tide."

"Okay, women, just let me get this straight," Magda says. "We're gonna go up a sewage pipe while the tide's changing and crawl around someplace in the pitch dark until we find some damp place anybody could get to, so we can't really hide anything there anyway, for why?"

"First of all, Ruth can get Danny's tide table."

"No, Isabel. I'm not stealing anything else from Danny or my mom. Not for you, anyway." Ruth walks backwards now, facing them and moving away into water higher than the rolled-up cuffs of her jeans.

"Will you two just listen? It can be our secret cave. We can stash anything we can carry under there. We need a place to hide."

"Get real, Isabel. You don't have anything to hide from. Stop being so melodramatic."

"How would you know that, Ruth? You're the only one of us whose life is perfect."

"Seriously, Isabel? You float in and out of my life like it's your own personal daydream. You can't even see the blood and guts through your rose-colored glasses."

"Why are you so judgmental, Ruth? Who died and left you

God? We are older than you, you know."

"No you're not; you were just born first." Ruth keeps backing away, shouting through cupped hands. Her shadow stretches across the waves towards Magda. "'How's Danny, Ruth?' 'Oh, he's fine, Isabel. It's really nice that you asked.'"

"I'm sorry." Isabel actually looks it. "I thought you hated Danny. I don't see why you care."

"You don't see anything but yourself, Isabel O'Sullivan. There's a mirror where your heart's supposed to be."

None of the shouting takes away the tension all around them. Magda can still feel it, pressing against her ribs and stopping the air like a rag in her throat.

"So I guess we're going to go into Underground Highbone and get trapped in a tunnel collapse or something. Great. That'll round off this week nicely."

"Come on, Magda, it's an adventure. We're *us*, we have to go under there at some point. We can't leave town without checking it out, can we?"

Magda squints out onto the water. The outline of Ruth arches up against the sun then disappears. "She's in the water. Naked. Look, those are her jeans up there."

"I'm not getting her out," Isabel says. "I've been underwater with her once this week. She's a fucking mermaid, that woman. That's not her jeans, it's her human skin. I'm telling you."

"Fine, I'll go. It's gonna be dark soon and the water's freezing. She might cramp up and we won't see her."

It hits again just as Magda drops her shirt on the sand. She feels her body spinning around and into that tree. There on the beach, she can see the texture of the bark right in front of her eyes. She turns in a circle, looking for a way out. She can still make out the dark smudges on her arms, and the scrape down her thigh. Her body is a loud stranger, saying things to her that she doesn't want to hear. She throws it at the cold, green water and dives. There is one beautiful, blank minute when she can't breathe or think.

Darkness under the first wave, and the taste of salt under the second. The scrapes on her legs sting and then go numb. She comes up and rolls over onto her back, gasping at the first star that's winking now over the smokestacks. Then the burning cold subsides, taking everything away with it. Everything that's written on her skin is carried up and erased in the darkening sky.

twelve

ONCE RUTH UNSCREWS the bulb on the O'Sullivans' kitchen porch light it's hard to see in their backyard. There's no sound either. No one is out this late on a Thursday night. Friday morning, technically. It was one o'clock when Ruth left her house. She climbs down off the picnic bench and puts it back by the table. There's no need to rush. She has time to do everything that needs to be done before the sun comes up.

Virgil Mackie said the reason you have an imagination is to give you a map for making things real. He said she shouldn't be scared of anything she thought. At night sometimes, he comes to stand under the window, like Isabel did. When Mackie comes, though, Ruth stays inside and just leans out. They talk, sometimes for hours, to each other and the darkness. Mackie comes back again. Isabel doesn't.

Now Ruth stands against the O'Sullivans' house under the mudroom window, waiting for her pupils to open up and adjust to the darkness. The shadows soak into her skin, making her less visible, muffling the sound of her. Mackie showed her how to see herself like a candle with the light burning towards the inside, how to burn and hide at the same time. He said she was right to be mad at Isabel, anyone would be.

They talked about fighting back, about how justice works, about war and fire and women. Burning, hanging, or drowning—those used to be the choices outlaw women had, back when Highbone was first built. Mackie said the way you became the judge instead of the outlaw was to appoint yourself. Nothing else to it.

It might be hours later when a bull raccoon stalks along the top of the chain-link fence at the back of the yard, using his grasping little hands around the pole. He's the size of the dog that stays chained in front of the biker garage. He doesn't even realize Ruth is there, watching him from her shadow. It's his neighborhood at nighttime; he's not expecting human girls in the backyards at two in the morning. There's a cloud of moths in the streetlight on the other side of the neighbor's house. The light shrinks her pupils and she turns away so she'll stay open to the darkness.

She puts the matches and the pint of Old Mr. Boston in one hand so she can use the other to cut the window screen with a safety blade from Danny's razor. At home she practiced soaking rags and lighting them on the back steps. Crappy gin works best.

She has to pull the bench over again so she can climb up and through the window onto the top of the O'Sullivans' dryer. First she takes her sneakers off, thinking of the big, hollow sound she used to make when she was little, sitting on top of the dryer at the laundromat, kicking her feet. Even in her socks, though, her feet make a resonant boom like the voice of someone else's god. She freezes and waits again. Night is full of time. She's been learning that lately.

There are towels folded in a basket. Ruth tries to imagine one of Isabel's parents doing that and can't. Moving through the dark house, she can picture Isabel and daytime in all the rooms. Memories of them in front of the TV, them in the kitchen making soul coffee, them coming in the front door with Henry riding Isabel piggyback, sleeping.

In the upstairs hallway she studies the ceiling. She has walked under it to get to Isabel's room a thousand times and never looked up. Like she thought, the O'Sullivans are the kind of people who have smoke detectors, and she's glad about that. She likes Mrs. O'Sullivan.

There is Isabel, sleeping on her back with her arms flung out, one hand hanging over the edge of the bed. She isn't scared of what's under there; she isn't crying or talking now. She sleeps with total confidence, a person lying in the middle of a world that belongs to her. There are dark puddles of clothes on the floor and papers tacked to the sloping ceiling. The window has no curtain, and Ruth can see the branches full of new leaves, darker than the rest of the darkness against the sky.

Ruth's drawing is invisible in the shadows at the far corner of the room. The fire could start there. She imagines the flower on the wall igniting, the light of the fire coming not from her hands but from the corner where that flower waits in the darkness. She can see Virgil Mackie smiling in the shadows. He might be waiting like that now, under her window. Her imagination stretches on a wire from Mackie to that drawing on the wall, a wire full of sparks and energy, pulling her tight and balancing her. Ruth crouches down to put the rag on the floor and opens the pint of Old Mr. Boston, wondering if the smell will wake Isabel up.

When a hand comes down on her shoulder it doesn't startle her. She hasn't heard a step behind her, but Mrs. O'Sullivan's touch is too light, too full of love, to frighten anyone.

"Come downstairs," she whispers, and takes Ruth's shoulders in her hands, lifting and turning her away from the doorway.

At the bottom of the stairs she pulls Ruth gently towards the den at the back of the house, pushing her into a chair by the sliding glass doors to the yard.

"They don't hear me back here," she says. "I can stay here talking all night."

"I was just looking," Ruth says. "I lost something. I hope I didn't scare you, Mrs. O'Sullivan."

"I know why you're here, Ruth. It's okay."

"Who do you talk to all night?"

"Everyone. No one. Myself. Do you read, Ruth?"

"Not like Isabel."

"I don't know what Isabel is like." Mrs. O'Sullivan sighs. "Here, put the afghan over you. Do you read, though?"

"Yes, but I'd rather draw. I never found a book that said what I needed it to. Do you know what I mean, Mrs. O'Sullivan?"

"Of course I do."

"Really? You mean that?" Ruth leans forward. It doesn't feel awkward or surreal, the way talking to people's parents usually does. After you try to burn down someone's house and they're not even mad at you, you're already way past that.

"Why do you live here, Mrs. O'Sullivan? I like your house, but it seems like you could be somewhere else, you know?"

"What, take off like Irene Warren? No, Ruth, I'm not that brave. And I keep thinking I might be able to stop my children from falling. Or burning."

"I'm sorry, Mrs. O'Sullivan. I don't think I would have hurt any of you, really. I almost hurt Danny and I was so scared."

She doesn't even ask who Danny is.

"Danny, he's my mom's boyfriend. I almost got him killed. I'm scared of myself, Mrs. O'Sullivan."

"I can see that, but you don't have to be. I can help. Look through my eyes, just for a minute. Let me show you."

"No one thinks you notice anything," Ruth says. "No one thinks you're paying attention."

"Sometimes I'm not, for days at a time. Sometimes I look down and I'm wearing something different than I was a minute ago, but I can't remember changing. I stay up at night, though, so I can watch when everyone else is sleeping. I see the raccoons and catch the kids who come in through the mudroom window." Mrs. O'Sullivan laughs a twinkly laugh like a little girl.

"You know how I can tell you are paying attention? From the wallpaper. I get it, Mrs. O. I get the wallpaper. That's how I know you're awake. You're telling people what it's really like in this house. You're saying something. Somebody heard you."

"Thank you, Ruth."

"Magdalene calls it Castle Gloom, this house."

"Ha, ha," Mrs. O'Sullivan says. Her voice is flat. "I like it. She doesn't need anyone's help, that Warren girl. Now, Ruth, look at me." She pulls Ruth around in her chair so that her back is to the glass. "Look right at me, Ruth," she says.

Ruth looks straight into Mrs. O'Sullivan's eyes that have no color in the night. She can see the wisps of hair making shadows on her face and the tendons running down the sides of her neck.

"You don't have to be crazy," Mrs. O'Sullivan says.

It's like someone just punched Ruth in the ribs, or spoke straight to her for the first time in her life. She doesn't answer, but her breathing comes fast and hard now.

"Whatever you do, don't marry anyone," Mrs. O'Sullivan says. "Don't have any children. Don't live in a house like this. Are you listening?"

Ruth nods.

"The children will hollow you out. You won't weigh anything anymore. You'll push against things, but they won't move. You'll be like wind that can't blow."

"That's already happening. Half the time I feel like I'm under-water or ten feet off the ground. I don't seem to be solid like other people. I'm so sorry, Mrs. O'Sullivan. I wanted to make all of it go away."

"So did I, lots of times. Don't worry so much about all that."

"I thought if things were turned to ashes I could breathe them in and no one would be able to take them away from me. I wanted to hurt people so they would stop ruining me."

"Try it, Ruth. Go upstairs now and try it. I'll stay here. I won't stop you."

She's telling the truth. Ruth can see that, but neither of them moves. Mrs. O'Sullivan looks past her, out into the yard, seeing the moths in the streetlight and the raccoon stealing the neigh-bor's snow peas. Ruth can see what she sees, the picnic table and the fences attached to fences attached to fences in a rolling grid under the sky. When she turns back to look at Ruth again, all of that is gathered into her eyes.

"Listen to me. Don't get trapped, honey. I don't think I can do anything for Isabel; I don't know where she is or what she's done now. But you, I can help. You, I recognize."

"She's your daughter, I know she is, and we all love her, but she doesn't love us back. I wanted to hurt her. I'm so sorry."

"You won't hurt each other, Ruth. That's just the part of you that's lying to yourself, telling yourself scary stories and making yourself believe in monsters. In the real world, girls don't hurt each other. Boys hurt each other. Girls hurt themselves."

"I get what you're saying, but sometimes we do, Mrs. O. Seriously, we do."

"You get what I'm saying. I knew you would. You know what book I liked? *La Bâtarde*. That was a book I loved. And *Summer Will Show*. You should read those. And *The Portrait of a Lady*. They go crazy, either a little or a lot, all those women. And then they come back down. Just wait it out, and don't grab on to things like a drowning person. It's a trick. Those are actually the things that drown you, not the things that hold you up. Teach yourself to breathe and wait it out."

There is no way to lie to someone like her, so Ruth just stays quiet.

"Please?" Mrs. O'Sullivan says. "Will you do that for me?"

They look straight at each other while everything between them settles into place in the silence. After a while the fight drains out of Ruth, and she slumps back in the chair.

"It's a trick, Ruth. Remember that, at least. Don't hold on. It's a trick."

"Isabel says you keep M&M's stashed around. Can I have some? I feel kind of shaky."

"Oh, yeah. I got lotsa stuff stashed around, kiddo. I'm like a Girl Scout doing wilderness training in this place."

She gets up and goes behind the freestanding green aluminum fireplace they had put in last year. It has a circle of white rocks around it, the only thing glowing in the dark room. There's a low bookshelf, where she moves some things and brings out a bottle of Rémy and some candy. She doesn't make a single wasted movement in the darkness.

"Drink from the bottle?" Mrs. O'Sullivan waves the cognac at her. "Or are you too stuck-up?"

Ruth laughs a little, breathless laugh then, feeling full of emptiness and relief. Nothing but space inside her.

thirteen

FROM WHERE SHE sits under the wooden playground, Isabel can see the engine house of Danny's boat. She can see the bench at the bottom of Main Street where Lefty sits, chattering to himself in whispers. Danny's boat is leaning drunkenly with its keel in the mud, but Lefty has perfect posture. Ruth ducks in and sits facing Isabel with her back to all that.

"Where you been? You're late, Carter. And I thought Magda was with you."

"Magda'll be here," Ruth says. "Henry was shouting at her when I was on the phone, wanting to come with us. She had to tuck him in early and read him a story."

"Well, she better hurry up. Low tide's in fifteen minutes."

"Listen, Isabel, something's the matter with Magda. I tried to tell you the other day at school, but you weren't paying attention to me."

"What do you mean, something?" Isabel says. "Something more than usual?"

"She went all, sort of, I don't know, quiet lately. I know her, Isabel. There's something she's not saying. Trust me."

Over Ruth's shoulder, Isabel can see Mr. Lipsky and his dad, passing by Lefty on their way into the park. It's one of those nights when the air is so heavy it's almost shining. When a cop pulls into the space at the end of Main Street acid rises in her throat and the ground slips out from under her. Here they are again, in another moment like all the moments lately. Full of sick fear and ridiculous beauty at the same time. The cops don't get out of their car. They aren't looking for her. Not tonight.

"Magda broods, hon. It's what she does. We love her for it. She's the inscrutable one."

"I'm serious, Isabel. The other night at the beach, when we got out of the water, she had bruises on her. A huge scabby one on her leg, and big streaks on her arm like finger marks."

"So, you saying she got beat up? Bad?"

"I don't know what I'm saying. We need to get her to talk. Give me a Lark."

"I only have three left. It happens to her, Ruth. You know this."

"This is different than the usual Magda. *She's* different than the usual Magda. Have you actually looked at her lately?"

Isabel is looking at everything, all the goddamned time. It's all so bright and sharp. Her eyes need a break, is what. Everybody still accuses her of not paying attention and not caring.

Mr. Lipsky and his dad are making their way down along the water's edge, the two of them throwing one long shadow sideways onto the grass. Ruth is checked out, thinking about something else, so Isabel just watches them until Magda's head tilts into their hiding place.

"Let me ask you women this," Magda says. "Do you have candles? A flashlight?"

"We have a lighter, see?" Ruth holds up the hula girl and spins her around until she's naked.

"Yeah," Magda says. "I found you by the cigarette smoke, secret agent girls. Well, I have everything."

Lefty is talking about schools of fish when they climb around the rocks and down onto the mud. The two Mr. Lipskys are on the steps of the bandstand, with pipe smoke curling over their heads. The air coming from the mouth of the drainpipe smells like the inside of big, dead things.

"Are you sure this isn't a sewage pipe, Isabel?" Ruth speaks with her hand over her nose and mouth.

"Yeah I'm sure. It's the seaweed that stinks at low tide."

"Danny says the seaweed lives on the crap from all these boats. It smells like Linda Blair's breath. Let's go in before I puke."

"You can't smell Linda Blair's breath, Ruth. *The Exorcist* is a film."

"I'll say it again. You don't know what I can do, Isabel."

"Hey, Lefty!" Isabel calls up in a shouty whisper. "Catch!"

She throws two Larks up to Lefty and puts a finger to her lips, inviting him into their conspiracy of silence, then goes into the tunnel last in line. Ten yards in, the tunnel is pitch dark. Magda stops to take out three hurricane candles and hold them up for Ruth to light. The drainpipe is big enough to stand up in, but they have to go single file. Once they're moving, all in a row down the tunnel holding candles, Isabel feels like she's back in rehearsals for first communion, or at midnight Easter Mass. Or maybe they're like medieval monks, processing through some crypt full of saintly bones.

"I think we're about under the diner now." Magda holds her candle forward, looking for whatever it is they're going to find down here.

"Wow, what would we do without you, Saint Magdalene of the Eternal Compass?"

"Quiet, Isabel. We're going uphill a little, that's good."

At the mouth of the harbor, the tunnel is cement, but farther in it's made of bricks. It gets narrower and their voices stop echoing.

"So, uh, not to be a spoilsport," Isabel says, "but what if there is no—"

"Holy shit. Look!" Magda points at the wall in front of them.

Isabel can't see until she stands on tiptoe to look over Ruth's shoulder. The drainage pipe curves off to the right, but the light from Magdalene's candle is falling on a door straight ahead. There are three steps up to it, and it looks like it could be anyone's front door.

"There's even a doorbell." Magda raises a finger to it.

"Don't push it, Magda. Jesus." Isabel backs away. "Can we just sit here for a minute? I need to get used to this before we open that door."

"How many blocks have we come?" Ruth asks.

"One? Two?" Magda says. "No tunnels to the left, just that one we passed on the right."

"And we would have had to crawl to go down there." Isabel sits down on the little step and lights her last Lark. "I think I'd need a bigger incentive before I'd do that."

"Do you think smoking down here will suck up all our oxygen?"

"I don't know, Ruth. Maybe we'll fall into a beautiful sleep and not wake up for decades. We'll never even realize it's happening. It'll be like a fairy tale."

"Yeah, one of those surprisingly violent and bloody ones where some girl has to sleep for a hundred years in a moldy hole, drowning and undrowning every twelve hours."

Magda rolls her eyes at them and turns the doorknob. They step over her into a room, but Isabel stays where she is, staring at the tide mark on the wall.

"Get up, woman. We need to shut the door." Magda yanks her shirt.

Up the steps and through the door there is a room with an old piano, ivory veneer peeling off the keys. Isabel touches them with one finger, and at first there is nothing. When she runs a scale, a few of its notes are there, with silences between them.

There's a bar, with shelves full of old plates and cups behind it, and a bunch of broken chairs. At some point a fire has blackened one corner of the room. Once there was a mirror on the wall, but only the frame is still hanging. There are splinters of mirror glass all over the floor, some of them covered in soot. Ruth sits herself right down in the middle of all that broken glass.

"You know what's spooky? It doesn't seem like anyone else has been here."

"Well, they have or we wouldn't know about it." Magda tests out a stool by the bar, then sits on it. "Your sister's been here; you said so."

"I know, but why haven't any assholes carved their initials in the bar or left their Boone's Farm bottles lying around?"

Isabel walks a circle around the room, stepping over Ruth on the floor, shining her candle into shards of mirror glass. Magda rolls a joint on the bar with one of Matt's buds.

"It's like there isn't any time here," Ruth says. "I could actually see the enchanted sleep thing happening."

Isabel tries "The Entertainer" on the piano, but most of the notes are missing. It's like the sentences she keeps trying to make lately, the things she's trying to say. Half the words it would take to say them are missing.

"Can I just ask, what are we gonna do with this weed besides smoke it?"

"Hello, Isabel? I tried. So far I'm the only one who has. We can't sell it to anyone we know, because Matt and Charlie know them too."

"If we roll it up and sell joints at school, he'll know right away. We'll be dead. What do you think, Ruth?"

"I thought Matt would suspect my mom and Danny of being in on it, but he definitely didn't. Mom was going over there the other night to cheer Matt up. He owes the money, though, you guys. He's scared. It's messed up."

"Isabel, what about your brother or your sister?" Magda says. "Can't we sell it to them to take back up to college?"

"Oh yeah, I'll just tell them I have a hookup in Colombia now. They won't ask any questions. I don't think so, hon."

"Magda, did you even hear me?" Ruth holds up her candle and flashes a piece of mirror at them like a beacon. "Matt owes the money to the guys that fronted it. What if something happens to him?"

"All right, all right." Magda puts her lighter back in the inside pocket of the toolbox coat and passes the joint to Isabel. "I'll figure it out. Again."

"Well, I helped you steal it and it was my idea in the first place." Isabel talks without breathing, like someone squeezing through a tight space. There isn't enough air in the world lately.

"Yeah, it was your idea, Isabel. I was just the one trying to fix it, so we don't all get killed or go to jail. You want credit for that? Be my guest."

"Of course she does." Ruth sits against the wall with shards of mirror sparkling around her, staring at Isabel with cutting eyes. "You relax, Isabel. I'm sure it'll all be fixed up and rosy just in time for you to wake up and take a bow."

"You guys, we should get out of here," Magda says. "It's after nine o'clock. The tide was dead low at eight fifty-five."

Isabel can hear the metal clinking in Magda's pocket when she puts her lighter away. She looks over at Ruth holding a shard of mirror glass in one eye like a monocle, flashing light back.

Nothing between any of them seems to be working anymore. The engine is banging, something's come loose. These are supposed to be the two people Isabel can say anything to, so why hasn't she? They all look back and forth at each other, frozen and trying to feel their way forward. Isabel hits the same piano key three times, low like a tolling bell, then she and Ruth both speak at once.

"I don't have to be crazy," Ruth says.

"I think I killed someone," Isabel says.

"Take it down a notch, you two." Magda looks at her like it can't possibly be true, and she must be exaggerating. "Isabel, what are you talking about?"

"I'm not daydreaming all the time, Ruth, trust me. The cops came to my house. I don't know if he's dead."

She can hear her own voice, low and flat as her mother's. She isn't crying, or even breathing hard. After all that time holding it in, it just comes out now without her even trying.

"He, who? You need to sit down and start at the beginning." Magda pulls her over to the bar, pushes her up onto a stool, and says, "Talk, woman."

"He grabbed me and put his dirty fingernails up under my Navy sweater and Charlie only wants to fuck me if I pretend I don't want him to. What the hell is that about? I had to burn my Navy sweater at the beach. I really loved it."

"Charlie?" Magda says. "Charlie is not dead, Isabel. You need to calm down. You're stoned. You're just freaking out."

"Not Charlie, the greasy one from Dunkin' Donuts. The one with the napalm jacket. You saw him. You were there."

Isabel looks at Magda, but really she's talking to Ruth. She can't tell if Ruth is listening, though. She just sits there against the wall, turning a piece of mirror over in her hands so it sends the candlelight into Isabel's eyes. Soon Isabel is blinded and there is nothing but the sound of her own voice. When she gets to the part where the vet with the napalm jacket walked towards her across the parking lot, Ruth drops the piece of mirror and stands up. She doesn't even look interested. She just moves past them to the door, feeling her way along the damp wall, then turns back from the doorway with her foot held out over the space above the steps.

"I don't have to be crazy," she says again. She steps down and closes the door behind her, leaving Isabel alone with Magdalene and the broken mirror and the story filling up the room.

When Isabel stops talking, Magda just says, "Okay, let's go."

That's it. She doesn't look disgusted or worried or proud, or even disinterested. It's like Isabel didn't say anything at all.

When they get back into the tunnel it's much darker than when they came in, but it also seems quicker. Isabel holds the sleeve of Magda's coat, feeling like a tall version of Henry, tugging on her for comfort. There are a few inches of green water at the mouth of the tunnel, and their feet get wet. Magda pokes her head out, looking from side to side and then up at the starry sky.

"So that was Underground Highbone," Magda says. "Are we impressed?"

Isabel lets go of her sleeve and takes a step back.

"You go, Magda. I'll stay in. If I go back up to the piano room, I'll be above the tide. No one's gonna find me in there. You can bring me some stuff tomorrow."

"Listen." Magda grabs both of Isabel's shoulders and looks her in the eye. "One: you have a right to defend yourself. Two: if the guy was dead the cop wouldn't have said assault. Think about it. Three: if they could have, they would have arrested you already. The most important thing is to act normal. Haven't you ever watched a single movie, woman?"

"Normal? Magda, we are not normal. Nothing about any of us is normal. Don't you get it?"

"Yes, Isabel, I get it. It is normal. Your reaction was extraordinary, but the shit that happens to us is everywhere, happening all over the place, all the time. That is the actual definition of normal. The *idea* of normal is just something people invented to control us. Now get in front of me and walk out there. Look straight in front of you and move."

She gives a little shove, and Isabel stumbles and splashes out onto the mud.

"Okay, see?" Magda says. "Sky still up there where it's supposed to be. It's all good." Isabel looks up, but it isn't comforting. The sky looks like it could drop down on her at any moment and pierce her with thousands of sharp stars.

"Stop trying to be chipper, Magda. This is serious. My life is over. Someone else's too, maybe."

"I am being serious, Isabel. Let's concentrate on the task at hand. I can't say that was a boring excursion, but we're no closer to world domination, the overthrow of Highbone, or the ultimate destruction of the American way."

"Oh, well." Isabel looks down and laughs. "Maybe next time?"

"On second thought, maybe we are closer to world domination. Who'd have thought it would be you that hit back? Everyone always expects it to be me."

fourteen

"THE DEAD SUFFER from a lack of pockets. Where will they keep their matches? It's dark there. How will they see? See, I can't C if I don't have my ABCs. Then there's the one I always leave out when I'm naming the seven seas."

Lefty's voice is quiet and he's upright on the bench facing the docks at the end of Main Street. He's looking down at where the water would be if the tide weren't on its way out. Now there's only mud that smells brackish, and whiffs of methane and diesel.

The mud is soft and shiny. It's silt, like silk. Girls are whispering inside the tunnel underneath him. The short one is scared. He can hear it in her voice. That voice is not tall, it's frightened, it's lightened, it doesn't stay on the ground at all. It isn't tall.

The bookstore man is walking by with his shaking father. His earthquake old father. Soon the flaking father will lose all his pockets and the bookstore man will need a hanky. Where do you get a hanky when your father has no pockets? Where is the woman who makes the handkerchiefs for them? Where is the lady with the needle in their lives? Dead, dead too. But women never have pockets, not even when they're alive.

"Listen," Lefty says to them in the same soft, shouting whisper as those girls, but the loneless homey old men don't. Don't listen. They look straight at him and smile, though. That is so nice, so . . . nice. Lefty smiles right back with every tooth in his head. He works so hard that every tooth smiles individually, shines up at them. Golden gifts for them, hanky-less but never cranky. They deserve a prize.

The little boy is following, but the girls can't see. Henry the fourth, fifth, eighth. Oh Henry behind them, back of the line. Henry in a different time. The old men shedding their pockets don't see. Only Lefty can see the secret boy. Not bookstore men or candle girls.

The girls drop something clanky, not cranky, in the tunnel. More shouty whispering. Not steps, not echoing steps, they have soft shoes. Just their voices, three loud, loud, feathery loud voices moving right under his bench now. Then Henry the Fourth voice climbs down the rocks after them.

"Little mountain man," Lefty says. He waves back, that lovely little poem of a boy. He belongs to his holy harlot sister. The one who's carrying things behind her eyes.

"Little mountain man, little poem on the stones, your sister has a tall voice. She's not the short one." It's hard today. Something keeps happening in between his head and his mouth. The back of his head and his mouth. Mouth in his head, of course. He has got a brain in his head and a . . . a mouth, but words are tangling up in there. That little joyful mountaineer will not hear. Will hear, but not get it, catch . . . it. Won't know his sister is the one on the left. The one who went left.

"Under the bench, little man. Their voices are under the bench." But then he does! He catches it, gets it. Miracle . . . aculous, beatific boy.

"I know. Thanks, Lefty," he says with his little butter-flying voice. "Don't tell on me, okay?" says that curly little one with so many pockets left.

"Go left!" That has been a miracle and Lefty is going to sit right here and digest it. Little Lazarus boy climbing down the rocks and into the mouth of that tunnel. Little child savior coming right behind those shaky, smiling, old ones, and those feathery girls with things behind their eyes. Everybody waving, Lefty in the middle of all that smiling and waving at the bottom of Main Street.

Not one golden hair on that diamond boy, dark and curly around his little voice. Just like his dark big sister, his spark of a sister with the soul leaking right out of her eyes.

It is clear. He, Lefty, is clearly here. He is the pin at the center, of old ones and little one and girls in the middle, all smiling and waving. Not one has seen the others, but he has seen them all. The world is a wheel and he is the axle. Everything is turning and he'll have to stay right here in the very precise centrifugal center and let it spin around him. It is clear as a ringing bell in the golden air, this is the exact center of the world, holding everything down. If not for him the earth comes undone. He is the one. As soon as it's all the way dark everyone will be able to see that. Once the sky starts spinning with night.

Once the sky goes dark and starts that slow turning, he will come clear as the man at the middle. Everyone will know it by the spinning stars.

RESURRECTION

one

RUTH WALKS THROUGH the tunnel until Isabel's voice dies, then stands with her eyes closed, breathing in the salt and iron air. She leans her face and one flat palm against the slimy crust of the wall. Is that Magda's voice, vibrating back through the concrete?

Weird how the sky opens out as it darkens, bigger than in the daytime. It was nicer in the tunnel, where the dark was honest and complete.

She makes her way through the squelching mud and up the rocks onto the dock. There it all is again, waiting. There is Highbone Village, looking like a movie set waiting for them to play the next scene and then turn into the people they really are when they're not acting. Because they don't actually do any of the things they've been talking about. Magda, Ruth, and Isabel don't rob perfectly sweet guys, or threaten to burn down each other's houses or cause near-fatal accidents. They don't fight back when slimy bastards grab them in the shadows. They don't fuck each other. Other people fuck them, and then they get angry and stoned and try to make beautiful things out of the leftover pieces.

There are still people under the yellow bulbs in the diner, and more people parking and going into Flannagan's. Others are wandering away from the harbor into the darker sky up the hill. There is a world underneath them, and none of them knows it. Ruth rounds the corner; Mrs. Hancock is coming out of the alley behind Main Street. What is she doing, sneaking down behind there in the dark? She turns her back to Ruth without seeing her, heading up Main Street towards Flannagan's. Then the alley is empty, like a memory of the tunnel.

Could she draw what happened under there? Could she freeze the exact moment where something was uttered and everything changed, like in the Rembrandt painting where all the anatomy students are staring at the real truth inside someone's body?

I think I killed someone. Jesus.

There are footsteps on the gravel, crunching their way down from the direction of Attic Antiques. She doesn't turn her head, just rests it back on the wall and blows smoke up at the planets in the sky. Mackie sits himself down and rests his back on the wall next to her.

"Well, well, now. Been busy?" He doesn't pronounce the *w* in *now*.

"You sounded southern just then."

"I told you, my parents are crackers. So? Tell me all about it."
It isn't a question.

"Mrs. O'Sullivan said I'm not crazy." That isn't exactly what
she said, but it's close enough.

"Did she, really?" He cocks his head at her. "That true, you
think?"

"Yes." No. Maybe.

"And, uh, when did you have this heart-to-heart with *Mrs.
O'Sullivan*?"

Mackie leans his head sideways into her until she can feel the
heat of him and smell the warm linen of his trench coat, intimate
and a little menacing. He takes out his pocket watch and holds it
in his open palm with some screws and a little scrap of cassette
tape.

"I was at Isabel's house. I was so mad, Mackie. Virgil. I was so
mad, I thought I could hurt people, but I couldn't."

"Why not?" he says. "You look tough enough to me."

"Is that what it takes, Mackie, toughness?"

"What else?"

"She beat some guy, Mackie. Isabel beat some guy, maybe to
death. Some lecherous bastard from the VA hospital. He tried to
feel her up and she maybe killed him for it."

"So, she got there first, eh? Second place for Miss Carter. I had
my money on you. Shame." He pulls his Chuck Taylors under him
and slides up to stand against the wall. "Hand up?" He reaches
down to her, but she stays where she is.

"What's gonna happen to her, Mackie? Will she get busted for it?"

"Search me, darlin'." Mackie shrugs the shoulders of his coat.

"What's gonna happen to me?"

She can feel a cold wind blowing through the sudden empty space around her body.

"You'll work it out. Like Mrs. O'Sullivan said, you don't have to be crazy. Not as much fun for me, though." He kicks up some gravel and walks away up the alley with his watch clinking against the screws in his pockets.

"Good-bye, Virgil Mackie."

He just lifts up his hand and keeps walking.

As Mackie's figure shrinks into the distance, everything else falls into perspective around it. She can see Main Street, and Castle Gloom up the hill, casting its squares of colored window light over the ribbon of the road, tree branches dark against it. She pictures the town like an old map, yellowed and crisscrossed with boundaries. Everything but the sea and the sky is marked with the name of its owner. And there is Virgil Mackie, walking east across the map, on the road out of town. His coat flaps out behind him like the wings of a crow and his sneakers don't make a sound. He hits the highway and throws a long evening shadow back over Highbone.

When Ruth comes around the corner onto Main Street, Magda and Isabel are in the doorway of the deli. She can see their legs stretched out across the sidewalk, and hear their voices dipping and falling against each other. It sounds like home. Comforting and stifling, like home.

And what about Isabel? Well, she came down to earth with a crash, didn't she?

Ruth folds herself into the corner by the window, held in by Magda's coat, feeling sick and safe. When a shadow falls on them it takes her a minute to realize it's Mrs. Skopek, smoking a cigarette and carrying a cut-glass ashtray in her other hand. She's using the ashtray instead of flicking her cigarette on the ground.

"I'm lost," Mrs. Skopek says. "Can you show me how to get to Normandy Street?"

"It's back up out of town, Mrs. Skopek," Ruth says. Isabel stares back and forth at them, wide-eyed. "It's pretty far, could someone give you a ride?"

"No, I had to run away."

"Gosh, why?" Isabel says in some kind of Pollyanna voice. She thinks Mrs. Skopek is funny. Mrs. Skopek leans over and whispers.

"There were Orientals. They killed my husband and now they've come for me. They're pretending to be neighbors, but I know they're from the camps. Can you hold this, dear?"

She's shaking now, glancing from side to side much too quickly. She looks like a nervous person, but speeded up on a jerky film. Ruth takes the ashtray from her and Mrs. Skopek reaches into her handbag. When she pulls out a pair of sewing scissors Isabel shrinks farther back into the doorway.

"Ruth," she whispers through closed lips. "What the fuck?"

"Mrs. Skopek's my neighbor. Aren't you, Mrs. Skopek? You

know me, don't you? My mom is Caroline, Caroline Carter."

"Oh yes, thank goodness, dear. Your mother misbehaves with that Hancock, doesn't she? Hancock."

"Crap." Magda mutters to her knees.

"I don't really know, Mrs. Skopek." Ruth shrugs. "Couldn't tell you."

"You'll help me, won't you, Ruth Carter? I can't let them recognize me. Help me, please, dear. Just hold that for a minute." And she reaches up and pulls what turns out to be a wig off of her head. Underneath it, her head is covered with green netting and pins. Under all that, there are some wisps of gray hair. Now she starts cutting the wig with her sewing scissors.

"Okay, we need to go now. Our friends are waiting for us." Isabel slides up and out of the doorway, trying to stay out of scissor range. Ruth looks at the ashtray in her hand and shakes her head. She stays put and so does Magda.

"Um, bye, Mrs. Skopek. Nice talking to you." Isabel heads up the street. Checking for Charlie, no doubt. Mrs. Skopek doesn't notice. She's busy working on her clever disguise.

"Mrs. Skopek, listen to me," Ruth says. "It's dark; there's no bus. Go into Flannagan's and ask them to call you a cab. They'll do it for you. They're safe. Don't worry."

"Oh, I knew you'd help, Ruth Carter." She replaces her wig and retrieves her ashtray from Ruth with precise movements, businesslike, then turns to cross the road.

"See, problem solved," Ruth says. "So, now they're both gone. They've taken their crazy shit up the road. You wanna tell me what's wrong with you, Magda?"

"Nothing's wrong with me. We need to help Isabel."

"Stop bullshitting me. And also, no, I do not need to help Isabel. I've known you all my life, Magda. I want to help *you*. I don't owe Isabel anything, trust me. You don't know the half of it."

"You do and you will, Ruth. You're not that kind of person. You're the person who knows what to say to make the wig lady feel better. That's who you are."

"Oh, really? Am I? Tell me you're not just a little bit terrified of Isabel O'Sullivan right now."

"A little, but I'm not mad at her. Ask yourself this, Ruth. Was it wrong, what she did?" Magda nods up Main Street towards where Isabel is standing in the flower beds in front of the bank.

"I don't know! I wasn't there. Isn't the guy some crippled head case? Could he even defend himself?"

"The scumbag tried to rape her, Ruth." Magda sounds like she might cry. Even when they were little, she never sounded like that before.

"That's not exactly what she said. You're exaggerating. He tried to feel her up. It sucks and it's gross and it's wrong, but how many times a day does that happen? We kill everyone who does that, the human race'll be extinct in twenty years."

"She didn't kill him. The cop said assault. If she killed him, they would have said murder. Anyway, when are we gonna start hitting back, Ruth? We need guns and swords and fucking grenades. I'm sick of this shit."

"Ask the guys in the park how that works out, Magda."

"Don't give me that hippie crap, Ruth Carter. Isabel did what needed to be done. Period."

"I want to talk about you, anyway."

"No, you don't."

"Is she gone?" Isabel is skipping back towards them with her hands full. She drops a rain of rose petals down over their heads. "Look, it's spring!"

"It's practically summer," Ruth says. "Why are you tearing up other people's flowers?"

"People shouldn't *own* flowers. Especially not banks. Does that woman really live near you, Ruth? *What* is her story?"

"She's terrified, Isabel. Weren't you listening to what she was saying?"

"Yeah, wow."

"Well, that's *her* freakin' 'inner life,' Miss Bohemian-Arty-Type. She walks around the block like that all the time, with the cigarette and the ashtray, and sometimes a beer in her hand too. Put that in your Balkan Sobranie and smoke it."

"What's with the whole weird racism thing?" Isabel sits cross-legged on the sidewalk in front of them.

"The Heos, that live next to the brake repair shop, they're Korean. Mrs. Skopek keeps freaking out 'cause her husband got killed in the Korean War. She called the cops and told them the Heos were communist spies who came to kill her."

"What do the Heos think?"

Magda snorts. "I'm guessing they think: 'Welcome to America. Everyone warned us it would be like this.' Come on, women.

We need time to regroup. We need to breathe." She stands up and takes out a pocket watch to check the time.

"You have a pocket watch in the toolbox coat?" Isabel makes a grab for it. "No fair you guys always getting cool stuff from the Attic when I'm not with you."

"It's my dad's. It was his dad's, too. He doesn't know I have it. He'll never notice. You could empty out the whole house, as long as you don't touch his study."

Someone is shouting in the park, and an alarm goes off behind Main Street. Ruth uses the wall to pull herself up.

"Magda, can you stop this circus town from spinning?" Isabel whines like a kid. "I'm dizzy. I want to get off and get some cotton candy."

"I said, come on. We can't stop it, but we can lie still and let the sky turn without us for a minute. Things are getting complicated. We need a little distance."

Magda jumps ahead and makes like a matador, flourishing an imaginary red flag for them. In her head, Ruth can hear the sound of Mrs. Skopek's scissors, scraping like nails on a blackboard.

That night Ruth sleeps for the first time in weeks. At first, when she closes her eyes she sees fire and stars and tunnels full of darkness. She just sinks down through it all into the pillow. Near morning she dreams of climbing the water tower alone. In her dream it's easy to do the scary part where you duck out of the ladder cage and throw your leg over the railing with a hundred and fifty feet of space below you. She stands up on the railing and stretches out her arms, balancing with the muscles working in the arches of her feet.

Then there are Magda and Isabel, sitting with their backs against the tank like always. Magda flicks a cigarette butt out over the railing, and the glowing end arcs out and falls. It hits the trees and bursts like a red comet, showers of sparks flying out.

Magda and Isabel gasp and shout while Ruth stands on the railing with the sparks flying past her. She is waiting to let go, to just rotate halfway around the railing and drop off into the empty sky, not hitting anything until the trees. She sees herself burst like those sparks, and then she is one of the stars. The stars feel brittle and frozen, even though they're balls of fire. They're like shards of broken glass, cold as the void of space, but they fill her with power. There is no more language and nothing left to touch. She opens out wider than death, with the sky sliding through her skin. She'll never heal over, never be separate and whole again. Her limit is meaningless now. She lets go of the railing and glides down through the air, arms outstretched. Then she explodes into a shower of red sparks, shooting upward from the trees.

two

IN ISABEL'S DREAM it is raining. She's under a skylight in a boat, and the drops are fat and loud on the glass. Everything is in slow motion, and she remembers she was drinking the night before, on a beach with her mother. That's right, there they are, she and her mother, drinking, and they're sinking into the sand. Her mother looks just like she does on the living room couch, with a glass of Dubonnet in her hand. At the same time, she is also Ruth's mother, which is why they're on the beach together. Her mother is laughing and looks younger as she disappears into the sand. But no, Isabel is on the boat now, under her skylight. Through the skylight she can see her little houseboat chimney and the fat drops slowly falling. No, they're birds landing, bird feet scratching on the glass.

It's someone throwing pebbles. Isabel is in Castle Gloom. Still there, still scared, holding her breath and wondering when the cops are going to descend on her with guns and badges and folders full of forms from Social Services.

Magda is below her bedroom window, wearing a face Isabel has never seen before. She is actually crying, and the next thing Isabel knows, she's in her backyard in socks and underwear and her brother's college sweatshirt, and Magda is lying curled up on the grass.

"Magdalene, honey, you have to get up."

"I can't move, Bel. I can't move anymore. I don't know how I got here."

"Everyone calls me Bel these days. Listen, sweetie, just until we get into my room. If anyone sees you, you're going to have to talk to them. You don't want to do that, do you?"

Just tears.

"All right, Warren. I'm gonna hold you up. See?"

"You actually come through in a crisis, don't you?" Magda says.

"I love you, Saint Magdalene of Sycamore Avenue. Stop thinking about what a selfish bitch I am and let me get you inside."

Once Isabel has Magdalene curled up on her bed she can put some jeans on and make Sleepytime tea. It's the only thing she can think of, but Magda won't drink it.

"If I could get some booze from my parents, I'd give you that. Dubonnet doesn't seem right at eight o'clock in the morning. Or ever, come to think of it."

"Henry isn't in his bed," Magda says.

"Are you supposed to be babysitting him? Should we go to your house and get him? I'll help."

"Henry never went to bed last night, Isabel." Magda is sobbing again, and she has the sheet in her mouth. "I can't. I really can't. This can*not* be happening."

"Slow down, honey. Are you saying he isn't in the house?"

"He isn't anywhere. I don't think he was there when I got home last night, but I didn't check. I didn't look in his room, Isabel. I just went to sleep."

"Okay, first, whatever this is, it isn't your fault." Isabel puts out a hand to lift up Magda's chin. "Come on, drink the tea. It seems to matter. People always make it when you can't cope."

Magdalene still won't take anything, so Isabel feeds her the tea like a baby, holding the teaspoon to her mouth and wiping Magda's eyes with the sleeve of her brother's sweatshirt. "Now try to start at the beginning."

"He's gone. That is the beginning and the end. Henry's gone. He isn't in the house; he isn't in the yard. He isn't anywhere on the block. I've been looking since six thirty. My dad is still looking. I got up to pee and I remembered I didn't check in his room last night, so I opened his door and his pajamas were kind of folded up on the pillow. But, you know, Henry folded up, not really folded up."

"Listen, he'll be somewhere close by, hon. He will. Should we call Ruth and go help your dad?"

"No! I can't go home. I might not ever be able to go home. Imagine what he's gonna do to me. And I can't go home if Henry isn't there anyway. I love him, Isabel. He's mine."

"We love him too, Magda. And he isn't going to be gone very long. Seriously. I just know it."

"I know the other thing. The feeling in his room. It was just . . . empty."

"Stop it." Isabel tries to sound like Magda would sound if they traded places. "I'm gonna call Ruth and tell her what's up. We'll go over there. I think Ruth is first lieutenant. Without you in the driver's seat, *I* can't be the one making decisions."

Ms. Carter is groggy and pissed off when she answers the phone, but once she hears Isabel's voice she gets Ruth without saying anything. Mrs. O'Sullivan is already stationed on the couch when they go past the living room on the way to the front door of Castle Gloom. Out on the street it's almost hot, almost like a summer morning.

"Well, there you go, Magda. My mom is on the couch and not behind it. See? Things are looking up."

"I can't make jokes right now, Isabel. I get that you're trying, but I can't."

They have to stop three times on the way to Ruth's because Magda's legs won't hold her up. She just sits down wherever she is and starts crying. When they finally get there, Ruth is out front, sitting on the shiny new front end of Danny's car, smoking and waiting for them. The sun is all the way up now and the glare from the white car blinds them. Ruth is just an outline against it, wearing a tank top and one of her mother's Indian skirts.

"All right, you two, get inside." Ruth sounds like she's in charge, like she just came back from being away and took over. It's only now that Isabel realizes she's been gone. Checked out, but she's back now.

"Go straight to my room," she says. "It's cool with my mom. Me and Danny are going to Sycamore Avenue to scope out your dad. Henry's probably back already. Isabel, get that fucking coat off her and get her a glass of water. Whenever I cry, my mom makes me drink water. Things seem worse if you don't."

Ruth's room is in the shade at the back of the house. Out the window, Isabel can see the edge of the trees, where she woke up two Saturdays ago. Looking at it now, you'd never know they'd been there.

"That's cool, isn't it?" Isabel says. "Danny's better."

Magda looks grubby and about twelve years old, but at least she's drinking the water.

"It's like we all have oceans inside us, isn't it, Magda? Water tables that need to be full. When we cry it's like the ocean coming out of our eyes, that's why it's salty. And we have to take it back in. It's like the tide."

They're on Ruth's bed, listening to Danny's car pull away. Magda holds the glass of water in her lap and leans her head on Isabel's shoulder.

"He won't be there," she says. "Why would he fold up his pajamas? He was going someplace."

"I'll put some music on."

"Isabel, I'm hiding. I can't hide."

"But I think you're right about not going home. Should we go to the cop shop?"

"What are you, nuts? *You* want to just walk into the police station right now? You?"

"Your dad'll call them anyway, and then they'll come looking for us. They'll want to know why you're not at home helping."

"I talked to them. They've been at my house since seven thirty this morning. My dad called as soon as I woke him up. And I'm not at home looking because it isn't helping. He's not goddamn there! Looking harder isn't gonna make him materialize."

"Okay hang on, let's make a map. We need a method." Isabel gets one of Ruth's colored pencils and stands with it poised to the wall. "Where are the places he could be?"

"I don't want to think about the places he could be, Isabel."

three

"YOU MAYBE SHOULDN'T have said that to Professor Warren, Ruth." Danny puts his key in the ignition and turns the engine over, pointing the wheels out onto Sycamore Avenue.

"Yeah, I know. I'm supposed to pretend Magda's dad is not a self-indulgent, raging asshole. I'm never supposed to tell regular people the truth about themselves or the world at large, least of all Ivy League types. I go to school. I know the drill."

Danny has made Ruth put her seat belt on, as usual. But she isn't usually in the front. Everything today is weird, even the fact that it doesn't feel weird to be riding in the car with just Danny, having a conversation like people. It isn't like talking to Mrs. O'Sullivan. He doesn't get her secrets or anything, but it's comfortable right now. Danny's car smells good. Could this be what his house smells like, like salt and tobacco and leather? But he lives with two landscapers, who probably don't smell good at all. Anyway, Danny is never at his own house.

"So, the guy asked me a straightforward question," she says. "Why isn't Magda there? What other answer could I give him? When she's in mental agony, her own father is the last person she'd go to for sympathy. Them's the facts, buster. Don't we have better things to do than worry about Professor Warren's delicate feelings?"

"I'm just saying, the guy can't find his kid right now." Danny turns off Harbor Ridge and heads up the hill on Seaview Road, towards the elementary school.

"Uh, Magda is his kid, Danny. Remember?"

"Good point too, flowergirl. Just givin' you the other point of view."

On the football field behind the elementary school the sun has begun to burn, but the grass is still wet. They've decided to look in a few places where they usually go with Henry, places he might go to hide.

It's obvious there's no one on the field, so they decide to search the scrubby trees that border two sides. On the other side of that is a development full of sixties colonials with dogs and swing sets in the backyards. Without talking about it they start at one end and take up lines five yards apart. There is something acidic moving through Ruth's veins, the reality of what they're doing is fueling her, even while she makes small talk with Danny. She feels a little like throwing up, but it's no effort at all to keep her mind from wandering. Things are clearer than they've been in weeks.

"I'm sorry about your car, Danny."

"Why should you be sorry? Shit happens, flowergirl."

"No, I just mean, I'm glad you're okay."

Turns out, that's actually true.

"Um, Ruth, I like your mom. I'm not gonna do anything mean to her or anything."

"Reality check, Danny. Me and you are never going to have this conversation. Stop now or I'll start screaming. All the dads will come pouring out of these backyards and kick your ass without waiting to check what's up first."

They wouldn't, of course, but it seems like a credible threat.

"I'm saying, I get that you're a little pissed off. That's just part of it. That's cool, you know."

"Okay, Zen guy. Good for you. Do you realize what it is we're looking for? I mean if Henry was back here playing or hiding or anything, we'd have seen him by now. There's only one thing we'll find by this method. This is not the time to talk about your deeply philosophical attitude to your love life. Show some respect."

"That's kinda low, flowergirl. And the little guy'll be cool. I got a feeling. Don't worry too much."

"I got a feeling too, Pavlich. It ain't good."

Whatever it's going to be, they don't find it behind the football field. The park seems like the next logical place. All roads in Highbone lead there, if not in a physical sense. While they're stopped at the red light by the Halfway Inn, a knock on Ruth's window makes her jump against the seat belt. It's Lefty. She heaves a sigh at Danny before rolling the window all the way down.

"The little poem," Lefty says.

"Um, we're kind of in a hurry, babe. Emergency today, no time for a poem. Maybe another time?"

"Yes." He looks excited. "Emergency day. The little poem that's the boy. He went under . . ."

The light goes green and the guy in the Lincoln behind them leans on his horn. Lefty jumps.

". . . behind you."

"Yep, there's a guy behind us. We can't sit here, Lefty. See you another time, all right?" Ruth moves Lefty's hand so she can roll up the window. "I am so not in the mood for Lefty today."

"Yeah, but you know, respect him, though. Who knows what Lefty's tapping into? His head could be like some kind of consciousness radio. We're all wrong the way we think about crazy people. They used to be magic and sacred and stuff."

"Yeah, Isabel says that, too. Actually, they used to be chained up like animals, living on piles of straw in their own shit. Don't kid yourself."

"My dad's crazy," Danny says. "Sort of, a little."

"Oh. Sorry, Danny. I seriously didn't know."

"No, it's cool. I've talked to your mom about it. He was in the war, in a prisoner-of-war camp in Germany. When I was little I thought, you know, he was always older than me. Always a grown-up. But I'm in my twenties now and I get it, that somebody eighteen is just a kid. My dad had never been off Long Island before, and it was much more of a hick place then. Farms and stuff. None of these developments full of commuter executives. My dad had never been to another state, let alone another country."

"Old people always say that, about LI before it turned into suburban hell. Old Mr. Lipsky said Wisteria Avenue used to be a dirt road. Weird, huh?"

"Anyway, my dad saw some serious things. Starving Jewish people getting shot in the head on the side of the road for no reason at all. Guys right next to him blown into pieces flying through the air when a shell fell in a foxhole."

"Jesus, he told you that?"

"Nah, my mom did mostly." Danny stops to stretch his arm along the back of the seat and twist his head around, backing into one of the angled spaces on Main Street. His voice is thin coming through his twisted throat, but he keeps talking. "A couple times he didn't come in off the water all night, even though the tide was in, and she'd be freaking out. It came out then, how sometimes he just couldn't deal. That stuff just broke him. He hardly showed it, though."

"What's he like now?"

"He just repeats himself a lot. He's got, like, two stories he tells, and he just repeats them over and over."

It's so hot they stop for iced teas in the deli. Danny is buying, so Ruth gets a large. In the Highbone deli they make lemonade into ice cubes and drop them into the iced tea. Two lemonade ice cubes in a large; when you get to the bottom you can pull them out and suck on them. They walk down the sidewalk towards the harbor, side by side with straws in their mouths.

"Um, Danny, can I tell you something and you won't tell anyone?"

"Yes you can, flowergirl. Scout's honor."

"If you were a Scout, big guy, I'm gonna be president. Seriously, by everyone, I mean my mom and all."

"Seriously. By yes, I mean yes."

"Right. Something's been wrong with Magda. Wait, so Magda's dad, he's a real bastard. And I don't just mean I think he's a bastard 'cause he's a stuck-up grown-up with a house on Sycamore Avenue. I mean sometimes Magda gets slapped around and stuff."

"Right."

"'Right,' Danny? That's your response to that?"

"Well, right is what it isn't, Ruthie. But those are just words. I mean right as in, right, keep talking."

"Right, so when I say something's been wrong with Magda lately, I mean something more than the usual wrong. She's, like, all quiet and she's not bossing us around so much. Which I kind of miss, actually."

"Don't hit me or anything, but people your age go through a lot of changes. I used to get all quiet and my mom used to freak out about it. I think she was scared whatever my dad has got passed on to me. I got through it."

"Please don't make me feel like it's pointless talking to you. This isn't some boring teenage life change. This is for real. She actually seems sad, wounded, kind of. You don't know how weird that is unless you know Magda. Saint Magdalene of Sarcasm does not do sad. She does eye rolls. She does biting commentary. She does bossy. She doesn't do meek and feeble. Not ever. Did you see her standing in the front yard with streaks on her face, looking like her legs were gonna give out?"

"So Magda's worried about something, is that what you're saying?"

"I'm saying something's made her change, and I have no idea what it is. Stuff freaks me out, yeah. I woulda thought that was obvious. But Magda is the queen of keep-it-together. And that's mostly because of the little Hank-man. She never lets go, because of looking out for him. If he's not around, that girl will fall a-fuckin'-part, I'm telling you."

"He's around, Ruth. It's gonna be okay. Have you thought about getting her to tell you what's wrong?"

"Are you kidding!? Man, get to know Magdalene Warren for a minute, then come back to me and say that again. I asked, but I didn't push it. You wouldn't either, trust me. Anyway, what I'm thinking is, let's do the math here. She goes all weird a week or so ago. Two nights ago at Fiddler's Cove I see these big-ass bruises on her. I mean bad, Danny. Scrapes all down the side of her and finger marks on her arms, like. Now Henry's missing, and she's in a puddle on my bed with no one to take care of her but Isabel O'Sullivan."

"Isabel looked like stepping up to me, babe. They'll be cool back there, and your mom'll check in between jobs. So are you saying you have an idea where the little guy is?"

"I don't know. I just think it's all too much of a coincidence.

Maybe Magda knows already, that's why she's freaking? It just seems like if Henry went on his own exploration mission and got his little ass lost, she'd immediately snap into commander general. She'd be directing search party traffic and putting pins in maps and shit. This person who looks at a mess and just falls over sideways is not Magda."

They're standing by the floating dock looking at Danny's boat. It bobs in the tide and the rake is piled up in sections by the side of the engine house. No place there for anybody to hide, not even someone as small as Henry.

"When we want to do stuff without people seeing, we go behind the bandstand. So does everyone else but, you know, the cops and the tourists can't see back there."

In the park, there's a village cop making nice with a family of tourists and some water rats scurrying in and out of the rocks at the edge of the grass. There are almost no shadows anywhere with the sun straight overhead and the glare coming off the harbor. All the boats are white. The dock is white, the bandstand. Ruth feels blinded by whiteness, like she's in the Arctic without those wooden Eskimo glasses. *Fade to white*, she thinks.

four

IT'S HOT IN the back of Ms. Carter's Pinto and Magdalene can feel dust blowing into her eyes from the open window in front. Ms. Carter is telling Isabel and Magda about one time when she lost Ruth at the ferry in Port Jefferson. Ruth was only four, and Ms. Carter got so scared she froze up and cried, but it turned out Ruth was by the stand that sold fried clams. She just wanted some and wandered away to ask the guy. She was too young to understand about money.

The story is supposed to be comforting. The clam guy was nice, and he asked Ruth where her mom was, then sat Ruth up on the counter with some clams and sent somebody to find her. Ms. Carter talks with her eyes on the road, loud enough for Magdalene and Isabel to hear in the back. The story makes Magda want to throw up.

"Can you drop us off here, Ms. Carter?" she says. "Please?"

"I thought you and Isabel were going to look for Henry at the beach."

"We can walk from here." If she doesn't get out of the car in the next minute, Magda will definitely throw up.

"I'm not helping, am I? Magdalene, it *will* be okay. I promise." Ms. Carter gives her an earnest smile in the mirror.

"You can't promise that, Ms. Carter." For a minute Ruth's mom looks like Magda slapped her, then her eyes go soft.

"Just tell me you're really going to the beach," she says. "You're not gonna do anything crazy, right?"

Once they've climbed out of the backseat, Isabel leans away from Magda into the driver's-side window and says under her breath, "It's okay; I'll take care of her."

They act like it's something Magda shouldn't hear. Even in an emergency, people are still stupid. What is anybody going to say that could make things worse than this? Or better.

"I need to go inside here." She points at the Stella Maris Chapel.

"What, the church? Are you serious, Magda? The church?"

"It's a chapel, not a church. I only thought of it while Ruth's mom was talking. We should go in."

"Why?" Isabel rolls her eyes now, because everyone is playing everyone else's part today. "You think God's gonna help?"

"Not remotely," Magda says, "but it's what my mother would do right now. Why are you even making me explain?"

Her mom never took her to the Stella Maris Chapel. They

went to Saint Ignatius on Herman Road, and only during Lent and on Christmas Eve. She went for the singing, that's what she always said. Uncle Tony would come with them, and her mother would disappear up the stairs into the choir loft while they found a pew. When Magda was really little, her mother would put a special piece of lace over her hair before she went inside the church, black with a round pattern that fit the top of her head and sides that hung down. Later, she stopped doing that. When the singing started, Uncle Tony would lean down to her and say, "Listen, Magdalene. Can you hear your mother's voice?" But Magdalene knew that voice coming down over the railing wasn't really her mother's. Mom and Uncle Tony were playing one of their tricks. That's why her mother was hiding upstairs, just like Uncle Tony did when they played hide-and-seek at home. She knew her mother's voice, all the ways it sounded. It was never like that.

The Stella Maris Chapel has a painting of the Virgin hovering over a sinking boat. There is a statue of Her too, with a star over her head and a collection box at her feet. It's empty, no priest to give them a creepy smile like they've decided to come back to God and he'll personally take them into his loving arms. Magda takes a candle without making a donation and kneels down. Isabel is sighing and breathing loud, pacing back and forth in the gloom behind the pews.

During Lent, all the statues along the aisles in Saint Ignatius were covered with purple cloths. You weren't allowed to see them again until after Easter. When the statues were covered, her mother stayed downstairs with Magdalene and Uncle Tony.

Whenever they went to church, her father was mad. When they came back in the front door, her mother made her go straight to her room to play while her father shouted. That was just part of the routine, part of the ritual. Voices singing and shouting and people all dressed up, going up and down stairs. Anyway, it was a lie. Nobody's voice comes down from above. Nobody is saying anything.

The smell of frankincense is faint. It's been weeks since Easter Mass, since people filed in from the midnight dark holding candles and singing. When Magda was little, Monsignor Tappi used to come to their church on Melville Road just for Easter Mass. He'd swing the burning incense down the aisle to make them all feel dizzy and holy. The rest of the year the blocks of frankincense stayed under a bench in the vestry.

Even though it's May now, the marble floor in the Stella Maris Chapel is as cold as January. The cold goes right through her jeans and her skin and kisses the bones of her knees. Magdalene lights the candle and concentrates as hard as she can, just in case someone is listening.

Fuck you. Fuck you. Fuck you.

Then she stretches herself flat out, facedown, laying her cheeks against the marble, one side and then the other. Outside, the sunlight blinds her and she sinks onto the porch.

"Come on, Magda. You're doing good. Let's keep going."

"No." Magda reaches for Isabel's cigarettes and then gives up. It's too much effort.

"No? What do you mean, no?"

"That's it. That's all I got."

"Oh, no you don't, Magdalene Warren." Isabel grabs hold of her hands and leans back with all her weight, pulling Magda up and over. It's easier to just give in and follow.

At Fiddler's Cove people are acting like it's already summer vacation. The beach is half-full of blankets and kids are in the water with inflatable balls. The asphalt is hot enough to burn the bottoms of their feet. It's so different from Thursday night when they were here last, not just the people but everything. Magda tries hard to block out the burning sun and the shouting kids, to see through it all to the beach and the parking lot they were at two days ago. They just need to get back there, back to when there was a plan, and they all knew what their parts were.

"This is pointless, Isabel."

"Magdalene, I don't know what's wrong with you, but—"

"You don't know what's wrong with me?! You don't—"

"All right! But this is not the time to stop being Saint Magdalene the Direction Giver. You are the exact person we need right now. Wherever Henry's at, he's lost somewhere, and I'm telling you, the only thing he's thinking is, 'Magda will know what to do.' It's what *I'd* be thinking if *I* was lost."

"What happens if I want a day off?"

"A day off!? Your brother is lost, woman. Have a day off tomorrow when he's home sleeping. Me and Ruth'll take the watch. Right now, your job is to be you."

"I can't, Isabel. I'm not me anymore. You don't get it."

She can't explain because there aren't any words for it. Something is grinding them through some kind of fatal play, and it isn't that empty silence in the chapel. That silence is just cruel. And pointless.

"I don't need to get it," Isabel shouts at her. "Just step up, Magda. These are the great American suburbs. Soak up a dose of the ambient denial and let's move."

The water in the shallows is cool, but not cold. It isn't really a marsh, it's an estuary, full of reeds and runnels of clear, brackish water. Crabs are scrambling over their feet, all heading in the same direction—out of the sun, maybe. It's named Fiddler's Cove because of the crabs. Fiddler crabs have one huge arm and they run sideways. Well, maybe they don't, but it looks like sideways to Magda.

"Is there quicksand in here?" Stupid questions seem to be some kind of tactic Isabel is using to try to help.

"No, there's no quicksand. Isabel, what if there really is karma?"

"Woman, stop it. This is not, in any way, shape, or form, your fault. Henry has actual parents. Not to mention, they are also your fucking parents."

"No, stay with me. I'm just thinking about Matt. Why did we do that to him? Matt has no parents at all, basically."

"He has a mom, but she's worse than mine, apparently."

"Whatever. He's us, pretty much, isn't he? Stuck in a cookie-cutter house, trying to focus on shit that matters, trying to keep an eye on the flowers and learning the names of the stars and whatever. And we screwed him, totally. Not just because of the weed or the money. We stole his escape plan."

"You said it's a big, dirty machine, remember? There's no way we're not gonna get some stains on our souls, you're the one who told me that. I believed you."

"I was wrong, Isabel. Isn't that obvious at this point? Ruth says some scary guys from Nassau County are out to get Matt for the money he owes."

"Wow, you really aren't you. You just said you were wrong. For real, though, this is not the time for you to suddenly develop self-doubt."

"It's my fault, is what I'm saying. What if this is just instant karma?" But it isn't even that, is it? Karma would mean there's a point to everything.

"You don't have room to think like this right now." Isabel grabs her shoulders and shakes. "We have to get out of this town, woman. Think about it. My mom hides behind the couch for days on end and my dad won't even call her a doctor. The one road to opportunity is working for the mob in a topless bar. Every time you go to the bathroom in Dunkin' Donuts, you get felt up by some diseased creep in a napalm jacket. You can't spit in the park without hitting some guy who got his brain put in a blender in Vietnam. Ruth's mom is the coolest parent we have between us, and she has to clean the toilets of a shallow bitch like Mrs. Hancock. Your little brother gets lost in the middle of the night, and you can't even count on your dad not to take it out on you. No, no, no. We do not belong here, and this place will crush us, Magda. Has it escaped your notice that the main road in and out of here is freakin' called the LIE? It's a pit of untruth, you can't climb out without getting some on you. You thought of it because it was necessary. You are the patron saint of the necessary. There's nothing wrong with that."

"I think we should put it back." It only occurs to her as the words are coming out of her mouth.

"What?"

"Matt's weed," Magda says. "I think we need to break in there and put it back."

"Jesus. You are not thinking straight, hon."

"I am. You want necessary? It's necessary. We need to put everything right if we want Henry back."

"Okay, listen. A: we've already smoked kind of a lot of it. B: if we put it back, what happens to us? Our escape plan is shot. And C: how the hell are we going to even do it? We'll get caught."

"Duh, in the opposite way we did before? Robbery on rewind. But we need to do it soon. Tonight."

"Did you hear that? That thud? That is the sound of my house-boat hitting the mud, of the wheels collapsing under the bus of your dreams, man. No, Magda."

"Are you saying you'll trade Henry for some weed, Isabel?"

"Not fair. If we put the weed back, we're all trapped, Magda. Henry, too. It was all for nothing."

"Maybe. Or maybe it's the leap we have to take. From here, nothing means anything, unless we make it mean something. Maybe this is the test."

They're on the other side of the estuary now, and only the high-pitched screams of the kids in the water make it across to them. Ms. Carter drives back in and parks up, with a cop car behind her. She's out of her car, leaning on the roof, shading her eyes and scanning for them before the cops have turned off their engine.

"Shit." Isabel looks around for an escape route.

"No, Isabel. We have to go over there. If we don't, it's on Ruth's mom. That's not fair."

"Why is everything we need not fair?"

With their jeans rolled up and their hair tied in messy knots, they look like girls on a beach vacation. For a minute Magda imagines them in a different life—a pair of girlie virgins reading books by Judy Blume and going to their mothers' Mary Kay parties. There is nothing to tell them from anyone else at a distance. Life only looks like what it is from the inside. They pick their way through the runnels of fresh water and the scurrying crabs back to the parking lot.

"Are you Magdalene Warren?" the cop says to Isabel.

"No." Isabel points. "She is."

They've picked Isabel out as the WASP of the pair. Kids named Warren who live on Sycamore Avenue mostly don't look like Magda. Officer Kemp is married to their Health teacher. Magda doesn't recognize the other one. He's young and wearing hippie clothes, a poncho even, but with a cop hat. Is that supposed to be some undercover disguise? Don't they realize what a small town they're in?

"Do you know where your brother is, Miss Warren?" Officer Kemp asks in his stern but benign voice.

"No." Isabel gets between them. She may be clueless, but lately it turns out she is kind of brave. "Uh, that's why we're looking for him."

"I was asking Miss Warren. You are?"

"Isabel. I'm her friend. I'm trying to help."

"Isabel O'Sullivan?"

Crap.

"It's all right, Isabel," Ms. Carter interrupts. "They just want to ask Magdalene some questions, so they can try to find Henry." She doesn't even look nervous. She's an actual hippie. Plenty of practice dealing with cops.

"He's gone." Magda's voice comes out flat, like nothing's bothering her. The Patty Hearst effect again.

"When did you last see him?" Officer Kemp is running the show, doing all the talking while the young one in the ridiculous disguise leans with his arms on the top of the cop car.

"I saw him last night," she says, "when we went to bed."

"And you didn't go anywhere? You didn't take him out?"

"No! I told them this morning, I read him a story and then shut his door." Magda's voice cracks a little and Isabel's eyes slide away from her.

"You were seen in town last night, Miss Warren. What were you doing?"

Oh.

"I went for a walk. Henry was in bed."

"Get in the car with us. We'll drive you back to your house. Your father wants you at home."

"She's with us; you can't make her go with you!" Isabel shouts. "What are you, arresting her?"

"Don't worry, Isabel," Ms. Carter says. "They just want to take her back to her father. They need to be sure they look everywhere and talk to everyone. Magdalene should be at home right now, no matter what."

The pretend hippie opens the back door of the cop car and makes a gesture like some kind of bodyguard, inviting Magda in.

Magda looks back at Isabel. "Get Ruth. Go to Matt's. You guys have to do it."

The back of the cop car smells like nothing at all. How do they do that? For a minute, Magda thinks maybe she's being carried off into a featureless world, a navy blue absence where her blank exterior will fit right in. But she never has been that lucky. They're taking her home.

five

FADE TO WHITE, Ruth thinks.

She shakes the blinding afternoon light out of her eyes and walks up the bandstand steps into the shade. She twists her hair up off her neck and fans it with one hand.

"I could tell this morning it was summer rolling in," Danny says. "You see the fog before you even notice it's warmer."

"Jeez, man, what time did you get up?"

"I went out last night after me and your mom got back from the movies. I slept on the boat, raked for a while, and came in with the tide to offload before the sun came up. That's the life, flowergirl. Time and tide and all that stuff."

"That's what Isabel wants, you know, to live on a boat, but not on the ocean. She wants to live on some cute little tugboat being a surrealist with her typewriter and her bohemian friends drinking absinthe and shit."

"Yeah, what's wrong with that? You don't sound convinced."

"God, you are, like, Mr. Contentment, aren't you? Everything's cool with you. Nothing's wrong with it, it's just not realistic, is it? Know how she wants to save up the money? Working in the Lagoon."

"They don't hire underage girls," Danny says. "They couldn't get away with it."

"Yeah, she's got the whole long-term plan going, but it's still a stupid idea. Okay, yeah, so she's all in charge of her own body and stuff, but she has no idea, is my opinion. I mean, do you know Vicky, who works in Dunkin' Donuts?"

"Yeah, I know her big sister. Why?" He looks worried. "She a friend of yours?"

"What if she is, man? She's a person."

"She's a person in over her head, Ruthie."

"Do NOT call me Ruthie. And yeah, I get that. I'm not stupid. My point is that Isabel is. Would you look at Vicky and think, 'cool, amazing, I want to live her life'?"

"Don't think I'd make a lot."

"Oh, ha, ha." Ruth stops to call out Henry's name.

They even get down on the ground and look through the latticework on the bottom of the bandstand. It's so dark under there that Ruth has to cup her hands around her eyes to block out the glare of the sun. It takes a minute for her vision to adjust, but then there are just syringes and empty bottles of Jack Daniel's and Boone's Farm.

"So what about you?" Danny's voice comes through the littered darkness from the other side of the bandstand.

"What about me, what?"

"What's the long-term plan?"

"Don't have the foggiest. I mean, the thing I love most is drawing, but where's that get me? I don't want to be all pompous with arty Village friends who drink nasty green stuff made of herbs, and I don't think I have the kind of chutzpah it takes to be Magda, so I need to think sort of . . . I don't know, not smaller, but less dramatic. Sometimes I think going away with Magda is just a cop-out."

"Going away where?"

"Oh yeah, well, the plan is to buy a van and drive it till we can't go any farther. California, basically. Keep your pants on, we're not going till high school's over. Magda's gonna work for a year while she waits for me. And don't get me wrong, I love the idea of it. I want outta here, for definite. It's just, the thing about Magda is, you don't have to decide anything. You just let her do it."

"You don't seem to me like someone who can't find your own way."

"Don't be fooled, man. Even when Magda's not here, she's in my head, pointing. Until today, anyway. Today is just twisted."

"Yeah, well. Everything happens for a reason."

"No, Danny. It does not. You're doing good here; don't blow it with stupid clichés. Save that for your transcendental-meditatin' yogi friends."

"I mean, Henry will come home and you will be different. Deny it or whatever, it's a truth."

"I am kind of different recently. I mean, I think I might not be Sidekick of Saint Magdalene anymore. I still love her, but there's stuff going on I don't feel like talking to her about, and that's weird. The other day I was upset, and I didn't call her up. I can't remember that ever happening before."

"Come on." Danny pulls out his keys. "Let's get back to your mom's. They might have heard something. Upset why?"

"Nah, the details aren't important. You know, someone gave me something amazing and I should have known I couldn't keep it. When they took it back, it was like being kicked in the stomach. I felt like I'd been run over, bruised everywhere. Couldn't breathe for a minute, you know?"

"Must have been some thing."

"Yeah, but it doesn't matter. Point is, the way to keep it is to keep it to myself. Not to tell Magda. I couldn't take her rolling her eyes at me over it. Lately, it's too much space inside me. Like, you know"—Ruth gives a sarcastic smirk—"emptiness or something melodramatic. I feel too light, like I might blow away. I know that sounds nuts, but sometimes it's good."

"Listen to me not saying people go through changes at different times in life."

"Whatever. When I'm drawing they come together: the driving west and the keeping stuff to myself. All I want to draw the past couple of days is space. Big giant landscapes, deserts, planets in the void, the ocean: space, space, space. I've always been scared of my own drawings. Like they were bigger than me, like they come out of me but they're not really mine, you know? But now I get it. I can just let go and it'll be all right."

The two Mr. Lipskys drive past them heading down Main Street. Manny waves at Ruth, leaning around his son.

"Crap, Danny, I forgot I'm supposed to clean Old Mr. Lipsky's apartment."

"Should I come back and get you?"

"No, thanks though, Danny. Tell Isabel I'll be at Mariner's. Pop the trunk. I need my bucket."

"Well, anyway, it was good talking to you, Ruth."

"All right, Pavlich, don't get comfortable." But she laughs when she says it and suddenly her lungs seem big enough to breathe with for the first time in weeks.

"Maybe you could go to college for art?" Danny says.

"Yeah, I could." She leans in the passenger window. "I might. But not around here. This place is poison for Carter women, man. Um, no offense."

"None taken, flowergirl."

Ruth reads the sign on the door of Mariner's Maps and Books that says, *Out to lunch. Back at Three.* It's way after three already. The alley in back is empty, and she stops to smoke a cigarette before she knocks on the door.

"The little movie star!" Manny Lipsky says when he opens

the door and sees her standing there. "What are you doing at the back door?"

"Shop's closed. You ready for me?" She holds up her cleaning bucket.

"I'll get you some iced tea," Old Mr. Lipsky says. "Come on up."

In the kitchen there is a board made of brown cork tiles on the wall, with pictures on it. Some are the pictures everybody has, father and son with a fish, everybody opening presents in faded color around a table. There's one that must be Young Mr. Lipsky, wearing a prayer shawl and a yarmulke and pimples. They're all in the muted colors of the past, surrounded by white borders.

Old Mr. Lipsky puts a braided candlestick down on a rubbery plastic cloth with yellow flowers on it.

"My son says this isn't a tablecloth, it's a fire hazard."

"I like it," Ruth says, because she can tell he does.

"My son's a snob. Did you notice? I like it, though. You can just wipe it with a sponge. Cuts down on the laundry. Laundry makes me feel like an old woman."

"Are you suggesting that old women wash their clothes and old men don't? Ewww." Ruth laughs and he does too. It's like having a granddad.

"Go through to the living room. I'll bring you an iced tea in a minute, Ruth."

He lights the candle, then bows his head and covers his face with his hands.

In the living room, there is a glass coffee table and modern furniture that looks like it came off *Star Trek*, white with a big brown stripe down it, made of something that hardly weighs anything at all. When Ruth sits on the couch, it feels hollow. She can hear Mr. Lipsky in the kitchen, mumbling into his hands.

Old people go back to living in apartments in the end. When they have kids, they're all obsessed with their house and their yard. Parents like the O'Sullivans act like stuff has to last forever. It isn't permanent though, not at all. Ruth can see that someday everyone will be in an apartment like this one, fading out of the picture.

Old Mr. Lipsky comes through carrying two glasses of iced tea.

"So you believe in God, Mr. Lipsky?"

"Not really." He doesn't use a coaster on the glass table, so she doesn't either. "It's called a havdalah," he says. "The candle."

"It's beautiful."

"I believe in people. I think it's good to remember them. Parents, children, grandparents. They make life good. I'm thankful, even though my son calls me an old woman for lighting Sabbath candles. It's supposed to be a woman's job, when there's one in the house."

No one in Ruth's life does anything at the same time every week. That's the exact reason people think her life is great. But a granddad who lights candles and speaks another language would be cool, too.

"A house without women is a sad thing, Ruth. How's the little Buonvicino?"

"Magda? She's not having such a good day, Mr. Lipsky. Things are bad right now. Isabel is coming to get me when I'm done here. Isabel O'Sullivan, my other friend?"

"I knew the Buonvicinos, the little one's grandparents. They had a great little place on 25A. It was on my route. Delivered them plenty of Asti and Sambuca, back in the day."

"I remember them. Magda's grandparents. They were sweet. Tiny and sweet, and always trying to make you eat figs."

"Anthony and Carmelinda did all the cooking themselves and the waiters were always somebody's *paisan*. In the summer you could sit under the grape arbor in the back. Nice people. Anthony's dad came from Italy around the same time my wife's people came from Russia. They could have landed at Ellis Island the same day. Irene Buonvicino was only little back then. I remember when she used to do her homework at the table in the back. Her and her brother, Tony."

"Well, I should get started, Mr. Lipsky."

"Manny."

"Manny. You did all the dishes already? I would have done them. I'll start in the bathroom."

The candle keeps burning the whole time she's vacuuming, and she's not sure whether to move it to wipe the tablecloth. The pictures on the corkboard keep her company, and for a minute it feels like this could be her house. Her mother is way too much of a hippie to have a plastic tablecloth, but she likes Old Mr.

Lipsky as much as Ruth does.

"Pop!" It's Young Mr. Lipsky, shouting from the bottom of the stairs.

"All right!" Manny cups his hands around his mouth to shout back. "Gotta go, honey. Time for the postprandial stroll. He's a snob, but he's a good kid. Thanks for the visit. Come back and see me again when you're not cleaning. Miriam would have liked you, and I'm not getting any grandkids of my own, obviously." He jerks his thumb towards the stairs and smirks.

"Pop! Let's go."

"All right, all right." Mr. Lipsky picks up a pipe from a side table and the box of matches from the kitchen.

"Are you supposed to leave that burning?" Ruth points at the kitchen table.

"I always do. I feel like it keeps Miriam company, even though I know that's nuts. Don't tell Samuel."

"Pop!"

Ruth waits for Isabel in the doorway of Mr. Lipsky's store. The sign is still there. She rests her head against the glass underneath it, like it's a label for her. *Out to lunch. Back at Three*, that's me. She laughs and touches the bay window where Gaius Pollio is patting the other side of the glass with his paw.

"Mr. Lipsky says the other grown-ups on Main Street think he's a joke"—Isabel stands over her, looking at the sign that's almost five hours out of date now—"because he closes the store in the middle of the day."

"Has he met Mrs. Gellaghtly? She leaves Attic Antiques wide open and sits downstairs drinking tea while we clean the place out. Capitalists in this town are useless."

"Ruth, what if Henry is . . . I don't know, I mean, what if they don't find him or something?"

What if he isn't even there anymore? Like he wasn't old enough to stay put in the world. Like they just wafted his little body back to wherever it came from. Ruth pictures Henry laughing his laugh, and the laugh is like a bubble, carrying him up and away.

"Do you ever think people might just start disappearing, Isabel? I mean like maybe Henry is the first of us to go. Maybe the reason all of us are different from other people is because we're not solid enough to stay in place? We're not really here in the way other people are."

"Henry isn't one of us, Ruth. Don't lay that on him."

"I mean, I don't really think that, but I feel like that sometimes, you know?"

Isabel looks at her sideways. "I guess."

Ruth closes her eyes and breathes, filling the new space inside her with ocean air. She can still feel Isabel without looking, but she can feel the rest of the world, too. Full of long roads and a thousand possibilities and a million kinds of light.

six

IN MAGDA'S CARRIAGE house Ruth can feel Mrs. Warren, smiling her sad-eyed smile at them from the shadows. The smell in here has been the same for years, long-gone hay and horses' breath and the sawdust from things eating through the wood. This is the place where Ruth first learned the truth about shadows and gravity. Now it's time for them to work the magic Magda asked them for.

"Take the dress," Isabel says from the doorway. "Just take all of it."

She is a silhouette against the big opening, looking out into the night and whispering back over her shoulder. Isabel doesn't feel anything here. This is just another place to her.

"I can't do that, Isabel!"

"Woman, there are still cops driving around. Can you just hurry up?"

Ruth creeps up to peer over Isabel's shoulder at a police car across the street. A guy in uniform is talking to some lady on the front porch of her house.

"The smell in here reminds me of Magda's mom shouting," she says. "For some reason it scared her if we came in here. We were supposed to play in the backyard, where she could see us from the window. If we were quiet for a while, she'd come looking. If she found us in here, she'd get really upset. The carriage house creeped Mrs. Warren out. She could sense stuff."

"Be quiet," Isabel hisses.

The cop walks back to his car, parked in front of the Warrens' house.

"It was always Magda's idea to come in here and pretend to be bandits hiding out, but I always seemed to be the one coming out the door when Mrs. Warren came around the corner of the house. Magda would have already disappeared into the trees, and it would just be me standing there, knowing I was wrong, and Mrs. Warren saying, 'I told you, Ruth!'"

"Do you have it?" Isabel says.

"She was so beautiful. I would always just stare up at her while she was telling me off and think, 'Be my mother. I want to run away with you.' When she left, my first thought was, 'She left without me.' How weird is that?"

"Ruth! Do you have it?"

"Yes. I stuffed Mrs. Warren's wedding dress in a gym bag. Happy? This is just so wrong."

"Yeah, but is the stash in there? I mean, they must have searched in here today. That cop's gone, but more will just keep coming back all night."

"Yes, it's here! Listen, Magda's probably inside, Isabel. Maybe we should try to talk to her?"

"No, Ruth. It's Magda's day off. Me and you are on it."

They leave through the little woods at the side of the carriage house. The moon isn't up yet; they have to keep their hands in front of them, to feel their way. The house behind the Warrens' has lamps on downstairs. They skirt around a yellow square of light and out into the road. People live in boxes. Even the light their lives give off is square.

"You know what I think, Isabel? I think we have no idea what we're doing. We just make shit up and we expect the world to be rational or something."

"It's not rational. It's magical. People just don't notice."

"Really, Isabel? That's what you're saying? Right now, today, you're saying, 'Wow, man, the world is, like, such a magical place'? Sunshine and daisies, yep."

"You are so wrong about me, Ruth. You have no idea."

"Yeah, you're actually a violent head case. You told us, remember? Do I have to carry the stash all the way?"

"It's okay. If anyone stops, I'll do the talking."

"Oh, good. That makes me feel better."

It seems like everyone they pass on the sidewalk knows it all, like it's obvious what's in the bag, and it's only a matter of time before some washed-out cop comes and proves himself on them. So Ruth leads Isabel the back way, off the road, in between things. Loading bays and scrubby woods, alleys full of rats and people who don't want to live in square houses. There must be routes you could take through the world where you never come out of the in between.

Behind the twenty-four-hour supermarket four guys are sitting with their legs hanging off the loading bay. Their white T-shirts look green in the security light. A murmur starts up as soon as Ruth and Isabel come into view. The guys straighten up, coming to attention, and the shouting gets louder.

"Look at the tits on that one."

"Fuck off, you no-necked piece of shit," Isabel says, like she's so tough now.

Ruth slaps her arm. "This really isn't the time to play street kid. Just keep walking," she says under her breath.

"Come on, honey, just a quick one. I got five bucks."

The four of them are passing a pint of vodka one way and a joint in the other direction. They're already beyond the tipping point. They've had enough to drink and smoke so they can pretend they're not responsible for anything they do.

Ruth and Isabel will have to pass that loading bay to get through to the gas station. They can't turn around and go back the way they came, because it's an alley no one can see into. Every few seconds there is a blur and a rush as a car slips by the gap between the buildings.

Now one of the jocks is standing up and passing the pint bottle to his friend. "Where you going so fast? Look at that one. I could just lift her right up."

"She's little, but she's got a body, man."

"I'm not taking the skinny one again."

"You're not taking anything, sweetie," Isabel says in some kind of pretend Vicky voice. "Sit yourself back down."

"Isabel! Seriously. *Shut up.*"

The vodka bottle comes flying over and smashes at their feet, broken glass all around them, and Isabel has no shoes on. Blood blossoms from a vein on the top of her left foot, like the stigmata they saw on the news. Ruth imagines a nail passing through Isabel's feet, and her mind gets stuck like a scratched record on the image. She stares at the blood and the picture is so clear it takes her a minute to shake it free.

There is only one way out and they both realize it together, without saying anything. They turn at the same time and run out between the cars on 25A, fast enough so it looks like suicide to run after them. On the road, everything is headlights and the separate, specific wind from each rushing car. The only way to do it is without thinking at all. Someone swerves into the Dunkin' Donuts parking lot and someone else slams on their brakes and burns a set of tire marks into the road. Then they're in the side street that runs behind Dunkin' Donuts.

"Hey, Jayne Mansfield!" Doris is sitting alone in the sidecar of her boyfriend's pink trike. "That how kids get their kicks around here? Actually playing in traffic? I thought it was just an expression."

"Jocks." Ruth is breathing hard. "Behind the supermarket."

Doris looks down at Isabel's bleeding foot. "Well, you got the battle scar. You otherwise unscathed, girlies?"

"Yeah. This is my friend Isabel." Isabel just stares at the trike, or maybe at Doris's impressive thighs. Ruth has to slap her arm to get her to respond.

"Hi. Really good to meet you."

"Let me tell you the secret," Doris says. "Put it right out there."

"Excuse me?" Isabel is trying to take in Doris's hair now. There seems to be too much blond for her tiny mind to contain.

"Sex," Doris says. "Men are actually terrified of it. All this crap about libidos and blue balls and frigid housewives—it's a scam. Trust me. Never been with a guy who wanted to fuck more than I did. Acting like you don't want it just helps them feel in control. Is that your mission?"

"No!" That's it. Isabel is hooked. Doris is her new guru. She'll be following her around now, repeating everything Doris says. Next thing you know, she'll be bleaching her hair.

"So, put it right out there. Wear that shit on the outside. Nobody'll bother you unless they already feel up for it. They won't need to cut your feet to get their hard-ons back."

Well, that's bullshit, but it seems to impress Isabel. A couple weeks ago, Doris seemed like the answer, or at least a signpost that pointed towards transcendence. Maybe she is, in a way. Here they are, doing the stations of the cross, putting one bleeding foot in front of the other, trying to get to the sacrifice that will save everyone. Doris is here on the side of the road to wipe their faces while they take a break between illusions.

Five minutes later, they come out through someone's front yard, still breathing hard, and see Charlie heading straight at them down the sidewalk.

"Jesus," Isabel says under her breath. "What is with this night?"

"Hi, Isabel. What are you doing over here?" Charlie almost sounds like a nice guy.

Ruth slings the gym bag farther onto her back, trying to look nonchalant and sure she's failing. "*I* happen to live over here, Charlie. Just like you."

Charlie looks at her like she's only just become visible. Like he didn't try to jump her behind the brake repair shop just last week. Everyone is doing that lately, looking at her like she's just flickered into reality, materializing out of dots of light like someone on *Star Trek*. They're all astonished, as if it's a magic trick, her acting like an actual person.

"So what are you up to, then, Isabel? Coming to work later? Vicky's on tonight, too. So, you know, tell me now if you're coming."

"We don't have time, Charlie."

"Oh, right."

"There's stuff going on. It's a long story." Isabel stares down at the sidewalk while she says it.

Ruth looks at Charlie, and she can see straight through him, like he's perfectly transparent with the night shining through from behind. Charlie's not bad or good, just a person with a set of empty actions to perform, just an extra. It's almost hard to focus on him, to make him stand out of the background. He stares at the cuts on Isabel's feet, but he doesn't ask about them.

"Uh, listen, tell Magda I said sorry. I kind of went off on her the other day. A little, you know. For a second, I thought . . . well, whatever. She'll know what I mean."

"Charlie, we gotta go. Sorry." Isabel looks up now, straight into Charlie's eyes.

And now it's her who has just materialized. She looks taller and more solid, and a lot more like the person who hits back at creeps in parking lots in the middle of the night. No one is who she thought they were last week. Everyone is reincarnated. Maybe it's Isabel who will float away out of here, up into the sky with the blood falling from her feet like rain. That is the thing Ruth will draw, as soon as this is all over. *The Assumption of Isabel*. She can see it perfectly.

seven

BY TEN O'CLOCK, Isabel only looks small and bored. They stopped at Ruth's house, and Henry is still missing. No clues even, as far as her mom and Danny can figure out. Now they're in the trees at the back of Matt's neighbor's yard, have been for almost an hour. They can't smoke, even, or someone might be able to tell where they are. Does it occur to Isabel that they are out in the woods at night, alone together again? Does it even register? Apparently not; she's just staring at the yard Virgin.

"Do you think there is such a thing?"

"Shh, Isabel. Not so loud. Such a thing as what?"

"You know, people pray to the Virgin and they get healed and whatever. Magda was doing it today. What is that about?"

"That's the power of the human mind, Bel. It can make anything happen. If you need to, you can make yourself disappear.

Trust me. All this, the ground and the grass and the trees and the houses, it's transparent. It isn't actually solid until you make it solid with the power of your mind."

"Why isn't everyone just floating around, then?"

Does she really think they're not?

"Not brave enough," Ruth says. "Easier to pretend all this is really here. That part is only hard work for some people. People like Lefty."

And me.

"Ruth, what if the cops come again? What if the napalm guy dies?"

"Then you're screwed."

"Thanks. Good to know you've got my back."

"I don't. Guess what? Everything on the planet is not specifically engineered to make Isabel O'Sullivan feel better. Deal."

Finally, Matt and his friends are leaving on the Saturday night beer run. They all pile into an old, beige Chevy II and head off to fill the trunk with cases of beer and boxes of Pop Tarts for when they get the munchies after *The Twilight Zone*. Their voices and the slamming doors sound different in the summer air. You can hear the heat in the way noise travels. In the winter, sound is small and brittle, but in the summer it's like liquid. When they pull away, the engine sounds like Danny's boat when you're underwater.

Ruth and Isabel hop the fence and come around through the backyard. There's a light on in the neighbor's living room, but he's an old man and his wife and kids are long gone.

"Last time, that window was open." Isabel points up at the side of Matt's house.

"Yeah, it was me that opened it, remember? Watch the bag." Ruth throws and Isabel only half catches it. Mrs. Warren's wedding dress is spilling out through a gap in the zipper. There's a rim lock on the kitchen door and it takes Ruth about half a minute to pop it with her library card.

"Skills of South Highbone. Doubt me some more, why don't you?"

"All right," Isabel says. "We're assholes from the right side of the tracks. Let's get this over with, woman."

"Actually, you know what? Magda taught me how to do that."

Matt's house smells like decay. The garbage hasn't been emptied and no one has opened the windows to let out the cigarette smoke. It's hot and stale. Ruth wants to run back to her mother's kitchen and bring some basil and peppermint and incense, anything that will cover up the smell of neglect in here. She opens the window over the sink.

"What the hell are you doing? He'll know someone was here."

"Uh, duh, Isabel. Pretty sure he's gonna know that anyway." She pulls the bag out of the garbage pail, stuffs in the overflowing milk cartons and beer cans, and ties it up.

It only takes a minute to go through and put the pot back, dumping it out of the wedding dress onto the bed where Matt will see it right away. The bed is full of laundry, so they put it on the top of the pile. Matt's room smells like Tide and Thai stick. He has glow-in-the-dark stars painted on the ceiling, looking half-charged and sad.

The sound of breaking glass makes them hit the floor like 'Nam vets in the park on the Fourth of July. They can hear a car squealing away. Not muffled and summery at all. Angry, like something from a movie soundtrack. Ruth crouches with her head down until everything's been quiet for a few, long minutes, then she creeps out first.

The living room window is smashed and there's a bottle on the rug with a burning rag hanging out of it. She can smell the gasoline, but the flame is already petering out. Whoever it is doesn't actually know what they're doing, as usual. Ruth jumps in and smothers it with the wedding dress while Isabel is still in the doorway, taking everything in. She looks around at the daisy curtains and the sagging couch and the bong, like it's some kind of habitat at the zoo.

"Come on, Isabel. It's not a museum. People live like this. Get over it."

"Ruth, you could have blown up."

"There's gonna be cops in about two minutes, Isabel. Let's go."

It's smoky in the room and Isabel looks like someone walking through clouds. There's an empty pizza box with a constellation drawn on it in blue pen. The names of stars are written in, then crossed out and written in again.

Isabel has cut her feet again, and she wants to wipe up the trail of blood on the kitchen floor, but Ruth won't let her. There isn't time.

They wait in the woods behind the neighbor's house,

listening for the cops. They never arrive, and Matt doesn't come back, either. Neighbors pour out into the street and stare for a while, then they leave again. Long after Ruth stops shaking, Isabel is still frozen, staring at Matt's house.

"The whole thing could've burnt down. We saved it. Christ, how did Magda know?"

"Um, I saved it, Isabel. And Magda just knows. Trust me. She's been like that my whole life. You get used to it."

There are sirens, but the sound is coming from far away in the village. Ruth moves away to sit with her back against a tree, while Isabel talks and talks, dealing with her nervous energy by babbling on and on, as usual. After a while she's running through some kind of fantasy about absinthe and lace and cities in Italy. There's no need to hear the separate words. If she just lets go, Ruth can turn the sound of Isabel's voice into wind and water, melt it back into the elements it came from anyway.

"I said, he thought it was cool. Hello, Ruth! Are you listening?"

"Nope. What?"

"Charlie thought it was cool. Sexy, even."

"You told him it was us! Why didn't he say anything when we saw him? Wasn't he mad?"

"Mad? Why? Ruth, pay attention. I'm talking about me and you, the other night."

"You told Charlie what you did, in my backyard?" Ruth can feel the bark of the tree, scraping against her back. She can feel the leaves under her feet, the air on her skin.

"What I did? What we did, you mean." She laughs. "Yeah, I told him. He thought it was cool."

"You know what, Isabel? Tell people whatever you want. It doesn't even bother me anymore."

From 25A, she can see a cloud of smoke filling the sky above the harbor, darker than the western sky. When a car goes by, she feels the rush and realizes she's off the sidewalk, standing in the road. She looks at Isabel, staring past her towards the village.

"Why are you still here?"

"What? We fixed it, like Magda said. Now we have to see what happens. This is where we're supposed to be, Ruth."

"Job done, Isabel. You don't have to keep following me."

Is that black cloud really there? Can Isabel see it, too?

"Look, how was I supposed to know you'd be pissed off? I'm sorry, all right? Jeez."

"I'm not pissed off." She reaches out to touch Isabel's arm, just to prove she can. "I meant it; I don't care."

Another car swerves at them and they both jump back. It's Danny though, pulling over with Ruth's mom.

"Get in, you two," her mother says. "Something's happening at the harbor." She doesn't even ask where they've been.

That's why the cops never showed up at Matt's house. The cloud of smoke is real. There is something else burning in Highbone.

eight

ISABEL SEES SPARKS, flaming ash and bits of wood and paper, made lighter than air by the heat. When Danny turns onto the top of Main Street she sees them dancing against the Maxfield Parrish color of the sky. The thing is, it doesn't seem wrong at all. Isabel can tell Ruth understands it too. It's obvious from the look on her face. Finally, all the things they know anyway are real. Everybody can see them now. This is how it is, burning.

The world has let out its flaming breath at last.

Main Street is closed off, with a village cop car parked across it. County is pulling up as they get there, and there is already a fire engine at the corner of Baywater Avenue. The volunteers have run a hose down the alley behind the stores.

Danny drives around and down the alley on the other side, behind the diner. The whole world seems to be standing at the end of the road by the harbor. Mr. Lipsky is there, and his old dad is sitting up in the back of an ambulance with an oxygen mask on. Magdalene is there, but they can't go over and talk to her because she's with her father, standing next to a cop.

The fire is at the back of Mariner's Maps and Books, and it looks like it's spread next door to the craft shop. Mr. Hancock is there, and Mrs. Hancock, and the 'Nam vets from the park are in a huddle around the bench by the water. Ms. Carter climbs out and holds the door for Isabel. She leans on the roof, and Danny stands by her, leaning on the hood. All at once, in the heat from the flames, it's like all of their movements have come into sync. The Hancocks and both Mr. Lipskys and Danny and Ruth's mom are all part of the same world, like everyone is in the same movie as them for the first time.

"Isabel, why are Magda and Professor Warren here?"

"Everyone's here, Ruth."

"No, I mean shouldn't they be somewhere looking for Henry?"

"Oh. Maybe they think he's here somewhere?"

And then Ruth is running into fire for the second time that night. As if she could smother this one, too, as if she's some kind of angel. Which she is, really. It comes home to Isabel right then that they all are. Angels, stuck somewhere, and maybe fire is the rite of passage, the magic door. Maybe Ruth is escaping now, without her.

It's Mr. Hancock who puts an arm out to stop Ruth. He's standing there on the corner by the fire engine. He rolls her along his arm and folds her into his chest and she's shouting at him.

"Let me go, you dick! There's a kid in there!"

"There's no one in there, Ruth," he says.

The water from the fire hose is loud, and Isabel moves closer so she can hear them. She reaches out to pull Ruth away, then changes her mind.

"You don't know that. How would *you* know what's really going on? Let go. You don't even know me."

"Of course I know you, Ruth. I've known you all your life."

And now Ms. Carter stalks over and says, "Leave her alone, Harold."

"You can't make me leave her alone forever, Carol."

"Her name's not Carol, it's Caroline!" Ruth shouts. "And your soap opera doesn't matter right now. Henry might be in there."

"Try me, Harold," Ms. Carter says. They're both ignoring Ruth. "You've got the house and the club and the trophy wife. I've got my daughter. Try me."

Isabel could swear he says the next thing just for effect. Just because there's an audience.

"I'm her father, Caroline. I have rights."

Shit.

Ruth just sits down on the ground then, right in the road. All the expression slides off her face. Now Isabel is the only one left standing.

Old Mr. Lipsky is watching, too. He's trying to take the mask off and talk, gesticulating at his son. Mrs. Hancock is watching, but it's just the usual sneer on her face. Danny is still next to Ms.

Carter's car, looking at his sneakers and shuffling, with his cigarette in the hand that's holding the back of his neck. Isabel can
see this is beyond him. He has a bit part. Danny isn't made for
high drama.

Now Sam Lipsky bends down with his hand on Ruth's shoulder, saying, "There's no one in there, sweetie. The firemen looked
in every room. My father was the only one there. They checked."

Sweetie. It sounds weird coming from him. He keeps trying
to be all fatherly lately. She puts her hand on his arm, and that's
strange too.

"What happened, Mr. Lipsky?"

"I don't know, Isabel. The whole . . ."

Water sprays up over the shops and then stops. The cordon
is in the middle of Main Street, but people back up onto the far
sidewalk to keep from getting soaked. There are no more sparks,
but the smoke has turned black and it smells heavy, like if you
breathe in you'll be taking something solid into your lungs. There
is a minute of silence, and then the whole town breathes out. The
fire is gone from the sky.

When Isabel looks down again, everyone is facing away from
the bookstore, towards the harbor. She's too short to see what's
coming; there's just a bunch of backs and falling ash and the sound
of people gasping. It's like watching fireworks when you're little.
She is trying to slide between people when a cop shifts the crowd
around the ambulance and Lefty comes through. People's gasps
have turned into words now, but everyone is talking at once so it
still doesn't make sense.

Lefty is holding Henry in his arms. He walks through the huddle of 'Nam vets next to the harbor and over to the nearest cop car, carrying Henry like he's a hurt bird or a newborn baby. People back away from him instinctively, but the cop is still waving them away. Lefty looks like the Virgin Mother, holding Christ after they took him down from the cross.

Only Henry's not dead. His head moves, and when he sees Magda he smiles a little, weak smile. He looks filthy. There's slime all over his face and his clothes. When Mr. Warren sees Henry he doesn't shout or run towards him. Instead he turns around to Magdalene and slaps her. The cop standing next to them doesn't even flinch when she falls back against his car.

He just says, "Don't worry, Professor Warren. We'll make sure your boy's all right."

Danny gets to Magda first, before Isabel. When Isabel bends down and holds out a hand, Magda looks at her and says, "I don't know why he did it. I don't understand."

"Don't worry, flowergirl. You're okay."

"Not my father. Jeff. I don't understand what I did wrong, Isabel."

"Jeff? The guy from the beach? Magda, what happened?"

Then Danny leans close to Magda, telling her Henry is fine.

She puts a hand on Danny's arm and says, "Where's Ruth?" That hand is like a blessing and a dismissal. Magda's big, sad eyes have gone holy. She is about to rise up. "I need to talk to Ruth," she says.

Now Old Mr. Lipsky is there, with his son behind him saying,

"Pop, you need to sit down."

"You okay, little Miss Buonvicino?" He turns around and flaps a hand at his son. "Stop fussing, you old woman! I'm your father. You don't get to tell me what to do."

Magda looks up at Old Mr. Lipsky and they smile at each other.

"Your little brother will be fine, Irene's baby. Don't worry."

Ruth is shouting again, behind her. When Isabel turns around, a cop is handcuffing Lefty's one hand to his own. Ruth runs around them in circles, trying to make them listen.

"Mr. Lipsky." Isabel grabs his arm. "Stop them! He didn't do anything."

"You don't know that, sweetie." Sweetie again. They're all sweeties tonight.

Magdalene takes in a loud, slow breath. "Yes, we do."

It's like she got her bones back the minute she saw Henry. She's standing up straight for the first time in days. The real Saint Magdalene the Magnetic is back, pointing them to the center of everything. Isabel can feel the tension go out of her own body.

"We do know," Magda tells them. "He's just Lefty. Henry likes him. He's our friend."

Professor Warren glares at Magdalene like he might hit her again.

Lefty says, "I had to wait until the water was out." The cop sucks in his breath, and for a minute Professor Warren looks like he might throw up.

"The tide," Lefty says, struggling. "I had to wait until the tide was out and the fish were gone. He was in the dark behind the water."

"He tried to tell us." Ruth shouts over at Danny and pulls on the cop's belt. "Danny, he tried to tell us this morning, remember?"

Henry is in the back of the ambulance now, with a lady paramedic talking to him and making him sip something from a straw. He's looking through the crowd and smiling at Magdalene, just smiling like he won the game and Magda is the prize. Professor Warren is telling the police to do their job. Magda turns her back to him and walks over to the ambulance. Her father doesn't matter anymore because Henry is back.

The fire is out.

nine

DARKNESS HAS BECOME a substance with a feel and a smell, but it isn't as good as Ruth imagined it would be. Something heavier than an early-summer night is hanging over Highbone. Always has been, really, but now it seems like everyone can smell it and touch it, not just her. The falling ashes are like pieces of something that's been there all along, the precipitation of everything suspended in the air of Highbone.

Two hours pass before they'll let the Lipskys go back in the store. People spend it wandering in and out of the park and Flannagan's and the Harpoon Diner. Everyone in town is too wired to go home. Ruth follows Magda and Isabel around the back of Mariner's to look. It isn't falling down. In fact, it's weird how little damage there is. She leans against the wall on the other side of the alley and looks up. There is a hole like a hell mouth in the back of Mr. Lipsky's building, burned around the edges. You can see the stairway through it and the opposite wall is covered in soot. The firemen told Mr. Lipsky it's safe now, the structure is solid and it's okay to go inside.

"Hey, Irene's baby." Old Mr. Lipsky is holding five dollars out to Magdalene. "The Harpoon's open, making coffee. Go on in and get us five. Black for Samuel, mine's milk and two sugars. Maybe some extra milk if they got it. I think maybe my refrigerator might not be working so good right now."

"You're gonna have to come to my house, Pop."

"All right, Samuel, stop fussing for a minute while we get these little ladies something hot to drink. Look at the little movie star. She's soaking wet. She looks like a drowned kitten."

"Ruth, come with me?" Magda asks like she needs it, like it's a favor.

Everything is close and vivid, like they're tripping, but they're not. Anyway, the veil is gone from between her and Magda. Ruth can see her again, but she changed while she was invisible. She looks hurt and scared, for the first time in their lives.

Now Magda grabs the tail of Ruth's wet shirt and pulls her towards the diner. They have to stand in the doorway because there's a line of people waiting for coffee. They don't need Old Mr. Lipsky's five dollars. The Harpoon is giving out free coffee tonight.

"Magda, we did it. We went back to Matt's house and put everything back, and I think we saved his life, maybe. Isabel couldn't get how you knew. She doesn't understand you."

"Yeah, it worked. Ruth, Jeff hurt me."

"What?"

"He's like my dad, but worse, and I didn't even see. Every time he went away, I couldn't wait for him to come back and touch me again. Then he hurt me. Maybe he was mad about the weed, or about me. I don't know."

"I knew something was wrong. I never thought it was that. Why didn't you say anything? You just sprung him on us. On me. I tell you everything, Magda. I used to tell you everything."

"You know what? It isn't like that with us. I can't turn around and lean on you. Me and you aren't made like that."

"Maybe you can now. We're changing, haven't you noticed?"

"It doesn't even matter now, Ruth. Henry's not mine anymore. All of a sudden, my dad noticed Henry is here. Did you see that?"

Professor Warren wouldn't let Magda hold Henry. He put him in the car and took him home, told Magdalene she could walk. But Henry smiled over his shoulder at them and said, "Don't worry, Magda. I knew you would find me, and Isabel taught me how to not be scared."

Professor Warren just said, "Get your seat belt on, Henry."

Ruth watched Magda lean in to wipe the slime off Henry's face with her sleeve. She had to snatch her arm out when her dad put the window up and pulled away. Their car has automatic windows that make a sound like a table saw.

"It won't last," Ruth says now. "People come and go and come back again. You'll see."

"He's going to take him and teach him to hate me."

"No one can teach him that, Magda."

Back inside Mr. Lipsky's store it smells horrible, but it looks surprisingly normal. In the back room, Ruth can see that all the boxes are soaked. There must be dozens of ruined books, but in front everything is like always. Except for it's weird to be in here in the middle of the night. And except for the smell.

When they hand out the coffee Old Mr. Lipsky sits in the captain's chair and Isabel gets into her place in the bay window. Ruth and Magda sit on the floor, and Young Mr. Lipsky walks up and down between everyone, looking into the street and then back at the counter.

"You're in shock, boy-o," his dad says. "Don't worry about it. You got insurance."

"Boy-o? *Boy-o*? Where have you been hanging out, Pop?"

"Where's Gaius Pollio, Mr. Lipsky?" Isabel calls from the window.

"Don't you worry, little Miss O'Sullivan," Old Mr. Lipsky says. "Cats take care of themselves. I bet you she smelled the smoke and took off right away. She'll stay away a week and then come back crying for food."

"Gaius Pollio's a she?" Isabel says it like it might matter. Like it's another one of tonight's crucial pieces of information.

"Oh, you're an endless source of comfort today." Young Mr. Lipsky says it to himself, staring out at Main Street, but Ruth can hear him, muttering under his breath at the window. He sounds like a sleepwalker.

When Ruth looks over at Magda she can see tears coming down her face, but Magda isn't moving or making a sound. She reaches for her hand, and there is no Isabel between them. She's in another world, sitting in the display window. Is this how it will be, then? Will it go back to how it was when they were little? Will they leave Isabel here and go away?

Later, they stand in the hole at the back of the store and Old Mr. Lipsky fusses about them walking home, but everyone tells him it's okay. There are still cops and people all over the place. When they come out through the burned back door and around onto Main Street, there's a chill blowing off the water. Magda wraps her coat around her and pulls out a pack of Larks. Her coat is silent, and Ruth reaches over to feel inside her pocket.

"Hey! Hands off."

"Where's all your stuff, Magda?"

"I don't know. I must have emptied my pockets at some point. I think I was looking for my father's watch."

Magda hands around cigarettes. She stands still with her lighter while they each try to use the giant flame without starting another fire, then they move on up the sidewalk together. The three of them are darker shadows in the night, carrying burning sparks up the hill out of town.

"Magda?"

"What, Isabel?"

"Lefty."

"Yeah, I saw."

Ruth grabs Magda's arm and feels a shudder go through her.

"Lefty knew, Magda. He tried to tell me and Danny this morning. He knew the whole time."

"What will they do to him?" Isabel says. "We can't let him get blamed."

"He won't," Ruth says. She only knows it's true when the words come out of her.

Tonight is the night when all the laws of force and motion reveal their secrets. It all clicks together like one of Magda's mechanisms, the Molotov cocktail and the bookstore, Ruth's cheap gin and Mrs. O'Sullivan's brandy, Lefty and Henry and the tide. The fire at Mr. Lipsky's, the blood soaking into the cement in the Dunkin' Donuts parking lot, it was all part of the pattern.

"We'll fix it," Magda says. "We'll fix it tomorrow."

ten

ISABEL IS STANDING by the window in her room when they come for her the second time. Her window faces the neighbors in back, and she sees the clanky cop Ford round the corner before she hears the doorbell.

She looks over at Ruth's flower that never became a tulip, René Char's poem held to the slanted ceiling with yellowing tape. The ashes of her Navy sweater that she put in a peanut butter jar next to the bed.

She can picture time stretching out and dust gathering. The room should have a clock with stopped hands, and a burned wedding dress like Mrs. Warren's. She doesn't have to go downstairs to know that things have caught up with her. When she sees this room again, if she ever comes back here, time will be piled up in drifts. It will all be cold and invisible.

She turns her back on Ruth's flower and heads down the stairs.

There are two cops this time, and the baby social worker. They're all working hard on their serious cop facial expressions. The baby social worker tries to make himself taller, standing in the hallway next to the cops. They're here for keeps. Hardball. Suitable metaphors for seriousness. She tries to care and can't manage it.

One cop has a uniform. County again. Is that because the Dunkin' Donuts parking lot is on the far side of 25A, or is it always county if you try to kill someone? Too much for the tourist board and the quaint little rent-a-pigs, murder. They say "serious assault" and then they say "attempted murder." They say "protective custody."

Her mother doesn't say "She's my daughter" this time. She says, "Can I make you boys some coffee?" Christ.

They sit down and ask her father about a lawyer for Isabel.

Isabel looks at the lamp by the couch, turned off now because it's still light outside. She looks at the empty depression next to it, where her mother usually sits, her mother who is in the kitchen now with the one in the uniform, acting hysterical about coffees.

"Dad?"

He isn't listening.

"Dad!"

"Isabel." He tries to pitch his voice lower than it is. Not for her, just because there are strangers here with uniforms.

"You have to let Ruth and Magda in my room. You have to let

them go through my stuff. Let them take whatever they want."

The baby social worker sits on the footstool by Isabel's chair, working hard to look concerned about her. Give him a few years, he won't even bother with that. Some girl will get arrested for doing what the cops won't bother to do and he'll stand there thinking about his model airplanes while they read her rights. They'll swallow him up in the end.

Someone is asking if she understands.

"Will there be books? Will there be pencils and paper?"

They don't even answer that.

eleven

"SIT DOWN, MAGDALENE," her father says.

Why are they in the kitchen? No one but Henry ever uses the kitchen table. Magda and her father eat in their rooms, or in front of the TV. It's coming, of course. This is it, the reckoning. Whatever it's going to be is here now. She stares straight into his eyes. It seems important to do that. Henry is watching *Gumby*; she can hear Pokey's swallowed words coming from the television in the den.

"I've been talking to Uncle Tony."

"What for? You don't even like him."

"But you do, don't you?"

"He's all right."

Where is he going with this? Does he actually think she's more scared of Uncle Tony than she is of him? She looks down at a box of kitchen stuff under the window by the side of the table, a set of oven dishes and a copy of *Let's Eat Right to Keep Fit*. Does it qualify as belonging to her mother because it's for the kitchen? Doesn't anything in this place belong to all of them? Held in common?

"You're obsessed with dividing things up, Dad. Some stuff is just everybody's, you know."

"Don't change the subject, and don't talk to me like that!" He takes a menacing step closer, but it might as well be happening to someone else. She's trying to care, trying to make her body feel like protecting itself, but it just won't.

"How will you throw out the wallpaper? Are you gonna cut the carpets in half?"

"You're going to live with Uncle Tony."

The whole sentence just drops into space. The dust that's floating in the light coming through the window stops moving. The sounds follow each other but they don't make sense.

"Did you hear me, Magdalene? I've decided it's better if you live with Uncle Tony."

"So, not the wallpaper, your children? You gonna put us in a box and chuck us in the carriage house till Uncle Tony comes to clear us out?"

If she had any sense of self-preservation, she'd stop now. She just doesn't care anymore. What's the worst thing he can do?

"Not *us*, Magdalene. You. The best thing for everyone is if you go out to Tony's. The schools are excellent and Tony will know what to do with you. Henry and I will stay here."

"Dad, why didn't you guys give me a middle name? You couldn't even be bothered to think one up, or what?"

"Magdalene! Did you hear what I said? You'll finish this year and go when school's over."

"Even you wouldn't do that, Dad. So, seriously, why just the two names for me? Henry got a middle name."

"I've done it, Magdalene. Tony's doing up a room for you and we called the school out there already. The guidance office here will send your grades over the summer."

"You can't do that! There's a law, Dad. There must be a law that says you have to take care of me. There's a law that says I wasn't allowed to leave till I was sixteen. What about you? You can't do that. Henry needs me."

"Law? You're talking to me about law, Magdalene Warren? You left Henry at the mercy of deviant street people, and your best friend has just been accused of murder."

"Isabel is not my best friend, Dad. Ruth is my best friend. Pay attention."

"Oh yes, Ruth. The one whose mother used to clean our toilets. That's better, then."

"Play that over in your head, Dad. You actually just said that, you complete snob. Anyway, they said *attempted* murder, which it wasn't. She was defending herself."

"I don't think that's how the police would tell it."

"She was defending herself from people like you!"

He doesn't hit her, even then. He found something worse to do to her.

"The fact is, Magdalene, you take after your mother. You belong with Tony. You're a Buonvicino. Henry and I are Warrens. He needs better influences."

"How the hell are you gonna take care of him?!" She's screaming and the look on his face is full of satisfaction. *See, she's hysterical*, it says. But she can't stop. Something is boiling up in the middle of her, something made out of anger and fear and blood and poetry. It's pushing up out of her throat and after it comes out she'll be clean and empty and she won't have to feel anything.

"What's his favorite book? How do you get him to stay in bed when he isn't sleepy? What do you have to do to get him to sit still at the barber? Where do his fucking socks go? You can't take care of him. Anyway, he won't let you. It won't work."

"He's young, Magdalene. How much do you remember about when you were six? The time to do this is now. I can't help you. It's too late, but I can raise Henry like a Warren. I can keep him off the street."

Magda looks down at the box of oven dishes and then up at the curtains her mother made on her fancy new Singer. The sewing machine is in the carriage house, but he hasn't taken the curtains down. Maybe he doesn't remember her putting them up and laughing at herself, saying, Susie Homemaker, that's me! This is what it's come to.

"I'm starting to look like her, aren't I? You're throwing me away because you can't stop my face from reminding you."

That is when he hits her.

twelve

ISABEL LAUGHS UP at the window by the bed. She had imagined a tiny one with bars, high up in a big cement wall. Something from *The Man in the Iron Mask*, basically. This is like a regular window, except you can't open it more than an inch, and there's wire mesh inside the glass. The door is just a regular door too, but the ones at the end of the hallway are locked.

She can only get two books a week, but the shitty TV in the common room is pretty much unlimited. There's supposed to be someone else in the bed across from her, but that potential girl hasn't been caught for whatever it is they'll catch her for yet. Give it time; they'll fill the place up. No shortage of anger out there. It's exciting, being in a building full of kids who refused to just sit back and take the crap that gets handed to them. It was always going to be this, wasn't it? This or the nuthouse. It was never gonna be a houseboat. Didn't everybody see that? They were always mad at her just for trying to pretend there was another future.

The baby social worker comes to visit. He said they'll send her schoolwork right away. She still has to do it in here; how ridiculous is that? Mr. Hazlett, the baby social worker, has her brother's name, Kevin. He looked confused when she asked him about his model airplanes. There's a girl who draws on the wall next to her bed with her own shit, and another one who cuts people up if they let her near anything sharp. She'll just go for anyone who walks by. You have to give her a wide berth and smile at her a lot from across the room.

Isabel wrote a letter to Mr. Lipsky at the store and asked him if he could maybe send her a book. Anything. She'd read the *Divine Comedy* if he still wanted her to, she said. Plenty of time in here. Enough time to think about all of it. She had to ask Kevin Hazlett to mail the letter. She has to trust a lot of people now who she knows can't be trusted. No other option. In the letter, she tried to explain to Mr. Lipsky. Turns out she cares what he thinks more than she cares what her parents think. Mr. Lipsky was at least paying attention.

She measures out two hours every day for going over it all, in between the group sessions and dinner. So far she hasn't found anything she regrets. Every hit of acid, every stolen thing, every minute spent under the water at the beach and in the air on top of the water tower, looking down on Highbone, every time they walked past and shouted "sucker!" at a wedding party getting their pictures taken on the bandstand. Every cut and every blow. She can live off all that for the rest of her life if she has to. Not quite seventeen and she's lived enough for a whole life. There are a lot of people who've never felt as scared as her, as high as her, never noticed the beautiful and the sublime and the terrible. Never held the power of retribution in their hands.

It's okay. It's enough.

thirteen

IT'S JUST RUTH and Magda now, like before, like always. When they get to the water tower, Ruth walks into the middle and lies on the grass. It's Thursday night; no one is out. No cars full of kids blasting Led Zeppelin and throwing Jack Daniel's bottles onto the road, no PTA moms driving their kids home from soccer games. Even the bikers, she hasn't seen since last Saturday.

No Doris, with her boyfriend's trike and her tattoo and her overly optimistic advice. There are worse things than being Doris, that's for sure.

The girders of the water tower are like a metal web around her, a spaceship or an alien creature with giant, mechanical legs. When Magda starts climbing, her coat falls out behind her like a cape.

"You look like the human fly," Ruth shouts.

"Shhh! You coming up, or what?" Magda stage-whispers down over her shoulder.

Ruth is second up the ladder, and second to make the leap from the ladder cage onto the platform. *Second place for Miss Carter*, Virgil Mackie said. For a suspended moment when she throws her leg over the railing, there's nothing beneath her, like in her dream, a world of lights and empty space. It feels perfect. Up here in the sky, everything is right again. The air holds her up and things below them are small enough not to matter. They are angels, come back to the sky, the two of them above everything, where they belong.

"Magda, do you miss Isabel?"

"I don't know. Yeah. She's us, Ruth. She just is."

"I guess. Will they keep her in that juvenile detention place, or send her to real jail?"

"You have to visit. If you don't, it'll just fade and then you won't want to and then everything will fall apart. Nothing means anything unless we make it."

"So, what's the point of that?"

"I really don't know, Ruth. I'm not the one who knows anymore. You need to figure stuff out yourself."

Well, she kind of knew that already anyway, but it would have been nice if Magda had let her say it. They sit with their backs to the tank for a long time, mostly silent, just breathing and smoking. It's been a month since they all sat at the back of the park burning the worst parts of their world, trying to get control of things by destroying them. Nothing they burned then even matters now.

"Nothing we believed was true, Magda. It's not like we failed; it's like the whole time we were playing the wrong game, moving the wrong pieces around."

"Yeah, robbing Matt was wrong. It turned everything upside down. You said that at first, and you were right, see? You should be the one deciding stuff. For yourself."

"Matt might as well be us. That's all I was trying to tell you guys."

"I get it. I got it then, even. I just didn't care. I thought we were invincible or some shit. I thought what we needed mattered more than everything else. I was stupid."

"Magdalene Warren, you have never been stupid in your entire life. I've been sitting right here watching for most of it, so you can trust me on that."

"I keep trying to imagine what it was like the other day." Magdalene uses her middle finger to flick her cigarette butt up and out and over the trees. They both smile tired smiles at the firework sparks, but neither of them shouts. "Did they come for Isabel with sirens, or just briefcases? Did she scream and try to get away, or just look guilty and stare at her feet? I feel like I need to know, like it's the only thing left I need to know."

The lights below illuminate silent driveways and empty porches, turning pockets of the dead world a sickly yellow. Up here in the dark blue before dawn, it feels like another time zone, like they're outside of the rhythms of sleeping and waking and driving in and out of driveways to school and work and hair-dressers.

"I'm gonna make the rounds," Ruth says. "I need to survey my queendom."

She begins the circle of the tower, counterclockwise with her right hand on the rail like it's a balcony. To the west, the harbor is hidden behind a downward slope of trees. North and a little east, the LILCO stacks rise up with their red and white colors showing in the safety lights that keep planes from flying into them. Over on the hill, Henry is safe in his room sleeping.

So, there were the things they thought mattered and then the real things that were there all along. Not exactly under the surface, but no one was looking at them. There's time and no time. No time is the same as forever. Every once in a while, one kind of time stabs its way through the other, and it's either a revelation or a wound. Or both. That's where they've all been, stuck at that intersection, skewered like insects in a case or Christ on the cross. Now everything is burned clean, pulled free.

And Danny, of all people, told Ruth if she can get into that art school in the East Village there's no tuition. If she's good enough to be accepted, she can go there for nothing. She'll still have to be able to live in Manhattan. She asked Vicky about a job so she can save up. Vicky said the manager at Dunkin' Donuts would give her afternoon shifts as soon as her sixteenth birthday comes. She put her hands on Ruth's shoulders, looked her in the eye and said, "He'll take it out of you, honey, but don't worry. I'll be here, too." Then she laughed, and it wasn't bitter. It was just, that's how it is and it's no big deal, actually it's kind of funny. Ruth still can't figure out if that's crazy. She can hear Vicky's laugh now, woven into the layers of sky around her. It blends with Mrs. O'Sullivan's laugh and Old Mr. Lipsky's. Even Doris's scraping bark. They were all her angels, her guides. Right now she could rise up on their laughter and take off into the atmosphere. No gravity, no friction. No sparks.

She lifts up onto her toes and shouts around the curve of the tank.

"Hey, we should get down before some little wifey wakes up and sees us." Her voice flutters out of her, lighter than it's been for a long time.

But when she comes around the bend Magdalene is standing on the railing, holding the side of the cage with one hand and looking out over the elementary school field.

"Get the hell down, Magda! You're gonna fall." And the voice has gone right back out of her, no air in her stomach to fill it. It comes out a squeaky whisper.

"I'm not coming down that way, hon. You have to decide stuff for yourself now. I've been watching; you can totally do it. You're ready."

"Yeah, right. What about Henry? Can he figure stuff out himself? Get a grip, Magdalene. Get the fuck down."

"Henry isn't mine anymore. I told you guys that, but you didn't believe me. You weren't listening."

Magda's Chuck Taylors are curved around the railing, and the bottom of her coat is hanging out farther than she is. Ruth can see the chain of her watch glinting, snaking from her pocket to the third buttonhole. Exactly like Mackie's.

"Magda, tell me about Jeff. Just talk to me about it."

"What should I say? He goes to Stony Brook. He fixes my dad's car. I liked him. Shit, Ruth! I acted like Isabel."

"Right, but you can stop now. Don't take it out on yourself. Take it out on him."

"I think we tried that, Ruth. Look what happened."

"Someone hurt you and I didn't know, Magda. You were standing right next to me the whole time, and it was invisible. No, it wasn't even invisible. I knew. I tried to tell Isabel, but I never thought it was that."

"I could hardly stand up. I could hardly move. How ridiculous is that?"

"Yeah, but we all just keep going. We're just ghosts; it only seems like things touch us. Really, you can just carry on no matter what, just like the guys in the park."

Magda laughs. "I don't want to be the guys in the park, Ruth. I don't want to be me. I'm the one who watches Henry. I'm the one who tells you what to do. I am not the one who misses some guy who backhands her and fucks her and leaves her bleeding on the mulch under the birch trees. I caught the wrong train. I went straight past the person I was supposed to be and got in the middle of someone else's life. This isn't me. I lost Henry."

"You didn't lose Henry. Your mom and dad lost Henry, Magda. Anyway, in ten years he'll be sixteen. You think he won't figure your dad out by then? Come on, you just have to wait it out."

"I don't actually miss him. Jeff, I mean. I miss the idea of him. The thing I thought he was before he did that. I miss *me*. And I will not hang around to miss Henry. I refuse to do that."

"Look, while we're sharing, the whole concept of guys totally escapes me. Why would any woman do what Isabel does? I'm never gonna do that. I need to figure what to do with my life that isn't that. You need to get down and help me."

"I can't, Ruth. I want to say I'm sorry, but I'm not. You need to climb down from here all by yourself. I'm doing you a favor."

"You know what? Mrs. O'Sullivan told me if I don't get married I won't go nuts. Think about it. She said Isabel was already doomed. She said not to grab on to things like a drowning person. You're the only thing I still want to hang on to. You're always there in my head, even when you're not there. Leaving me is not a favor. You need to get down and let me leave you."

It's almost daytime now. Soon the color of Magdalene's hair will resolve out of its blackness. If she climbed up next to her now, Ruth would feel the heat of her and smell the linen of her coat. It's a trick, like Mrs. O'Sullivan said. You just have to let go.

If Magda is going to get down, the slow way or the fast way, it will be by herself. They're all by themselves now. Whatever gravitational force kept them spinning around each other, stuck in repeating circles, it's gone. That doesn't mean they won't know each other, or even love each other still. It means they have three separate souls, weighed in the balance one at a time. Isabel's mom saved Ruth, so she'll need to be waiting to save Isabel. Magda's right about that; they need to be there while Isabel's in and when she gets out.

Ruth turns away towards the ladder. She imagines Magdalene falling, her coat fluttering out like a pair of dark wings. Mackie falling into Magdalene. Dark angel falling away from her, leaving her alone in the sky. Sparks flying up as Magdalene hits the trees.

Maybe that is how it ends. Maybe.

Ruth throws her leg out over the railing and into the ladder cage. There is the sudden feeling of the world again, rushing underneath her, the air and the salt from the sea, the crazy poetry of all those kinds of light mixing together, Lefty and Old Mr. Lipsky and Mrs. O'Sullivan's secret nighttime world. Ruth and Isabel and Magda are the people who can feel what all of it means. Why would you give that up? Their lives together, the things they've seen and done and felt, are already so much more than other people have. Whatever happens next, it was worth it.

Turns out the wave she felt coming that night on Seaview Road was a holy wave. Like all real visions it was terrifying and it was beautiful. It crashed over everything and washed them like beach glass, taking away their edges and their clarity. But in the end it left Ruth scoured and dazzling. She is empty and pure now.

There is a place for her, between the sun and the other stars.

Acknowledgments

IF NOT FOR Danielle Zigner at LBA Books, you would not be holding this novel in your hands. She didn't just rescue it from the slush pile, she believed in it, fought for it, and nurtured it through everything that came after that with heroic patience and good humor. Allison Hellegers at Rights People found the book its New York home, but much more important, she made me feel that it did what I hoped it would do.

Thanks to my friend Sally Mills for the lucky dime. For reading drafts, partial or complete, once or many, many times, thanks to: Shamira Meghani, Lisa Miller, MaryLee Miller, Maia Pollio, Mahine Rattonsey, Danny Reilly, and Angela Sherlock. Bonnie Zobell, Marko Fong, Eamonn Lorrigan, and everyone in the "Long Stuff" office at the Zoetrope virtual studio provided support and advice early on. The whole of my big, remarkable family has been behind me on this. I am so grateful.

Neelam Masood, woman of all automotive knowledge, explained to me how vintage brake systems work and how a girl might go about sabotaging one. Robert Lunsford of the American Meteor Society shared his stunningly detailed memory of meteor showers visible from Long Island in the spring/summer of 1979. It is not his fault that I later moved the Lyrids to an impossible date and time. Both Lisa Miller and JoAnne Buntich gave me legal and historical advice regarding property titles (it mattered at one point), juvenile detention law, and social work. Again, mistakes and misapprehensions are my own.

So after all that, you hope for an editor to notice your novel or, better still, like it. If you're pretty much the luckiest author ever, you get someone like Emilia Rhodes, who genuinely loves your book, understands what you want to say, and applies her remarkable intelligence and patience to helping you say it. I am grateful to Emilia and the whole wonderful team at Harper New York for being so excited about *Little Wrecks*. The feeling a writer has when that excitement comes across is indescribable. I won't try; I'll just say thank you all very, very much.